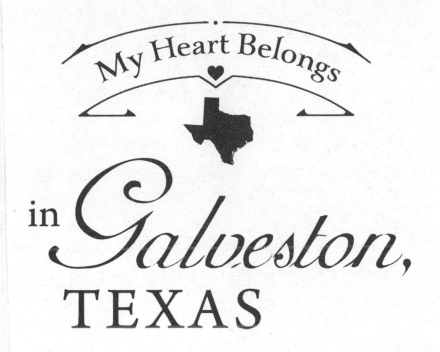

My Heart Belongs in Galveston, Texas

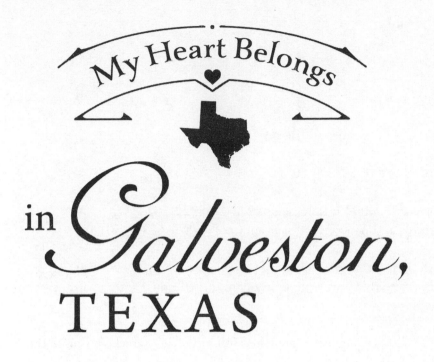

My Heart Belongs in Galveston, TEXAS

Madeline's Search

KATHLEEN Y'BARBO

BARBOUR BOOKS
An Imprint of Barbour Publishing, Inc.

ISBN 978-1-68322-500-3

Adobe Digital Edition (.epub) 978-1-68322-502-7
Kindle and MobiPocket Edition (.prc) 978-1-68322-501-0

All scripture quotations are taken from the King James Version of the Bible.

This book is a work of fiction. Names, characters, places, and incidents are either products of the author's imagination or used fictitiously. Any similarity to actual people, organizations, and/or events is purely coincidental.

Series Design: Kirk DouPonce, DogEared Design
Model Photograph: Lee Avison/ Trevillion Images

Published by Barbour Books, an imprint of Barbour Publishing, Inc., 1810 Barbour Drive, Uhrichsville, OH 44683, www.barbourbooks.com

Our mission is to inspire the world with the life-changing message of the Bible.

ecpa Member of the Evangelical Christian Publishers Association

Printed in the United States of America.

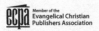

Dedication

To those who look at the stars and see their Creator;
To those who look at the sea or the hills or a bluebonnet in spring and know God exists;
And to those who wish they could.

Also for all the history nerds and those who are BOI.

But the LORD sent out a great wind into the sea, and there was a mighty tempest in the sea, so that the ship was like to be broken. Then the mariners were afraid, and cried every man unto his god, and cast forth the wares that were in the ship into the sea, to lighten it of them. But Jonah was gone down into the sides of the ship; and he lay, and was fast asleep. So the shipmaster came to him, and said unto him, What meanest thou, O sleeper? arise, call upon thy God, if so be that God will think upon us, that we perish not.

JONAH 1:4–6

Author's Note

I am a history nerd.
I want everything to be just right.
All the facts and just the facts.

However, sometimes the story calls for me
to "bend" history to make it fit.

If you're a history nerd too, be sure and read the special extra
chapter at the end of the novel to discover the inside
information on what is fact and what is fiction.

And if you have read the dedication and don't know about the folks
who Galveston natives call BOI, then that's the place to get the scoop.

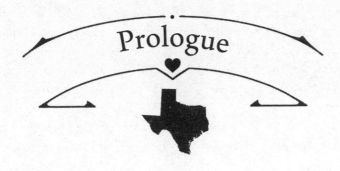

Prologue

Gulf of Mexico
September 19, 1855

The storm raged around us like a mad beast intent on taking our ship and all aboard down to the briny depths. The men assigned to the watch had given up and lashed themselves to their posts. At least two had already been lost to the waves.

For once I gave thanks that my wife had been too ill to travel with us. The illness that forbade her travel just may have saved her life.

Galveston lay behind us now, the storm's surge making it impossible to put in at port. So we sailed on, heading into the eye of the monster rather than out to sea where the waves would likely have already been stilled.

The reason for this decision, the cause for the choice to chance death and find a port to drop anchor, lay down below on a bunk in the captain's quarters. For tonight, regardless of the tempest that raged, a child would be born.

The child's father came to stand behind me, his face etched with nearly a full day and night of watching the one he loved endure indescribable pain. Behind him, the woman hired as nursemaid shook her head.

"So the child did not survive?"

A single tear traced my son's cheek. "The child, she is weak but alive."

"And Eliza?"

Again the nursemaid shook her head. This time she too showed tears. "Gone."

A groaning sound roared from the depths of the ship, and warning bells rang. We had been taking on water since an hour after sunset. I looked beyond these two to the man standing in the door.

He was waiting. No words were needed. The vessel and its occupants were done for. With only two small boats with which to evacuate, I knew what must be done.

"Turn for Indianola," I said. "We race the wind and hope for the best."

"But sir," my loyal crewman protested. "We will not make land in this vessel."

"We will get close enough," I told him.

And we did. The storm still raged farther south, but the winds were more companionable to sailing into port at Indianola. We did no such thing, of course, for to sail into that port in this ship would be to invite unwanted attention, even in this abysmal weather.

I ordered two small crafts sent out. One carried my son and the remains of his wife along with a loyal crewman to row. The other carried the child and her nursemaid. On this vessel, I sent my most trusted man to see to their safety.

"No matter what," I told him. "See that the child lives, even at the cost of your own life."

And he had vowed it would be so.

My son, a devoted sailor always, went on my orders but under a protest I understood. Even my answer, that separation from the child meant one might arrive safely if the other did not, did not dissuade him from his despair.

"Go and bury your wife," I told him as my crew fought to keep the ship from ruin. "Take rooms and wait for me here. Find a wet nurse for your daughter. I will come to you."

With that, I sent my son off into the night with the body of his wife wrapped in the same blankets where she had so recently given birth.

A moment later, I heard a sound like the mewling of a cat. I turned to see the nursemaid holding a bundle.

"She will live?" I asked her, for I knew I must make a report to my wife should the Lord allow us to be reunited this side of heaven.

"She will live."

I pulled back the wrappings to see wide brown eyes peering up at me. One tiny fist had found its way free of its prison and now shook at me like an angry fishmonger.

"Hello, little treasure," I said to her. "Go with God. We will be together soon."

And then I released my granddaughter to the waves and the wind and the care of God. Most certainly and especially the care of God.

Chapter One

New Orleans, Louisiana
March 14, 1880

Of all the assignments Jonah had been given since he joined the agency almost ten years ago, this one had to be the strangest. Though his career thus far had included putting his life on the line to bring in murderers, thieves, and con men, here he sat sipping tea in the fancy New Orleans parlor of a woman old enough to be his grandmother.

Or at least pretending to while he studied the distinctly feminine rose-scented room. His gaze landed on the mantel where mismatched crystal vases were filled with the pink blossoms. Larger vases on the bookshelves opposite the fireplace vied for space among the leather-covered volumes.

Given the fact it was early March, Jonah wondered if she had a greenhouse to grow the flowers all year, but he didn't ask. In fact, there was much he wondered about this room, but with the goal of getting out of this place as quickly as possible, he remained silent.

The only space that did not show some evidence of the owner's penchant for pink roses was the window seat that looked out through lace curtains onto Prytania Street. As if to make up for that grievous transgression, the seat had been wrapped in the same rose-strewn fabric that covered the walls and the two chairs where he and Mrs. Smith now sat.

When Jonah returned his attention to his hostess, he found Mrs. Smith, a tiny woman who had obviously once been a great beauty, watching him carefully. Her dark eyes twinkled as she regarded him with what appeared to be equal parts assessment and amusement.

Though she'd only yet offered him a polite greeting and settled him into this parlor, Jonah couldn't help noticing this elderly woman had the smile and graceful movements of a much younger person. And her voice, when she spoke, held the slightest trace of an accent. Whether it was the familiar Acadian French of his grandfather's people that he recognized in her tone or something else entirely, he couldn't say.

"So, you think I've lost my mind, don't you?" she said as she lifted the teapot to pour more of the fragrant brew into his cup.

He did, and he'd told the captain as much. However, the woman sitting across from him had apparently paid dearly for the privilege of hiring a Pinkerton man to solve her case, and she had requested him specifically.

"Ma'am," he said in the reverential tone he'd learned from his mama back home in Texas, "I take every assignment seriously."

A smile rose and then she chuckled, lighting her wrinkled face as she set the teapot back in place. "Well done, Detective Cahill. You've answered my question without actually giving me your opinion of my sanity."

"Begging your pardon, Mrs. Smith," Jonah said, "but I don't believe you hired me to determine that."

"True, I most certainly did not." She sat back and gave him an appraising look. "Yes, I believe you'll do."

Unsure how to respond, Jonah merely nodded. Whether she liked him or not was of no difference to him.

He shifted positions and tried to pay attention as Mrs. Smith abruptly changed the subject and picked up her teacup then began to tell yet another story about tending her roses. Though he kept his gaze attentive and focused on his host, Jonah couldn't help but wish she would move on to the topic he had come to discuss.

"I do hope you don't mind me prattling on," his hostess finally said. "I shall miss my roses once we've all relocated to Galveston, and good listeners are hard to find these days. You, Detective Cahill, are a good listener. I applaud either your parents or your superiors at the agency for training you well."

"Thank you, ma'am," he said for lack of any other response.

Mrs. Smith leaned forward, still balancing her teacup. "Do you have any questions for me, Detective Cahill?"

He paused. "I confess I have only skimmed the information you provided, but from what I recall, you wish me to find a young relative of yours, one Trésor Smith who was born in 1855 and who you believe is now residing in Galveston, Texas."

"Trésor is my granddaughter. And I believe you will find her in Galveston, Texas, yes," she said. "Indianola was the city of her birth, but as you know, most of the city was lost to a storm some five years ago."

"So you believe she is in Galveston?"

"I *know* she will be," she told him.

Jonah shifted positions. "Again, without consulting the full file, I must prepare you for the fact that as an adult, she may not want to be found. Or worse. . ."

"Yes, dear," she said gently. "I understand what you mean, and although I am quite confident you will succeed, I do lay this all at the feet of Jesus for His ultimate solution."

"Very well, then. I will give the file my full attention and be ready to begin the search when we meet again."

She leaned forward. "Am I correct in understanding you will not require lodging during our stay on the island?"

"You are correct."

She took a sip of tea and then regarded him with an innocent look. "Because you have family there?"

His brows lifted. "Yes," he said carefully. "I do."

"And you wonder how I knew this?" Mrs. Smith smiled as she set her teacup down.

"The thought did occur to me."

Even those he was closest to within the Pinkerton Agency had no idea of his connection to this city. Jonah's father had severed connection some twenty years ago for reasons unknown to anyone but himself and

Grandfather Cahill. They remained estranged until the day Father died. Even now, he had no idea if his grandfather still lived.

"The answer is simple," she said. "I knew your grandfather."

Knew. Past tense. A smidgen of grief arose.

"You wonder of my use of the term *knew*."

"I did wonder, yes."

She waved her hand as if dismissing the statement. "Truly, I cannot tell you whether Monsieur Cahill still draws a breath or not. Our acquaintance goes back many years but does not extend to the present."

Mrs. Smith sat back and awaited his response. For a moment Jonah had none.

Finally he found the words. "I see."

Mrs. Smith seemed to have sensed his ambivalence in regard to the old man. "He was a difficult man, but God has His ways of dealing with difficult men. Go and see for yourself."

Jonah let the comment pass with nothing more than a brief nod.

"Detective Cahill, I know there was much trouble under that roof while your grandfather lived," she continued, obviously not waiting for his response. "And apparently your father has overcome that trouble by finding a good life in Galveston."

"Yes, I believe he had," Jonah said.

"Had? So he is now deceased?"

"He is," Jonah said. "Lost to the fever some two summers ago."

"My deepest condolences, Detective Cahill. I remember him as the most precocious child. Please know your father was a very good man."

Jonah managed a smile as he tried to imagine his father as a boy. "I know he tried to be. I was blessed to be his son."

"Well, that is all the Lord really asks of us poor flawed humans, isn't it? That we try our best. The trick is to continue trying even once we've failed. That is the reason you are here and the whole purpose of my search for my granddaughter. You see, I failed in keeping her close. I wish to remedy this."

"Yes, ma'am," he said. "I will do my best to find her."

Mrs. Smith stood and so he did the same, their meeting obviously at an end. "Well then, I do appreciate you humoring me by paying a visit to me here in New Orleans," she said as she moved toward the door. "I look forward to seeing you again in Galveston when your assignment begins three weeks hence."

"About that," he said as he decided to raise a concern he hadn't known how to voice until now. "You know, you do not have to feel obligated to go along with me. I can easily send updates to you here."

Iron-gray brows rose. "You believe I will hinder your investigation?"

"No, ma'am, not at all. It's just that I wonder about the wisdom of a sea voyage, albeit not a lengthy one, at your. . ."

No. He wouldn't say it. To complete that thought aloud was to accuse a lady of being elderly, and although all evidence pointed to that fact, he'd been raised far too well to bring it up.

"Oh child," she said with a chuckle. "Your concern is touching. If only you knew what I know about sea voyages and. . ."

Then she seemed to have her own trouble finishing her statement. Instead, Mrs. Smith shook her head and then placed her hand atop his sleeve.

"Look here. Don't you worry, Detective Cahill. I'll get there just fine, and I assure you I will not be traveling alone. I'll be bringing a few of my staff along with me as well as my assistant. She has proven invaluable in helping me to write down my memories, and I am certain she will make an excellent traveling companion."

"If you wouldn't mind, I wonder if I might take a look at your assistant's notes. There could be information contained in them that will help my search for your granddaughter."

"Of course," she said with a nod. "I will arrange it as soon as we are settled in Galveston. Now do take care on your journey. I know I am very much looking forward to mine. It will be wonderful to be back on the island."

"So you've been before, then. Perhaps anything your assistant has recorded in relation to your previous visits will be of help in this investigation."

"Oh child," she said gently, "you'll find nothing in those notes about such a thing. Some memories aren't to be shared."

He paused before responding. "While I understand, I do hope you'll keep in mind that I have been charged by you with uncovering secrets." At her raised brows, he continued. "I have found, Mrs. Smith, that people do not go missing without secrets being part of the equation."

Her surprised look turned to one of satisfaction. "Yes, of course. Rest assured, young man, I will neither hinder your investigation nor hide any information I believe might prove helpful."

Jonah exchanged parting words and then left with a wave to his hostess and no doubts that Mrs. Smith would arrive just as fit and fine as she said she would. As to whether she was hiding something he might later need to know, that was yet to be determined.

He stepped out onto the banquette that ran alongside Prytania Street and checked his pocket watch. It was early yet, still several hours away from his appointed time to leave the city. Fitting the watch back into his vest pocket, Jonah gave brief thought to his dilemma.

Go.

He frowned, recognizing that nudge. Rather than stand outside Mrs. Smith's home and argue unsuccessfully with the still, small voice that had never steered him wrong, Jonah sighed and headed toward Esplanade Avenue.

He found the address easily enough. The white two-story home with three columns running across the front and a balcony that spanned the upper floor was now bracketed between two smaller dwellings that had been built since Jonah's last visit.

Three windows marched evenly across the second floor, their tops curved and their dark green shutters open to allow the midday sun. Two more windows matched their upstairs twins along the columned porch with the third spot held by a painted wooden door of deepest black.

Upstairs, a white lace curtain moved, but was it the breeze that caused it to shift or someone studying him as intently as he studied the stately residence?

Jonah paused for a moment, one hand resting on the smooth metal of the iron gate. To his right and his left a black iron fence, topped at intervals with the fleur-de-lis design that also appeared in his family's coat of arms, stretched to the edges of the property. The entrance for carriages must have been moved to the back alley when the property on each side was sold off.

Or perhaps those who resided behind this fence had no need for carriages any longer. Again Jonah sighed. Again the still, small voice said *go*.

Just as he was about to reach for the lever that opened the gate, he caught sight of a young woman walking toward him while looking down at something in her hand. Her cloak was made of fine green velvet just a shade darker than shamrocks, and her dark hair had been tucked up beneath a fashionable hat of a similar color.

She appeared so engrossed in whatever she held that she did not notice Jonah or act as if she recognized him until she was almost upon him. Oh but he knew her.

Even now as she appeared deep in thought, the old feelings rose. It had been the better part of a year since he'd seen her, longer than that since he trusted her.

And yet a small part of him knew if he wasn't careful, he could fall in love with her all over again.

The gate swung open beneath his hand, but Jonah did not step inside. Rather, he stood his ground and prepared for the next skirmish in what had become quite a battle with the frustrating female.

The woman walking toward him, a local journalist for the *New Orleans Picayune*, had ruined more than one Pinkerton investigation with her relentless snooping. She had also very nearly cost him his job and his freedom last summer.

What he would never tell her was that she had also broken his heart.

Though it appeared from Madeline Latour's lack of attention to anything other than whatever was in her hand that their meeting here today was pure accident, Jonah was skeptical. With this one, he was always skeptical.

He stepped into her path. "Hello, Madeline."

Chapter Two

Madeline jolted at the use of her first name, dropping her notebook in the process. Catching herself by grabbing the iron fence, she looked up into familiar eyes.

Regrettably familiar.

She sighed as she pushed away those old feelings that swirled around his memory. Of all the men to see today, it would have to be Detective Jonah Cahill of the Pinkerton Agency. What was he doing in New Orleans?

Gallant as always, the Pinkerton man reached for her notebook first. She couldn't help noticing his dark brows rising as he obviously spied the initials engraved on the notebook's leather cover: M.W. for Maggie Winston, the identity she had assumed in order to complete her investigation.

Each time Madeline took on a new identity in her role as an investigative journalist, she always added a few personal touches to give that persona the image of reality. The notebook had been the perfect accessory, so perfect that it had practically secured her the job that would give her access to an eyewitness that no one else had been able to interview.

"This can't be yours, can it?" he said with an infuriating quirk of his dark brow.

"Thank you," she said as his fingertips brushed her palm. "It's lovely, isn't it?"

"Quite," he said as his eyes raked the length of her. From any other man, the gesture might have seemed impudent, rude even, but this was a man with whom she had some history. Good history until she ruined it.

Had he chosen that life instead of this one, Detective Jonah Cahill might have made a daunting outlaw. He was of imposing height and build with eyes of silver gray and pitch-black hair that curled at his neck.

Jonah wore his ability to decipher people and stop them cold with a casual air. His face was perpetually fixed with an expression that seemed to assume he had already won the war before the battle began.

It had been almost a full year since she'd last seen the handsome Pinkerton. The last time they met, outside the courthouse after the McRee case concluded, she had made Jonah so mad he swore he'd have her arrested.

Worse, she'd broken his heart and she knew it. What he didn't know was he had also broken hers.

At this very moment, his expression told her he'd lock her in jail and throw away the key if given the chance. Not that she blamed him.

"Thank you, Jonah," she said as she carefully tucked the notebook into her pocket. "I would ask what brings you to New Orleans but I assume you'd tell me you couldn't answer the question."

His lip curled into what almost passed for a smile. "That was always your trouble, Madeline. You assumed."

Madeline forced herself not to allow Jonah to see that the truth of the hurtful comment had reached its mark. Instead, she nodded toward the house nearest them. "I was sorry to hear of your grandfather's death. Yellow fever, I believe it was?"

She could see by his expression that Jonah hadn't known. "Oh, I am so sorry. No one told you, did they?"

Any remnant of civility disappeared. "Goodbye, Madeline," Jonah said as he stormed inside the fence.

The gate slammed behind him, leaving her to decide whether to respond with a polite goodbye or just gather up the remains of her pride and walk away. Madeline chose the latter.

Besides, she had an appointment and could not be late. Her tears would wait for later when she did not have to explain them to anyone.

Not that she could.

Jonah stood on the porch and watched Madeline walk away. Sashay, as his mother would call it, for the infernal woman never could help looking like royalty. From her regal bearing to the way she seemed to be above it all even when she obviously did not mean to, she was nothing like any woman he'd ever known.

And that is how he'd managed to fall in love with her. It was why he'd fallen head over boot heels for the nosy reporter who he'd imagined would be his for life.

All he could hope as he watched her walk away was that the Lord had saved him from a pain worse than the one he felt right now. He'd trust in that and in his ability to forget Madeline Latour someday.

One last look at the frustrating female, and Jonah turned his back on her. His anger had led him as far as the front porch, but now he wondered about the wisdom of knocking on the door.

He hadn't been here since his grandmother's funeral, and now his grandfather was gone as well. *Go.* Yes, it was time.

Jonah knocked twicc, and someone called for him to come in. He stepped inside, allowing his eyes a moment to adjust to the dim light of the two-story foyer, then heard the swish of petticoats a moment before a woman called out.

"Who is that out there?"

"It's me," he responded. "Jonah."

Bess's cackling laugh reached him a moment before she did. Wrapping him in her ample arms, the woman who'd been with the Cahill family as long as Jonah could remember held him tight.

Finally, she released him and took a step backward. "I sure am glad to see you. What brings you to New Orleans?"

"Work." He paused. "I didn't know about Grandfather Cahill until today."

"Oh child," she said. "No reason you would have. He was a stubborn man. Never did forgive your daddy for marrying your mama, so it isn't surprising he didn't leave word for her when he was sick."

"She will be devastated all the same." He paused. "My mother never gave up on that stubborn old man."

"I know. I do love your mama so." She paused to give him an even look. "I am sorry, Jonah, but he left this home and everything in it to charity."

It took him a moment to realize what she was saying. "I didn't come here to get anything from him. I just wanted to know. . ." He paused. "I hope you've been cared for, though."

"Oh yes, Mr. Cahill was quite generous with me, but then I always knew he would be." She paused to give him a knowing look. "That man always did know I kept his secrets, and in return, he made sure I was rewarded. I'd say that's an even trade."

"What will you do? You know you're always welcome in Galveston. My mother could use the company."

"I do thank you," she said. "And much as I love your mama, I think I'll stay here until the charities take over. Then who knows? Maybe I'll pay your mama a visit. Say, how is that little sister of yours?"

"Susanna is ever the same. I wish she'd settle down, but she refuses."

"Now don't you go rushing her. She'll find someone in time and without her big brother's help."

"I suppose. She's beautiful, Bess, the image of Mama at her age from what I've been told, and a much better shot than I am."

"Either way she'll find a man, then." Bess laughed. "I credit your daddy for teaching the both of you to shoot well."

"That is true," he said. "He would be proud of how she turned out."

"I reckon he would be proud how you turned out too. Look at you, a fine Pinkerton man. I am so proud of you, Jonah Cahill." Her expression brightened. "But I can tell they don't feed you right up in Chicago. You give me a minute and I'll have you some shrimp gumbo on the table."

"That sounds mighty fine," he said, "but I've got a train to catch, so I can't stay long."

She shook her head. "Since when did it take you long to fill up on my cooking?"

"You've got me there, Miss Bess," he said as he hugged her once more, this time lifting her feet off the floor.

"Put me down, Jonah Cahill," she demanded between fits of laughter.

"You might be two heads taller than me, but it wasn't that long ago you were nothing but trouble."

"Some would say I still am," he quipped as he released her to follow a step behind as she led him into the dining room.

While Bess scurried to the outdoor kitchen to fetch his meal, Jonah settled on the chair she indicated. His grandfather's chair.

How many times had he seen Grandfather Cahill sit here with his spectacles on the end of his nose and a newspaper in his hands? And how many more times had he seen his father do the exact same thing in their kitchen in Galveston?

Too many to count.

He missed them both dearly at that moment, and that surprised him. But that was one news story the nosy reporter from the *Picayune* would never get.

❤

With only a few minutes to spare, Madeline arrived on the doorstep of McCloskey's Restaurant at Numbers 70 and 72 on St. Charles Street and ducked inside beneath a banner proclaiming their motto: "The best the market affords with prices to suit the times." Immediately she was ushered upstairs to a private family room.

Her hands still shook from her encounter with Jonah. It would not do to allow her brother to see, so she shoved her hands into her pockets as she stepped into the room.

Her brother Phil, technically Phillip Emmanuel Latour IV, had already helped himself to a meal and was dabbing at the corner of his mouth with a napkin as the door closed behind her. Where she had inherited her mother's fair Irish coloring—and some would say temperament—Phil was the image of their olive-skinned father.

"Sit and eat." He reached for a bell to ring for the waiter.

"No time," Madeline replied as she removed her cloak and then snatched a piece of bread from the basket in the center of the table. "I'm due back in half an hour," she said as she liberally applied butter and jam before taking a bite.

"Ah, the secret project," Phil said as he lifted one brow. "Ironic, don't you think, given our family's choice of occupation?"

Madeline chuckled. "You act as if we had any choice in the matter of our occupation."

Truly, choice was never given in regard to the family business. The Latour family had dealt in secrets for three generations, possibly longer, and with the birth of Phil's two sons the business was likely to continue on for at least another generation.

When anyone in New Orleans possessed a great need for discretion, a desire to find something or someone, and a vast amount of money with which to pay, the Latour family was always the first to be consulted on the matter.

Such was their reputation that there was no need to advertise the family's services. Rather, clients came recommended to them by others. Father sent son and mother sent daughter for over a century, most coming from families of bankers, men of commerce, politicians, and several, noble birth.

"I worry about you, Maddie," he said as he sat back to regard her with a measuring look. "What need have you to hide anything? It is just a newspaper article, isn't it?"

It wasn't, but still she ought to have shared the details with Phil. Something held her back, likely the fact that he would either dissuade her or beat her to the answer.

"Patience," she told him. "I promise I will tell you everything just as soon as my research is complete. But I will say that it may turn out to be more than just an article. I just don't know yet. It could be nothing."

Madeline punctuated the statement with a smile that she hoped would convince her nosy older brother that she was sincere. Depending on where the facts led in this investigation, the family might not like the notoriety it would bring.

Maybe she would write the story under a pseudonym. That would be a good discussion to have with Papa when the time came, for proving that Jean Lafitte not only lived after reports of his demise but also married again and survived to an old age would definitely catapult her, and by result the Latours, into the spotlight.

Borrowing a sentiment from Mother, she would cross that bridge when she came to it. She pasted on a smile and took a seat beside Phil within reach of the bread basket.

"All right," he said with a nod. "Then our discussion of your secret project is tabled in favor of the reason we're here, and that's for you to tell me what you've learned about our current client's request."

She waited until Phil retrieved his paper and ink from his case and then began. "It is amazing what men will say to one another when they believe the women are not listening," she told him after she'd given him the facts he needed to respond to railroad heiress Violet Chastain's request to investigate her fiancé's questionable business dealings.

With what she'd found, Mademoiselle Chastain would likely be ending her engagement. It always felt good to be part of something that actually helped someone, in this case seeing that an impressionable young lady did not ruin her life by marrying a man who was obviously only looking to increase his financial worth without telling her he had several other wealthy wives already.

Per their custom, the papers associated with this case were secured in a safe-deposit box. She handed Phil the key and rose just as the door opened and her father stepped inside.

"Papa?" she said as she crossed the distance between them to give him a hug. "I didn't expect you to be here. What a nice surprise."

"Madeline, Latours do not like surprises. It's the nature of our business, yes?" At her frown, the stoic Phillip Latour III actually grinned. "I am teasing you, my darling. Of course I am pleased to see you, although you are mistaken if you believe seeing you here was a surprise to me."

Her father extricated himself from her grasp to nod toward Phil. "I believe you were just leaving, weren't you, son?"

Phil gave Madeline a look, pocketed the key, and then shrugged. "Yes, of course." He winked at Madeline and then said his farewells to them both.

When they were alone, Papa nodded toward the table. "Do sit." She complied, and then he continued. "You know I have been patient with you in regard to your work for the newspaper. Your role as reporter serves the family well. However, do you have anything you wish to tell me?"

Her father never asked that question unless he already knew the response. Madeline paused. Now to decide exactly what her father must have discovered about the real purpose of her investigation into the elusive pirate.

"I just handed over the key for the Chastain documents to Phil, so that assignment is complete. Perhaps you could be more specific?"

Still he looked skeptical. "This widow, Madame Smith, she has no idea you are my daughter?"

Madeline pushed a strand of hair away from her face. "If she does, I would think she might have asked why I was using a different name. So no, I do not believe she knows. Why? Have you heard something in that regard?"

"I have not." Papa shifted positions. "Madeline, I am rarely comfortable when you misrepresent who you are, although I understand your work as a journalist requires it."

"My work with Madame is not only an assignment assisting with her memoirs, but it is also a kindness I hope is someday extended to me."

His thick brows rose. "I certainly hope not. Can you imagine what sort of things would have to be written about you should your memories be recorded?" He chuckled softly. "No, my darling, you are a Latour, and Latours keep their memories and their secrets to themselves. It is something we take very seriously. You know that, yes?"

"Yes," she said. "I know that."

"Good. I only wish you had offered the true identity of the woman for whom you are working."

"I didn't think it would be important," she said, knowing that this was only part of the reason. In fact, she'd feared that had she offered a name, Papa would have researched her and found what Madeline hoped to find—the link to the pirate Lafitte—before she did.

The truth of that shamed her. It would serve her right if he had uncovered the information.

"Have you discovered my employer's identity?" She lifted her gaze and knew he had. Of course.

His smile was surprisingly gentle. "Surely you are not so foolish as to assume I woud not wish to know with whom my only daughter was spending her time."

"What do you know of Madame?" she said carefully. "I ask because after recording some of her memories, I am curious about certain aspects of her life."

"She is from an old and well-respected family. Hers was a love match that her father did not approve. He hired our firm to investigate, and no, you may not see the records. They were destroyed at her father's request upon his death. I only recall because one of my first assignments when I officially joined the firm was to put them in the fire."

"Did you read them first?"

Papa chuckled. "Oh, but you are your father's daughter. No, I did not, but only because my father was standing there to see that I put the sealed papers into the flame."

Madeline sighed. "A pity."

"Indeed. We rarely have requests to burn the files, so I often wondered what might have been discovered had the documents been read. In any case, I have something for you."

He reached into his pocket and pulled out a key that had been threaded onto a thin gold chain. Papa placed it onto her palm and smiled. "This is yours now."

Madeline looked up into his eyes and saw love and kindness there. She glanced down at the key, seeing only the number fourteen. Carefully, her father wrapped her fingers around the key, allowing the chain to hang free.

"My next assignment?" she asked him.

"Eventually," was his cryptic response. "For now, keep this close to you and never take it off, do you understand?"

At her nod, Papa continued. "When the time is right, instructions will be given."

Madeline slipped the chain over her head and tucked the key into the bodice of her dress where it lay hidden from view. One more secret to keep.

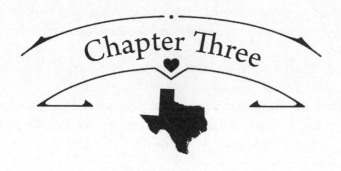

Chapter Three

New Orleans
One week later

"The elusive Miss Latour. Won't you join me?" *New Orleans Picayune* editor Ellis McComb ushered Madeline through the newsroom and into his office. "Where is my article?" he asked as he closed the door on the noise outside.

"About that," she said as confidently as she could manage. "I am still developing leads."

His bushy gray brows rose. "So you're here to beg more time and not to deliver my article?"

Madeline squared her shoulders. "I am here to offer a choice."

"I am listening," Mr. McComb said as he drummed his ink-stained fingers on the top of the papers that littered his desk.

She leaned against the door and recalled the words she'd practiced all the way here. "If you absolutely need an article from me for tomorrow's edition, I can turn in a sweet little story about an old lady who somehow manages to grow pink roses all year around before the end of the day today."

"Or?"

"Or I can deliver the story of the century." She paused to let that idea sink in. "A story that will change history."

Mr. McComb's expression never changed. Instead, he lowered his bulk into the chair behind his desk and steepled his fingers. "When?" he finally said.

"I wish I had a better answer, sir, but I can give you the story when I have all the details and can prove them." She paused. "I have good hunches but nothing to back them up. I couldn't allow the paper to print something so explosive without being absolutely certain of its accuracy."

"Explosive?"

"Yes, sir."

He seemed to be studying his hands. Then Mr. McComb looked up at Madeline. "All right, then. Get me the piece on the pink roses by three this afternoon. That gives you two hours."

Madeline let out the breath she didn't realize she'd been holding. "Really?"

"No. Of course not." He pushed his chair back and stood. "Go get that explosive story, and do not bring it to me until you have the proof of whatever this is."

"I will." She nodded and stepped out into the newsroom. "Thank you, Mr. McComb. You won't be disappointed."

"I'm counting on that. And keep in touch," Mr. McComb called over the noise as Madeline hurried to the door. "I want weekly reports letting me know you're still working on this."

Madeline waved in response and then hurried to her final errand of the day where the clerk at the Caffrey Stationer's Shop handed her the wrapped parcel containing a stack of bound journals that Madame had ordered. Though it had not been her true purposc in taking the position as assistant, Madeline had come to enjoy listening to and recording the old woman's stories over the past few weeks.

From tales of old New Orleans to stories of persons she loved being lost to hurricanes or other disasters, Madame had much she wished to be recorded. It had truly been enthralling to listen to the stories, and an honor to record them for posterity.

"How many of these have you gone through already, mademoiselle?" the kindly stationer's assistant asked.

"Three since I began working for Madame on the last day of

February," she told him as she handed him the payment.

"Perhaps I should offer a discount," he said with a chuckle as Madeline tucked the package under her arm. "I pity you having to do all of that writing," he said as she crossed the distance to the door.

"Madame has led a most interesting life," Madeline replied. "I am finding it fascinating to record it all."

And indeed the stories she had recorded in these journals had been fascinating. Every question led to another story and every story to yet another.

Still, her employer had not broached the one subject that Madeline most wished her to speak about, namely, her suspected connection with the infamous Lafitte brothers. Perhaps today was the day to be more direct with her and ask.

She thought about Papa's news that Latour & Sons had become involved in Madame's life many decades ago. Interesting how life had a way of turning about on itself to form twists and bends that led back to its beginnings. Madeline wondered if Madame knew of this investigation her father had ordered.

Though she wanted to ask, she wouldn't. Pretending not to be a Latour for the good of the investigation was bad enough. She simply could not speak of the Latours as if she knew nothing of them.

By the time Madeline reached the stately residence on Prytania Street, she had made up her mind. If her question angered Madame, then she would apologize and try a different way of asking on another day.

She found Madame in her sitting room, a sheaf of papers laid out before her on the tea table. "Oh, I am sorry," she told her. "I thought I might leave these new journals in here in anticipation of this afternoon's work."

Madame smiled. "I do prattle on, don't I? Come and sit with me. I have news."

Madeline did as she was told, settling onto the settee and adjusting a flower-covered pillow to suit her before placing the bundle of journals beside her. "Perhaps I should get my pen and inks?"

"No, dear. There will be time for that later. I have the most delightful news. These wonderful memories you've been recording have inspired me to find a dear one who was lost to me, my lost treasure, as it were." She paused. "Her name was Trésor, and I failed her once. I will not fail her again."

"I'm sorry, Madame, but I don't understand what that has to do with news."

"Oh, of course. You and I are going to find her. It will require travel, but my Trésor will be found."

Travel. Madeline forced herself to maintain a neutral expression. With Papa urging her to finish her work for Madame and Mr. McComb sending messages asking for updates on her article, this was not the time for travel.

Then there was the question of whether Madame was making an informed choice to go searching for this Trésor. At her age, was she thinking rationally or had her memories caused her to listen to sentiment over reason?

Madame appeared to study her closely. "You're smiling. Is that to cover your discomfort? Do you think I have lost my mind?"

"Not at all," she said quickly.

"But you are concerned," Madame said.

"Perhaps a little," she agreed. "This seems quite sudden."

"And impetuous?" She shook her head. "Perhaps it may seem so, but I have had this adventure in mind for quite some time, and I have hired the services of an expert to help."

"An expert? Well then, might I ask where this adventure is taking us?"

"Oh, of course." Madame grinned and leaned forward as if she was about to offer some secret tidbit. "Galveston Island."

"Galveston?" Madeline imagined the possibility of doing research on her Lafitte theory in the place where the pirate had been in residence some sixty years prior. "I think that's a lovely idea."

Madame paused as if assessing her, dark eyes alight with what appeared to be excitement. "Do you?"

"I do," she said with enthusiasm. "How soon do we leave?"

Her employer laughed. "Soon, but of course there are preparations to be made. You sound excited about this trip. Have you been to Galveston before?"

"Not that I recall."

"Ah, recollections are funny things, aren't they?"

Madeline nodded as she calculated how to bring up the Lafitte brothers. "Will this be your first trip to the island?"

"Oh goodness no. I consider Galveston like a second home to me," she said as she picked up a rose and inhaled its scent. "But it has been far too long since I was there. You look like you want to ask me something."

Madeline's heart raced. Now was the time to turn the conversation toward her reason for being in Madame's employ. "I have heard stories of pirate treasure buried in Galveston, specifically Jean Lafitte's treasure. Do you think those stories are true?"

"Well of course you have heard these stories," Madame said. "A person could not walk down a city street in New Orleans or take a meal in one of our fine dining establishments without hearing such tales. However, I am old enough to know that the truth has been lost in the telling and retelling."

She decided to be more specific. "So you don't believe Monsieur Lafitte left treasure there? Or perhaps he went back for it much later after it was safe to do so."

Madame sat back and regarded her with an expression Madeline could not read. "Much is said of Monsieur Lafitte. Do not believe all of it."

Not the answer Madeline had hoped for. Not an answer at all, really. At least the topic of Lafitte had been broached.

"Perhaps you might set the record straight on Monsieur Lafitte, then. Do you have memories of the pirate that you wish to be included in your memoirs?" She reached over to retrieve the bundle of journals. "Give me just a moment and we can begin."

"Oh my, you are quite curious, are you not?" Madame said with a chuckle.

Madeline stilled her motions and then slowly placed the bundle back on the seat beside her. It would not do to become overzealous and show herself as a reporter in disguise.

"I am. The topic is fascinating." Madeline took a deep breath and let it out slowly, putting on her most contrite expression as she returned her attention to her employer. "I suppose the excitement of this trip is to blame. Please forgive me."

"There is nothing to forgive, my dear."

Madeline offered a smile. "I offer it just the same."

"Then I shall accept." She paused. "You ask if I knew Lafitte, and yet you either must think me much older than I am or must not be aware of the history surrounding him."

"Neither, Madame." Madeline knew that history quite well. "I only wonder if you might have some insight. What he actually did and the details surrounding his supposed death is the subject of much speculation."

"Ah, speculation," she said slowly. "It is an interesting thing, is it not?"

"Well certainly," Madeline said. "But there is often a grain of truth in such speculation."

Madame reached for the bellpull on the wall beside her and called for a servant. A moment later, the maid appeared with a curtsy. "Please make the usual preparations for my departure as we discussed. Mademoiselle will be joining me."

"Certainly," the maid said. "And when will you return?"

Madame Smith winked at Madeline, drawing her back from her musings. "One cannot merely put a closing date on a treasure hunt, can one?"

Treasure hunt. Madeline smiled at the truth in those words, even if her employer was referring to a missing person and not missing coin or baubles. "No," she agreed. "One cannot."

After the maid had gone, Madeline tried again to turn the topic back to Lafitte and Madame's possible shared history with the pirate. "Madame, you did not say whether you wished to dictate any memories regarding Monsieur Lafitte."

"No," Madame said in a most distracted voice. "I did not say, did I? You know, I believe I will have my nap now. Perhaps later we shall speak more of this."

Later. Not the answer she had hoped for but still enough of a promise to allow Madeline to get her hopes up.

She wrote to Mr. McComb letting him know she would be traveling and that she hoped their travels would provide the documentation Madeline was hoping for in regard to her story. Then she made a plan for how she would break the news to her father.

Madeline waited until the day before her departure to finally broach the topic of her upcoming trip with Papa. As expected, he was less than pleased.

"Impossible! I cannot allow it," he fumed as he stared down at Royal Street from his office above the apothecary's. "Not now. Not after. . ."

He turned around slowly. Madeline recognized his expression. "What, Papa?"

Papa hurried to his desk and indicated for her to take a seat across from him. For a moment he shuffled papers until he apparently found what he was looking for.

"There has been a report of questions asked in regard to Latour & Sons," he said as his fingers drummed a rhythm atop the stack of documents. "I wondered at first what the cause might be."

"Perhaps someone heard you had forgotten to add your daughter to the company name?" she quipped.

Ignoring the long-standing jest, her father turned his attention to her. "This is nothing to make light of, Madeline. Questions have been indirectly asked in regard to our business practices in general and our handling of cases in specific."

"But why? We are a good, God-fearing family who run a lawful business and have for a century. We do nothing illegal that would require investigating. All the authorities here in New Orleans know this, many by personal experience."

Papa chuckled, but his laughter held no humor. "Indeed, I brought this to the attention of more than one well-placed friend of our family since I discovered this."

"And?"

He shrugged. "And I was told this was not a matter with which they could offer help, although every one of them did commiserate and offer to stand up in our defense."

"I do not understand," she said. "Then who is investigating?"

"It is assumed to be the Pinkerton Detective Agency. As yet I have not learned the name of the person paying for their services, but rest assured I will." He paused. "So perhaps your trip with the widow woman is well timed. The Lord, He makes plans that we do not always understand, you know."

"I do," she said. "But I am concerned for you and Phil."

"Do not be," he said as he waved his hand over his desk. "Let them investigate. As you say, we have nothing to hide other than our client list. That list and the details of cases associated with it, we protect with our lives."

"Of course," she said.

Papa stilled his movements and seemed to be contemplating something on the opposite wall. Slowly he began to nod. "Yes, of course. You shall go with this woman, Madame Smith. You have the key, yes?"

"I do," she said as she lifted the chain from its hiding place to show the key still attached.

"Good." He rose to come around the desk and then offered his hand to help Madeline to her feet. "I wish for you more than a life as a reporter and scribe to a widowed woman," he told her. "I wish a husband for you."

His statement stunned her. "Whatever would you say that for?" she asked. "I am perfectly content working for the *Picayune*. Once Madame's memoirs are complete, I will return to do more work for you. So no, Papa, I do not need a marriage."

Her father smiled. "So I said when the Lord brought me your mother."

She patted his hand and returned his grin. "Someday, Papa," she said. "When I am ready."

"When the Lord is ready," he corrected. "Now, go on and gather your things. Your mother will be planning a nice meal tonight to say goodbye."

Madeline thought of all the travel preparations that remained undone and stifled a sigh. A nice meal, as Papa termed it, meant hours of cooking, hours of eating, and a table filled with every Latour family member within twenty miles.

Making a quick exit, she turned down Royal Street toward home. Papa's warning about the Pinkerton investigation stalled her steps.

She had seen Pinkerton detective Jonah Cahill not so long ago. It appeared he had been visiting his late grandfather's home, but was Colonel Cahill's death the real reason the irritating detective was in the city? Given their shared past history, he certainly had reason enough to cause trouble for the Latour family, but did he dare sink so low?

As yet, she did not know, but Madeline Latour was not raised to let questions go unanswered.

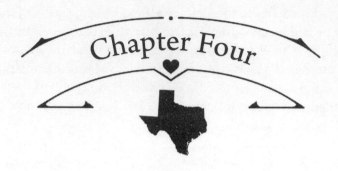

Chapter Four

Galveston, Texas
One week later

Some sixty years after Jean Lafitte fled Galveston Island at the strong behest of the United States Navy, Pinkerton agent Jonah Cahill stood on the property that once held the ruins of the pirate's home and waited to feel something. Anything.

While he waited, he looked out over the now-lush garden of the dwelling the pirate had audaciously painted bright red—the better to challenge those with weapons trained upon it—and settled his gaze on the bay beyond. Something startled snowy egrets fishing along the shoreline, causing them to launch upward against the wind on a backdrop of cloudless blue sky. A moment later they landed some twenty yards downstream and resumed their search for their next meals.

This side of the island faced the mainland, but the bay's depth and width gave it the same feel as the brown Gulf of Mexico on the other side. The only difference was the lack of sandy beaches here, the shoreline filled with marshes instead.

Jonah turned to face that wind, placing his back to the bay and his attention on the home in front of him. Finally his feelings thawed. He was home. Or at least he'd returned to the place where he'd been born and raised.

The place that, at least in part, made him who he had become.

Though all that remained of that daring red house, allegedly filled to the rafters with ill-gotten treasures and topped by cannon turrets, was the cellar and foundation that now sat beneath a rather modern and stately home, rumors abounded that Lafitte had left something of himself behind in hopes of returning.

This sentiment he understood.

The three-story frame building was a rather unassuming structure when compared to his maternal grandfather's grand residence on Broadway Avenue or his paternal grandfather's New Orleans home, but its pedigree as having possible pirate treasure buried on its grounds served to set it apart from any other home on the island. This fact had earned him instant admiration from his childhood friends.

Ahead of his time, Jonah's father built the home with the main living spaces on the second floor and the bedrooms a floor above. This not only gave protection from the high water that occasionally flooded the property, but it also allowed for a bird's-eye view from Jonah's third-floor window and ample space on the dirt-covered first floor to dig for pirate treasures.

His had been a unique upbringing for an island boy. Like all the others who grew up around him, his had been a life mostly spent at or on the ocean. Mama never verified Father's repeated statement that owing to their seafaring life, Jonah was named after the biblical character who ended up inside a whale. Rather, she would merely laugh.

And yet, unlike those other boys, he also had the benefit of a maternal grandfather named Asa Henderson whose first devotion was to science. Mathematics came in a close second, and all else including family trailed somewhere after. A minor celebrity in the city, Asa Henderson was hired by the Congress of the Republic of Texas to survey this land and create its symmetrical grid of streets and alleys.

At Grandfather Henderson's side, Jonah learned several things. Chief among them was the lesson of creating a straight line, the importance of walking a straight line, and the ability to see that not everyone agreed with the first two lessons. If pressed to admit it, those long hours spent in the dour old man's presence shaped his career as a Pinkerton more than any other.

Father taught him to fish and hunt, to live off the land and pilot any seagoing vessel. He also taught him to catch the delicious blue crabs that skittered about just beneath the water. Thanks to his father, Jonah was always well prepared for whatever situation he found himself in.

Jonah lifted his nose to the familiar scent of salt air and frying chicken as it drifted past on the wind. On cue, his stomach growled, and he checked his watch. Likely Mama was supervising work in the kitchen about now.

In his mind, Mama never aged when he thought of her. She had given him a different upbringing from the men who had shaped him. Her legacy then, as now, was to instill in him a strong sense of right and wrong and a strong desire to do something about injustice.

He suspected it might be something in her past that set his mama on such a crusader's path, but Jonah was never able to discover exactly what that was. Instead, he soaked in her stories of society and propriety, and in turn, she patiently stood by as he ignored them.

"You there."

Jonah turned toward the sound and spied a fair-haired man of average height and slender build hurrying toward him. There had been a time when he knew everyone on this island, but with the growth of the city's population, that was no longer true. Thus, he assessed the stranger as he would anyone he encountered in the course of his investigations.

By the time he arrived at the edge of Cahill property, the stranger's face was flushed despite the coolness of the spring temperatures. When the man reached into his pocket, Jonah instinctually placed his palm on his revolver.

Instead of a weapon, the stranger withdrew a small notebook and then lifted his attention to give Jonah a direct look. "You're a Pinkerton man, aren't you?"

Rather than respond, Jonah casually shifted back his coat just enough to show his revolver. To his credit, the stranger took a step backward.

"I'm sorry, Detective. Where are my manners?" He stuck out his free hand. "Walt Townsend," he said in a most agreeable tone, though his expression had gone wary. "You see, because I am relatively new to this fair city I pay a modest fee to the railroad folks for information on any stranger of interest who arrives on the island. Fortunately, I happened to be at the station when you arrived. Purely coincidence, but fortuitous, don't you think?"

"Do I know you, Mr. Townsend?" Jonah said as he ignored the man's outstretched hand but took note of the fact that he wore a gold signet ring and kept his hands clean and free of calluses.

"Well, I don't suppose you would." He gave up on trying to shake hands and shrugged instead. "As I said, I am new to Galveston, but do have extensive credentials elsewhere."

Jonah stood his ground. Either this man was selling something or he didn't have the good sense to realize he wasn't speaking to a man who enjoyed conversations with strangers.

"Yes, well, perhaps I should just get to the point," he said, his tone flustered. "I am currently in the employ of the *Galveston Daily News*. Perhaps you've read my work. Just yesterday I managed an insightful article on the reasons a fellow kicked a dog—it bit him—and on the arrest of that cotton broker fellow who swindled his boss."

A nosy reporter. A Pinkerton agent's worst nightmare. Jonah continued to stare. He said nothing.

The newspaperman tugged at his collar. "Yes, well, in that capacity I did some investigating and discovered a Pinkerton man had set foot in our fair city via this morning's train. I must wonder if your arrival in Galveston coincides with the recent criminal mischief at this address."

Jonah frowned but remained silent. Susanna hadn't written him about any incidents. He had to assume this man was fishing for information by throwing out facts that were anything but.

Townsend's eyes narrowed as a smile rose. "Oh, I get it. You can't say anything about an ongoing case." He winked. "You know, I thought of going the Pinkerton route. Didn't work out for me. Seems like once I find something out I must share it. Makes me a good reporter but a lousy lawman."

"As does expounding at length on dangerous topics. Or claiming facts that are untrue."

Whether the reporter understood Jonah's veiled threat was not certain. However, it was clear the man was not done talking.

"However, I do think there's a story here. I do hope you will agree and assist me." Townsend paused. "I cannot offer much reward for information, but I have a personal stipend from my own accounts that I can spend at my own discretion."

The sound of a door opening behind him caught his attention. Jonah ignored the reporter to look over his shoulder up to the top of the second-floor steps where his sister now stood in the doorway.

"Tell me what you know, Mr. Townsend," he said without looking away from Susanna.

"Actually, I was hoping you could tell me," he said. "Oh, look, Miss Cahill. Have you reconsidered my offer?"

Jonah turned back to stare down at Townsend. "What offer have you made to Miss Cahill?"

"Just to report her side of the story," he managed, though his voice did not hold steady. "My sources say local law enforcement is keeping this quiet, but if there's some sort of lunatic pestering these good people, then I believe it is the citizens' right to know lest one of them becomes the next victim."

"Leave," Jonah said through clenched jaw. "Now. And do not return."

"Well, I cannot promise that, Detective," he said with a nervous chuckle. "You see, I've got a job to do, and as part of that job I really must investigate the claims I've heard regarding events at this home. The pirate Jean Lafitte once owned it. Did you know that?"

Wonderful. Yet another outsider looking to capitalize on the Lafitte name.

"Go," Jonah said again, this time punctuating his demand by leaning just close enough to give the reporter an idea of exactly how angry he was getting.

"Please consider contacting me, Miss Cahill," he called to Susanna as he took two steps backward. "I have informed Officer Pearson that I will be assisting him in this matter, so speaking to me would be the same as speaking to him. Perhaps you would like to come down here and consent to an interview?"

Behind him, Jonah heard the unmistakable sound of a weapon being cocked. Susanna apparently wanted the reporter gone as well.

"Do as he says and go," Susanna said. "I'll speak to Officer Pearson myself should I have the need to do so."

"Mr. Townsend," Jonah said as he barely held his temper in check. "You have been warned. Should you ignore this final request to leave, I promise you will regret it."

Townsend appeared ambivalent and then a moment later hurried away. Jonah turned around to see his sister aiming her shotgun at the reporter, obviously keeping him in her sights until he disappeared around the corner.

"Welcome home, Jonah," she called with a laugh. "Better come inside before I have to shoot someone."

"As long as it is him and not me, I just might look the other way."

"I've missed you," Susanna said as she stepped back to allow Jonah inside. His sister, younger by five years, got more beautiful every time he saw her. While he had inherited his dark hair and silver eyes from the Cahills, Susanna was the image of their beautiful mother with honey-colored hair and dark blue eyes.

Though she was easily as good as he at handling a gun, the fact that she'd been frightened by some sort of criminal activity infuriated him. "Tell me what Townsend was asking about," he demanded as Susanna closed the door.

"Hush," she told him, setting the rifle aside. "Mama does not need to hear about this."

"But I do," he said softly. "What happened?"

She shrugged. "Nothing of any consequence. My guess is fools looking for pirate treasure again. There were a few holes in the ground."

Jonah knew his sister well enough to know she hadn't told him the entire truth. "There is more," he said. "What else has happened? I seriously doubt a reporter would be worried about holes dug on the property."

"Of course that one would," Susanna quickly responded. "Just yesterday he managed twelve paragraphs on a dog bite. Twelve," she repeated.

"So he mentioned, and yet I still don't believe you." Jonah studied her. "What else has happened, Susanna?"

"Is that my son I hear?" his mother called from somewhere in the interior of the house.

"Do not say a word to her, Jonah," Susanna whispered. "She does not need to worry about this."

Jonah gave her a doubtful look. "Once I have heard the entire story, I will decide what, if anything, I will tell her."

"I'm afraid so, Mama," Susanna said. "I pulled the rifle out, but Jonah got past me."

"Oh, you two." His mother hurried into the room to envelop him in an embrace. "I have missed you so, Jonah. Come now, Cook is making your favorite meal. I know you must be starved."

"It can't be fried chicken, can it?" he said, although he knew good and well that was exactly what would be on the menu. It always was when he came home to Galveston.

"All right now," she said as she released Jonah to hold him at arm's length. "Let me look at you. Oh, my son, you have not been eating well up in Chicago. I can see it. Come and let's eat."

Funny how her words echoed the ones Bess said to him on his visit to New Orleans. Much as he knew he was a blessed man, apparently the Lord had also seen fit to give him women in his life whose sole purpose was to feed him.

"Happily," he told her as he offered Susanna a smile.

Jonah followed the Cahill women into the dining room where a meal—more like a banquet for visiting royalty—awaited. Before he could protest, his plate was filled to overflowing and his family had joined him to enjoy the meal.

"I was in New Orleans on business recently," he said when the conversation lulled. "I stopped by Grandfather Cahill's house."

Mama set her fork down. "Has he finally succumbed?"

"To what, Mama?" Susanna asked. "Have you managed to get a response from all of those letters you sent him?"

"Whatever it was that the Lord decided to take him with," she said, eyes glistening. "And no, he never did respond to any of them. Not even when I wrote of your father's passing. He was a hard man to love but I did love him, as did your father."

"To answer your question, yes he has passed on, but not so long ago. Earlier in the spring," Jonah said gently. "Yellow fever was the cause according to Madeline."

"I see." She lifted the linen napkin to her eyes. "I do hope he took care of Bess. She was always loyal to him."

"She said he did," Jonah told her. "And she is doing well."

"Well, good." Mama rose. "Would you excuse me just a moment? I believe I have something in my eye. I will be right back."

"Goodness knows that old man was not kind to her," Susanna said. "But she never gave up on him."

"It is a lesson we all should learn." With Mama gone, Jonah seized the moment. "All right, tell me, Susanna. What else has happened?"

She looked over in the direction that Mama had disappeared and then returned her attention to Jonah. "The cellar shows signs of an intruder. We don't know if this happened just once or whether several attempts have been made."

"We?" he managed as he absorbed the news.

"Yes, while I refuse to frighten Mama, I did feel it was prudent to alert Officer Pearson. He investigated and has also been quite kind to patrol the area regularly ever since."

Jonah knew the man to whom she referred, and he was a good lawman, trustworthy and capable. Still, when it came to his mother and sister, there was no one who would care for their safety as well as he would.

He made a note to talk to Pearson tomorrow.

"And what was his suggestion to you? Does he think this was an isolated incident?"

She shrugged. "He suggested we change the locks and fortify the door and then offered to help. I agreed to allow it but made him promise he will come for dinner in payment."

Jonah nodded. "Pearson is a good man. I'm grateful he was able to help. I will have to thank him personally." He paused. "Believing we lived on top of buried treasure was good fun when we were children, but no one here really believes there's anything left of it. Why would Lafitte burn his home if he left treasure in the cellars? Does Pearson believe this rubbish?"

"No."

"But Townsend is curious. Has he been asking questions that have made interest in this topic rise again?"

"It's possible," she said. "I know he has been asking questions of me, so I assume he's asking elsewhere too. With him, it is hard to tell what he knows and what he is merely guessing at."

"Whether Townsend is involved or not, I am concerned," he said softly as he heard his mother's footsteps indicating her imminent return. "I will get to the bottom of this."

"And that is what makes you such a good Pinkerton detective." Susanna put on a smile as her mother entered the dining room.

"What is this I hear about your brother and the Pinkertons?" Mama regarded Jonah with a curious expression. "Have you finally come to your senses and left the Pinkertons? Is that why you have decided to return home to Galveston?"

Jonah chuckled. At some point during each visit, his mother would make an attempt to keep her only son within reach. Generally she would rail against the risks of the job, the excessive travel, and the fact that he had to associate with undesirables. Sometimes she flat-out told him she missed him. At least she'd broached the topic early in his visit this time instead of making him wait.

"With your permission, I will be staying here while I see to a matter I've been called in to investigate," he said. "I expect to be here a few weeks, perhaps less but not likely more. So no, I have neither come to my senses nor left the Pinkertons."

She shook her head. "Well, I had my hopes, but of course I do understand. You were meant for this life you have, son, and only the Lord can change you."

Jonah shook his head. "So you have given up praying for a change of career for me?"

"Not at all," she said, her blue eyes twinkling. "I have merely given up waiting for the Lord to act and begun expecting it."

"Then let us pray the Lord hurries," Susanna quipped as they all laughed.

Later, however, after the dishes had been cleared and Mama had gone out to the market to purchase yet more food for the next meal,

Jonah asked Susanna to show him exactly where the holes had been dug.

There were four, one in each corner of the back part of the property. "None of these are deep. My guess is the fools were either interrupted or decided there was no treasure to be had here."

"Either is possible," Susanna said.

"Now show me how you discovered the criminals had been inside the cellars."

Susanna led him to the back of the house where the cellar door bore deep gouges and one hinge appeared to be ruined. Stepping inside the murky darkness of the cellar, Jonah reached for the oil lamp hanging on the post by the door and lit it.

As the light blazed and an orange glow settled over the cellar, Jonah spied what appeared to be the beginnings of a hole near the easternmost wall. Apparently the idiots had been interrupted in their endeavors, because the shovel they used was still leaning against the wall.

"This doesn't belong down here, does it?" Jonah asked Susanna.

"No, I have never seen this shovel."

Jonah nodded. This would go into evidence tomorrow. For now, he would bring the tool upstairs to keep it from disappearing or being used again. He would also see that the cellar door was repaired before he laid his head on his pillow tonight.

"Exactly when did you last have to call out Officer Pearson?"

"Three days ago," she admitted.

"And have you seen anything suspicious since?"

She looked up at him, her expression serious. "I do find this particular hairstyle you're now wearing suspicious. I wonder why you chose it."

As Susanna giggled, Jonah felt his anger rising. "Stop," he managed. "You really need to take this seriously. Strangers with a shovel have been digging down here, likely while you and Mama were asleep upstairs. Have you not considered they could have chosen to walk in the back door and accost both of you rather than choose to do their damage in the cellar?"

She hadn't. Even in the dim light, he could see the sudden realization on her face.

"Townsend will have to be made to keep his nose out of this and his reports out of the paper," he said.

"There is no crime in writing newspaper stories." She paused to chuckle. "A pity when it comes to Mr. Townsend."

"True, but when those stories incite criminal activity, that becomes an entirely different situation." At his sister's skeptical look, he shook his head. "Don't worry. I will handle this."

"Thank you," she said softly.

Jonah snatched up the shovel and escorted his sister to the door. "It's what I do, you know."

Chapter Five

Jonah walked into the Galveston Police Department headquarters with a shovel and a bad attitude. He had been up most of the night deciding how best to handle the issue of the threat to Cahill property and possibly Cahill lives once he left Galveston.

If anyone were to truly find treasure on the grounds, they certainly would not take well to Mama or Susanna interrupting them. And if anything happened to either of them, Jonah would never forgive himself.

Officer Pearson ushered Jonah to a desk situated beneath an open eastern-facing window and piled high with papers that shifted each time a breeze drifted through. Jonah took a seat across from the police officer and waited until Pearson had cleared a spot and retrieved pen and paper.

"First, thank you for seeing to the issue at my mother's home," Jonah said. "Your presence was of great relief to my sister."

"Just doing my job," he said, "although I am happy to hear that I was able to ease your sister's mind about her safety. She's a very nice lady, and I don't like to think of her and your mother in danger." He looked away and cleared his throat then nodded toward the shovel now leaning against the edge of his desk. "So you've got new evidence?"

"Discovered yesterday by me during the course of my review of the crime scene," he said. "Susanna has confirmed that this shovel does not belong on the property, so I'm turning it over to you to be processed as evidence."

Pearson rose to examine the shovel while Jonah described the location where he found the garden tool. "Don't see any identifying marks on this." He looked over at Jonah. "It will be difficult to identify an owner."

"Yes," Jonah said, "but it is evidence all the same. What can you tell me about your investigation thus far?"

Officer Pearson returned to his chair and regarded Jonah with a serious expression. "I've got trespassing and property damage charges pending against the perpetrator or perpetrators. With your evidence and testimony, I can add breaking and entering and another count of property damage."

"If the culprit turns out to be Townsend, you can add harassment and irritating a Pinkerton agent."

Officer Pearson chuckled as he leaned back in his chair. "Townsend's a little enthusiastic, but he's harmless. Once he's been on the island for a while he will settle down and figure out how things are done here."

"I am going to have to respectfully disagree. Just the amount of irritation he caused me in the few minutes I had the unfortunate experience of meeting him has to be worth jail time."

"I will admit he's a trial when he corners you, but until I have proof he's more than just annoying, I cannot consider him a suspect in anything that's happened to your family." He let out a long breath. "However, I'll see that he understands to stay away from your mother and sister. Will that help?"

"Thank you," Jonah said. "Is there anything else I need to know about what's happened at my family home?"

The police officer seemed reluctant to respond. Finally he shrugged. "There is one thing that you should consider. Miss Cahill told me she did not believe anything had been taken, only that holes had been dug."

"Yes, that is true."

"Have you considered the possibility that whoever dug those holes has found something and that is why he keeps coming back?"

He had not. And yet, it was certainly something to think about. Finding treasure at the bottom of one of those holes would be a good reason to return and dig more. Of course, so was finding nothing.

"Every child I knew dug in that yard. My guess is the same happened in my father's time. Nobody ever found a thing. However, what is your opinion?" Jonah asked him.

"Truth is, I haven't formed one yet, Detective. There's just too little information and too many options." He shrugged. "I'd welcome any help, but you do have my word I will keep this case a top priority."

Jonah rose. "I appreciate that."

Officer Pearson stood but seemed hesitant to say goodbye. "Was there anything else?" Jonah asked.

The police officer glanced around before returning his attention to Jonah. "I wonder if you'd like me to keep an eye on Miss Cahill and your mother until whoever's been digging over there is found."

"I appreciate that, Officer Pearson, but owing to a Pinkerton assignment I have taken on here in Galveston, I will be staying there and should be able to watch over my mother and sister just fine."

His smile dissolved. "I see. Well, if you need some assistance, you know where to find me."

"I appreciate that. I'll let you know anything else I find that might help." Jonah took two steps toward the door and then realized what had just happened. Unless he missed his guess—and he rarely did—Officer Pearson was looking for a way to spend more time with his sister.

Susanna had spent all her time taking care of Mama since their father died. Maybe it was time for her to find a little happiness. And who better than another lawman to be the fellow who captured her heart?

Jonah turned around. Officer Pearson was still watching him.

"You know," Jonah said as he returned to his spot beside the desk. "I start work on a new investigation tomorrow. With my responsibilities to the Pinkertons keeping me busy at all hours of the day, and possibly the evening as well, I wonder if I might ask a favor of you. I wonder if you might look in on my mother and sister. Just to be certain all is well."

"Sure," he said, his expression brightening. "It would be an honor, Detective Cahill."

"Under the circumstances, maybe you ought to call me Jonah."

He grinned. "Then you'll call me Thomas."

"All right, Thomas, thank you."

As Jonah walked away, he couldn't help but grin. Susanna would either be very happy with him or completely irritated.

Either way, it would be fun to watch.

His mission complete, Jonah stepped out into the midmorning sunshine and then stopped short. Was that Madeline Latour going into the T. Ratto & Company Confectioners?

❤

Madeline's sweet tooth led her into the confectioner's shop even as good sense told her she should first complete her mission to mail a letter to Papa. She hadn't corresponded with him since she sent him the telegram letting him know she had arrived safely.

The interior of T. Ratto & Company Confectioners was filled from top to bottom with sugary treats of every type. To her left, a long counter ran the length of the shop with a mirror on the wall behind it. Displays of Crown and Messina oranges and Messina lemons were stacked on the counter near the cash register, and a display of bottles of fruit essences lined the shelves behind them.

The smell of cakes baking competed with the fragrance of sugar candies and roasting peanuts. Madeline inhaled deeply and then smiled.

The shop was thick with customers, and a dark-haired gentleman with an accent that sounded vaguely Italian was speaking with a housewife in an animated tone.

The door closed behind Madeline with a jingle made by a string of silver bells affixed to the doorknob.

"Good morning, young lady," he called. "I'll see to you once I've helped these kind folks."

"I am in no hurry. There are far too many choices, and I will need a few minutes to decide."

The Italian fellow went back to his customer while Madeline slipped past a pair of well-fed matrons and a harried mother trying to corral two young boys. The bells on the door jangled again as the boys began playing tag around their mother's skirts. One of the matrons walked toward her, causing Madeline to step out of her way behind a display of tea cakes.

She stepped back into the aisle, her eyes on a presentation of rock candy on the counter. So intent was her focus that she did not see the Pinkerton agent until he stood between her and her intended treat.

"Hello, Madeline."

She gasped and took a step backward, colliding with the display of tea cakes. Detective Cahill reached around her to steady the table, placing him far too near. She ducked under his arm and hurried past the boys and their mother to emerge onto the street.

Her heart racing, Madeline spent just a moment debating whether to duck into the post office and complete the mission that brought her to this part of the city or to hurry back to the home Madame had rented in hopes that Jonah Cahill would not catch her first. Unfortunately, she spent too long trying to decide.

"Hello, Jonah," she said when he stepped out into the sunshine and caught up to her on the sidewalk.

Without responding, the Pinkerton grabbed her elbow and escorted her away from the busy sidewalk and into the shadows of the alley around the corner. She might have avoided the private conversation by crying out in protest, but truly she was as intrigued regarding why Detective Cahill was in Galveston as she was annoyed that he might pose a threat to her investigation and employment with Madame.

Rather than tip her own hand, Madeline followed quietly and then waited for the angry expression on Jonah's face to translate to action—and conversation. While she waited, she pasted on a smile.

The better to irritate him, for a man in the throes of anger was a man who tended to speak before thinking. And men who spoke before thinking were a reporter's best source of information.

She considered retrieving her notebook and pen from her reticule then decided against it. Anything he said, she would have to commit to memory. It was far too dangerous to have a notebook containing important information pertinent to her Lafitte investigation near the hands of the last man she wanted to see it.

It was quiet here, the shadows cool and the scent decidedly more green and earthy than the nearby street. Sounds of horses clopping past mingled with snippets of conversation as they drifted by on the salt-scented breeze.

It reminded her a bit of the New Orleans courtyard where they had shared their first kiss. The thought jarred her, as did the Pinkerton's nearness.

Jonah released her and then began to pace. "Why are you following me?" he demanded.

"Following you?" She laughed. "You're the one who is following me, Jonah Cahill. First in New Orleans and now here. What is it exactly that you want from me?"

"The truth of why you are here in Galveston, Madeline." He halted his pacing and stood in front of her. Oh, but he was a handsome man, particularly so at this moment.

But he was Jonah Cahill, and they had a shared history. Worse, if Papa was correct in his theory that the Pinkertons were investigating Latour & Sons, then Jonah Cahill might actually be investigating her part in the family business.

Madeline smiled in spite of herself. "Jonah, you flatter me," she said as she watched those beautiful silver eyes lock on hers. "Why in the world would I want to follow you anywhere, let alone to an alley in Galveston? And remember, you're the one who found me. I was innocently shopping for a sweet treat when you barged in with your histrionics."

His dark brows rose. Like her, there was French blood flowing in his veins. Unlike her, that blood and its resulting disposition gave him quite the temper.

"Histrionics?" he managed. "I have been accused of many things, but that is a first."

"See," she said gently, "you're proving my point. My father, he is the same way. Accuse him of losing his temper, and he will have the same kind of fit you are having now. All the pacing and bluster, it is quite irritating but I manage to bear it. But you know that."

"Noble of you," he said through clenched jaw. "You haven't answered my question. Why are you following me? Are you here on business related to the *Picayune*?"

Madeline thought of several responses, none of which would get her out of this alley and away from the frustrating man as quickly as she wished. Rather, she smiled sweetly up at the one man who could ruin her

Lafitte investigation by being far too interested in her business here in Galveston and said the one thing she hoped would quench his curiosity.

"I am not following you, Jonah, although I do not doubt whatever brings you to Galveston would likely be interesting enough to write about. I am here as the guest of a woman for whom I have been doing some work."

"Who is this woman?"

Madeline pushed an errant strand of hair away from her face. "Jonah, unless you can give me a good reason for betraying that confidence, I am not going to answer that."

He squared his shoulders like a gunfighter waiting to pull his gun. "I could easily find out."

"Well of course you can," she said, doing her best not to consider the fact that he just might do that. "But what would be the purpose? I assure you my time in Galveston will be spent on pursuits that have nothing to do with you or the Pinkerton Detective Agency."

Madeline let out a long breath. Now maybe he would leave her alone. Then a thought occurred.

She paused to allow him to digest the information and then continued, her tone sweet and light. "So I might ask of you, why are you here in Galveston? Is there something I ought to be writing about for the *Picayune*?"

Jonah's change of expression told Madeline the question had hit its mark. "Do not cross me again, Madeline."

"I have no intention of crossing you, Jonah. In fact, my intention at this moment is to return to the confectioner's and pay for those tea cakes you knocked over."

"You will do nothing of the sort." He shook his head. "Look, if you are truly on the island for the reasons you've said, then I hope you enjoy your time here."

"Thank you."

"But if you have not been telling me the truth, I will find out soon."

"I have no doubt," she said even as she hoped he would not. "So shall we go back to the confectioner's and finish our business there? Or did you have more threats and ultimatums to deliver?"

Jonah almost smiled. "I think I've delivered all the ultimatums I need to deliver this morning. As to threats? No. Consider those promises."

Madeline managed a nod and a grin that she hoped would cover the lurch in her stomach. When would she learn that Jonah Cahill was not a man to be toyed with? Nor was he a man whose kisses she would forget anytime soon.

If only she hadn't just recalled them.

Using her best finishing school posture, Madeline turned her back on the Pinkerton agent and made her way up the alley to the street beyond. Turning right, she opened the door to T. Ratto & Company Confectioners and stepped inside with all the dignity of a woman who had not just been hauled out on the arm of an angry detective.

The shop was quiet now, the matrons and the woman and her sons having gone. Madeline gave thanks that none of those who witnessed their spectacle were here to see her return.

Before the door could close, Jonah followed her inside. He and the owner, Mr. Ratto, exchanged greetings, first in Italian and then in English. Madeline noticed the tea cake display had been repaired with no signs of any bad conduct having happened there.

"Two tea cakes and a peppermint please," she said, ignoring the fact that Jonah now stood directly behind her.

"Put that on my account," Jonah said as Mr. Ratto wrapped Madeline's purchases.

"Do no such thing," Madeline responded.

"Ignore her," the detective demanded as he reached around to set another tea cake on the counter. "And add this to the amount."

Madeline pulled her coins from her pocket and set them on the counter. "I will pay for his as well."

Mr. Ratto looked back and forth between Jonah and Madeline and then shook his head and threw up his hands. "Out. Both of you. And take your coins, young lady," he said as he handed her the coins along with her wrapped treats.

Jonah said something in Italian and then added in English, "I insist."

The confectioner would not be convinced. "Neither of you will pay me, do you hear? Now go, both of you. Carry on your flirtation elsewhere."

"I assure you flirtation is the last thing on my mind with this man," Madeline corrected. "Now if you will not take my coins, might I open an account?"

"Not today," Mr. Ratto told her. "Perhaps next time. Now go." He reached past her to hand Jonah his wrapped tea cake. "Before I call the law on the both of you."

The twinkle in his eyes gave away the confectioner's true feelings. However, he was insistent they leave, even to walking to the front door and opening it. "Hurry away, you two, before I change my mind and charge you both double."

"Thank you," she said. "But I promise I will be back."

"Not today, you won't. Young lovers plague me," he muttered as Madeline walked past.

"But we are not—"

"Go," Jonah told her as he pressed his palm to her back and urged her out onto the sidewalk. "It's useless to argue with Mr. Ratto. I've been losing arguments to him for longer than I care to admit."

"Well then," she said as she tucked the wrapped package into her bag. "It has been interesting, Jonah."

Once again, she straightened her backbone and walked away from Jonah Cahill. As before, she could feel him watching as she walked away.

So great was her distraction that Madeline walked right past the post office and was a full block down the street before she realized her error and turned around. By then, Jonah was gone.

She briefly considered going back into the confectioner's shop and attempting to pay Mr. Ratto. Instead, she decided to heed Jonah's advice and give up.

Giving up on learning what the Pinkerton detective was doing in Galveston, however, was something she would not consider.

Chapter Six

Jonah sat in the parlor of Mrs. Smith's rented home on Broadway Avenue and waited for her to join him. Like her New Orleans parlor, this room was also filled with vases of pink roses. Unlike the other parlor, the roses did not extend to the wallpaper or furniture cushions.

From where he sat, Jonah could see the Browns' home just down the block. Former president Ulysses Grant would grace the family with a visit next week, but today the grounds were quiet and the gardeners were busy pruning and prettying up the place.

With his maternal grandfather's home just a few blocks away, Jonah had spent many happy hours playing like savages with the Brown boys. While they were given the run of the expansive grounds to whoop and holler and do as they wished, the sacred space of Mrs. Brown's rose garden was forbidden territoy.

"Good morning, Detective Cahill."

Jonah rose to greet Mrs. Smith. Rather than looking tired from her journey, his elderly client appeared fresh as the roses surrounding her. "Good morning, Mrs. Smith," he said as he helped settle her on her chair and then offered her a rose-covered quilt for her lap.

"Don't fuss over me, Detective Cahill," she told him even as her smile clearly told him she enjoyed his attention. "Please sit and tell me what you've learned."

What he had learned was this sweet elderly lady had paid dearly to send him on a fruitless search for a person who might not exist. However, he would not give up so soon.

"The trail for this woman, if indeed she existed, is very cold."

"She did exist, and I agree, it is," she said, her bright eyes assessing him. "That is why I specified the agency send you. I followed the McRee case closely."

His gut lurched at the mention of the court case that not only nearly lost him his job, but also lost him the woman he thought he would marry. "I was almost thrown in jail," he reminded her.

Thanks to a nosy reporter who ferreted out secrets that the judge thought had come from him. The same nosy reporter who'd decided to plague him again.

"Yes, but you got the job done, and that is what counts." She paused to pick at a thread on the quilt and then swung her gaze up to meet his. "Do you not agree?"

A year ago, he might have said yes. Now he was not so sure.

"You look ambivalent, Detective Cahill," she said. "Do you not still believe any means to an end is appropriate?"

"I believe that every decision has consequences."

"Well done," she said. "You and I shall agree on that point. Now as to the matter at hand. You've had time to read and analyze the file."

"I have." He shifted positions. "I have not yet gone to Indianola to investigate that lead, but I plan to do that in the coming week." At her nod, he continued. "You offer a birth date for your son Samuel Smith, which I was able to confirm. Samuel allegedly married—"

"Not allegedly," she corrected. "I was there. It was quite legitimate, that wedding."

"Yes, all right," he said, deciding not to argue the point. "Samuel's wife Eliza, I find no concrete evidence she ever existed. No birth records, marriage record, or death records."

"I'm sure you'll be tired of hearing me say this, but she lived, I promise. Perhaps you would like a look at our family Bible?"

"Very much so," he said.

Mrs. Smith nodded. "I will send you word when my maid has unpacked it from my trunks."

"Thank you." Jonah leaned forward. "Now I'm afraid this is where the story gets complicated. You say Eliza Smith's daughter, named Trésor, was born in Galveston on the 18th or 19th of September in 1855, but I can find no record of a female Smith child born on either day. I looked for several weeks in either direction and found nothing to correspond to our missing person."

"I sense that is not all you have to tell me," Mrs. Smith said.

"No, it's not. I spoke to an old-timer in the city records department who recalls a hurricane coming through about that time. He says it is possible that is why there are no records of the birth."

"Yes, that could well be true. But there is more, I can tell."

Jonah frowned. He hated to give this nice old lady bad news, but a hurricane followed by a yellow fever epidemic, as the gentleman explained had happened, certainly lowered the odds that a child would survive.

"There were fevers after," he said gently. "Many died."

"And you think my granddaughter may have been among them." She gave him a sideways look. "Does that mean you are giving up the case already?"

"Not at all." He considered his next statement and decided to speak plainly. "Mrs. Smith, I will see this case to its end, but as of now, I cannot find any evidence that your granddaughter existed."

To his surprise, the elderly woman laughed. "Oh my," she said. "You are so very forthright. I do believe we will get along just fine."

"You understand it is possible there is no granddaughter to find."

Her expression sobered. "Yes, of course I understand. But Trésor Smith does exist, and you are the one meant to find her. I know it."

Jonah leaned back and studied her a moment. "All right, then tell me how I can find her."

She shook her head. "I don't understand."

"If you're certain she exists, tell me what makes you so certain. Were you present at her birth? Did you receive a letter of announcement from your son or his wife? Do you see what I mean?"

"Oh, I do see. I was given an account of her birth by someone dear to me. Someone whose trust is completely above question."

"Then give me the name of that person, please."

"His name was John, and he was my husband." She turned her attention away from him to look out the window beside her. "He died from yellow fever not long after the child was born, so I am quite aware of the fevers that killed after the 1855 storm."

He sensed he had lost Mrs. Smith's attention, for she was now looking out the window. Slowly she returned her gaze to meet his.

"That would be nearly a quarter century now. Oh, how that does make me wonder how it all passed so quickly."

Jonah let the silence fall between them, unwilling to speak until his host indicated she was ready to continue their conversation. Finally she sighed and turned back toward him.

"The world is a different place now," she said, her voice soft. "I do miss my husband so."

"I'm so sorry, Mrs. Smith." He rose. "I should go. Before I do, the last time we met you told me you would give me access to your assistant's journals. Would those be available?"

Mrs. Smith nodded and reached for a bellpull beside her chair. A moment later, a maid arrived. "Please ask Miss Winston to join us, and tell her to bring all the journals."

The maid hurried away, leaving them alone again. Jonah nodded toward the roses on the mantel. "My mother also has a fondness for roses," he told her.

"Beautiful flowers, aren't they? I am in debt to my dear neighbor Mrs. Brown for these lovely blossoms. She is such a hospitable lady."

Jonah smiled at the thought of Mrs. Brown being so free with her favorite flowers. "I have a different recollection in relation to Mrs. Brown and her rose garden. I am afraid her boys and I did our best to sneak into that forbidden part of the garden anytime we thought we could get away with it."

"Oh, but she always knew, didn't she?"

"Yes," he said slowly, wondering where this lady got her information, "somehow she always knew."

"Excuse me," the maid said, returning to the room. "Miss Winston has not yet returned from her errands."

"Well then," Mrs. Smith said. "Perhaps you wish to wait, or shall I send a message to you when she returns?"

"I have other leads I can follow today," he said.

"So tomorrow, then?" she asked. "I will see that Miss Winston has the journals ready for you in the morning. Perhaps the family Bible will be found by then as well. Call on us anytime after ten, would you?"

"I will," he said then said his goodbyes and made his exit. As he stepped out onto the sidewalk, he spied a familiar person standing across the street.

"Donovan, is that you?" he called as he waited on a horse and buggy to pass before crossing the street to join his fellow Pinkerton agent. "What are you doing here?"

"I'm here to see to the security arrangements for the former president's visit next week," Detective Donovan said.

"Since when is that a Pinkerton's job?" he said as he shook Donovan's hand.

"Since the Browns do not want to take any chances that the former president's security team might miss something." He nodded toward Mrs. Smith's home. "Is this where you're living now?"

Jonah smiled. "This is my client's home."

"Two Pinkertons working two different cases on the same block of the same street," Donovan said. "Wonder when that's ever happened."

"I'd say never, but maybe this can work to our advantage. I'm investigating a missing woman. My client doesn't have a description or any other identifying information other than her late husband told her the girl was born a specific date in 1855."

"Not much to go on," he said. "How're you going to approach this?"

"I'm still deciding," Jonah said.

Donovan looked past him toward the Smith home. "It sounds like you don't trust your client is being completely honest with you."

He reached over to clasp his hand on Donovan's shoulder. "That, my friend, is it exactly."

"Why take a case like that?"

"I've asked myself that ever since I sat in her parlor drinking tea and listening to her stories several weeks ago." Jonah shrugged. "There's something there. Some mystery that needs solving. I'm just not sure that it is the mystery she has hired me to solve."

"But you're going to get to the bottom of it either way."

"I am." He paused to glance back at the Smith home and then returned his attention to his fellow agent. "Something else I could stand to get to the bottom of," he said.

"What's that?" Donovan asked.

Jonah told him about the holes that had been dug on Cahill property. "That doesn't bother me so much. It has been happening for years. But the minute someone breaks a lock and gets into the cellar beneath the house while my mother and sister are home, that's when I take this seriously."

Donovan seemed to consider this a moment. "I agree."

"I would welcome any ideas you have. I need to be sure my mother and sister are safe, but I also need to approach this as a Pinkerton and not as someone who is too close to the subject."

"I would need to see the evidence."

"There's a shovel in police custody, but there isn't anything unique or identifying about it." He paused. "You're welcome to come out to my mother's home and take a look at the cellar and the marks on the door. I will have to arrange for my sister to take my mother out so she won't wonder what we are doing."

"So she doesn't know about this?"

"We haven't told her yet. My sister doesn't want to upset her, and so far I agree."

The sound of women talking came from across the street. Jonah glanced over to see the cause. Finding nothing out of the ordinary, he went back to his discussion with Donovan.

Then he heard the scream.

❤

A few minutes earlier

Madeline rounded the corner at Broadway Avenue then froze. There, standing across the street in front of the Brown home, was the Pinkerton detective Jonah Cahill. He was in deep conversation with another man, and neither of them was looking her direction.

Slowly, Madeline retraced her steps until she no longer stood in view of the Pinkerton agent and his companion. She certainly could not return to Madame's house by way of Broadway Avenue and the front door, so she ducked into a back alley and followed it all the way to the property's rear gate.

Though the serving girl's eyebrows rose when Madeline stepped inside the back of the house, she said nothing. Madeline offered a weak smile and then hurried up the servants' stairway to her room on the third floor. Dropping her wrapped package of treats onto the writing desk, she hurried to the window where she had a view of the two men still conversing on the sidewalk.

If she could get the window open, Madeline realized, she might be able to hear the animated discussion going on there. Several tugs later, she gave up on trying to lift the sash of the old windows. Instead, she stepped into the hallway and hurried to the floor-to-ceiling windows at the end of the corridor.

There she had better luck, although she soon discovered that an overgrown magnolia tree blocked her view. Worse, the sound of the breeze coming off the Gulf of Mexico sent any sounds from the street off in the opposite direction.

Not to be done in by this small obstacle, Madeline realized if she were to step out onto the small wooden ledge that traversed this side of the home, she might have access to a spot where she could hear the men and yet remain hidden by the foliage.

One careful step and then another, and soon she could hear Jonah Cahill's voice. "I would welcome any ideas you have. I need to be sure...," he said to the other man. "I also need to approach this as a Pinkerton and not as someone who is too close to the subject."

Madeline gasped and leaned against the downspout behind her. So Jonah Cahill was following her. Worse, he not only was participating in an investigation that involved her but he also admitted he had been close to Madeline.

And here he had accused *her* of investigating *him*. Of all the nerve.

"Miss Winston? Is that you out on the ledge?"

Madeline jumped at the sound of the maid's voice. Grasping the downspout, she narrowly managed to avoid falling three stories to the lawn below.

"Yes, Gretchen," she told the maid as her heart continued to pound out a furious cadence. "Did you need something in particular, or were you merely taking a census of the household staff?"

"Goodness, Miss Winston, I don't understand half of what you just asked me, but I am supposed to tell you that Madame Smith wishes to speak with you just as soon as you return from your errands."

A salt-scented breeze blew past, causing Madeline to tighten her grip on the downspout. "Well, as you can see, I have returned from my errands. Would you please tell Madame that I am getting a breath of fresh air and will be down shortly?"

"Didn't you breathe none while you were out?"

"I did," she said as patiently as she could manage. "However, that was on ground level. I prefer air at least three stories up."

The maid looked skeptical but nodded all the same. "All right, then. I'll see that Madame is told." A moment later, the window closed behind her.

"Gretchen, wait," she said, being careful not to speak so loudly that the men across the street might hear.

Unfortunately, Gretchen did not hear either.

Madeline inched her way back to the window, trying to ignore the dizzying difference between where she stood and where she might land if she fell. She tugged on the window sash, but it would not budge.

Letting out a long breath, she tried again. And again. Either the window was now stuck or the maid had locked it.

She rested her head against the glass and then began to knock. Of all the time for the staff to be away from their third-floor rooms, it would have to be now.

What to do? Madeline crept back to the other side of the drainpipe to reach the corner of the house. Though a palm tree hid her from view, if she took another step around the corner, she would be standing on the top of the second-floor porch that ran the length of the front side of the home. Anyone walking down Broadway Avenue could glance up and spot her.

So could the men who were still chatting across the street. Irritation flared. Eventually she needed to have another conversation with the Pinkerton, preferably with her feet on solid ground.

Looking around for a solution to her dilemma, Madeline reached out to yank on a palm branch. The tree was solid and easily the biggest of all the palms on the property. Another yank and she determined the branch might hold her weight.

The question was what to do once she'd grasped the branch and jumped from the roof. Would the branch allow her to sail across the distance between the ledge to the trunk of the tree, or would she be left hanging in midair?

There was only one way to find out.

Grasping the palm branch with both hands, she leaned forward as she prayed for a safe and preferably soft landing. Pushing off with knees that shook, Madeline closed her eyes and felt the ledge disappear from beneath her. So did her self-control as she cried out.

A moment later, she collided with the trunk of the palm tree just beneath the crown of fronds. Hanging on tight, Madeline dug her fingers into the trunk and contemplated her next move.

She was eye level with the second-floor windows, but as far as she could tell there was no one inside who might have seen her. Inching her way down the tree was an option, but Madeline's fingers refused to cooperate when she ordered them to move.

So she was stuck, arms shaking and her legs quaking. How long she could remain in this position was a mystery, as was what she could do to remedy the situation.

She lifted her gaze to the swaying green fronds above her and the blue sky beyond. *Lord, please send help* was the only prayer she could think of at the moment.

"Hello, Madeline."

Chapter Seven

Jonah Cahill's voice was unmistakable. Madeline froze.

"H–h–hello, Jonah," she managed.

"Come down, Madeline," he said, his voice oddly patient.

"Well, now," she responded as calmly as she could as a bee began circling her nose. "That's a bit of a problem."

"Just let go. I will catch you."

"No." Her hand was cramping and the bee buzzed past her ear, but both were preferable to facing Jonah Cahill right now.

The chain she wore around her neck had come lose from her bodice and now hung free, the key on the end of it blowing in the stiff breeze. "I can't."

"You have to," he insisted.

"Just go away. Please?" Again the bee buzzed past, this time alighting on her nose. Madeline swiped at it, losing her grip.

The world turned upside down and then righted again. The next thing she saw was Jonah Cahill's face.

"Again, hello, Madeline."

If she hadn't been equally embarrassed and irritated that Jonah Cahill had not only witnessed her fall but also provided a safe landing for her, Madeline might have thanked him. Rather, she scrambled out of his arms and hurried to adjust her clothing and tuck her necklace back into her bodice.

Her head still felt as if it were spinning, and her knees threatened to buckle. Though she took longer putting the pins back into her hair than necessary, she found Jonah still staring at her when she was done. "Truly, I am fine," she said. "Please just go."

"Not until you explain how you got up in that tree," Jonah demanded.

Madeline straightened her spine and prepared to ignore him. One look into the Pinkerton agent's eyes, and she changed her mind.

"All right," she said, "but can we go elsewhere to have this discussion?"

He shook his head. "I cannot think of a single reason why I shouldn't march you up to that front door and tell the owner of this home exactly what just happened."

Several responses occurred to her. Finally she shrugged. "You're right. There are none."

Jonah shook his head. "So no arguments from the reporter?"

"None," she said, calling his bluff. "Let's go. Of course, you would then have to explain why you were following me earlier. Perhaps my employer wouldn't be so happy to hear me tell that story. You know, the one where you were seen hauling me out of the confectioner's store and into the alley."

"And I doubt anyone at the *Picayune* would care," Jonah said. "And I had valid questions that did not need to be overheard."

So Jonah thought the employer she mentioned was the newspaper? Then she would not correct him.

"Just as I have now." She nodded toward the kitchen window where Gretchen and the scullery maid were openly watching. "So how do you want to do this? Either we can go to the front door and you can have your say or we can find a place where the two of us can have an uninterrupted conversation that does not involve an alley or prying eyes and listening ears."

"Fine," Jonah said. "Let's go. I know just the place."

He led her across the street and past the spot where he'd been speaking with the stranger a few minutes ago. "Donovan," he called as he stepped onto a path that led toward a gated garden.

"Hey there, I wondered where you went," a ginger-haired man called as he rounded the corner. "Oh, I see you've got company."

"Borrowing the rose garden for a minute," Jonah told him. "Thought

I better let you know."

"Hello, I'm. . ."

Madeline let the remainder of her words go unsaid. Jonah knew her name, but if any of the locals got wind of the fact that she was calling herself something different to the mistress of the house, things wouldn't turn out so well.

Jonah opened the black iron gate and ushered her inside. Here the scent of roses was much stronger than in Madame's parlor. Around the edges of the formally laid-out space were climbing roses that spiraled over the fence and wound through it. Bricks the same color as the home formed the path beneath their feet.

"This is beautiful," she whispered, unaware Jonah had heard her until he turned back and nodded.

"Mrs. Brown has spared no expense," he told her.

"So I see."

Next came sweeping sections of rosebushes of different colors and sizes, some trailing on trellises and others situated around them. Here and there spaces had been left for benches made of the same black iron.

Jonah guided her past a dolphin-shaped birdbath filled with water and dotted with multicolored rose petals toward the center of the garden. Madeline heard water splashing, and then they turned the corner.

There in the center of the garden was the grandest fountain Madeline had ever seen in a private garden. The dolphin from the birdbath had been replicated here but on a much larger scale. Two other dolphins of similar size burst from the middle of the pool of water, each pointing in a different direction.

Water rose up through the center of the fountain and caught the sunlight before splashing over the dolphins in a shower of rainbow-colored drops. The effect was breathtaking.

Though Madeline knew she stood just a few yards away from one of Galveston's busiest streets, she felt as though she had left the island entirely. As though there was no one else around for miles.

Well, no one but her and the Pinkerton detective.

That thought nearly ruined the moment, though she determined to ignore Jonah as long as possible. Finally, apparently tired of her gawking, he led her to a bench situated just out of the way of the splashing water and indicated that she should sit.

"All right, Madeline," Jonah said without joining her on the bench. "Before you say anything, I am going to talk. Then you may have your say."

"Jonah, truly you are being insufferable. I just—"

"Not yet."

❤

If he allowed himself, Jonah would have been seriously distracted by the image of Madeline Latour seated on that bench with roses all around her and sunlight illuminating her dark curls and angelic face. But he would not be distracted. Not by any of it.

Though the woman seated before him was a beauty, she was also a nosy reporter who had caused him trouble in the past. Worse, she'd invaded his dreams ever since the day he saw her on the sidewalk in front of his grandfather's house in New Orleans.

The woman he almost married had become the woman he most wanted to avoid. And now here she was.

"Madeline," he said firmly. "You are possibly the most exasperating woman on this planet. I asked you to stop following me this morning, and this afternoon you fall out of a palm tree into my arms."

"To be fair," she said, "I was not following you this morning, and I only landed in your arms because you insisted. And because the bee frightened me."

"The bee frightened you," he echoed. "Of course. That explains it."

"It is the truth."

"But what you haven't explained is why you chose that particular tree to fall from. Either you were following me or you are working on a story." Jonah paused. "Or both."

She rose to join him beside the fountain. "It might be neither."

Jonah stood his ground as he looked into her eyes. "I don't believe you, Madeline."

"So I noticed." Madeline leaned down to trace her fingers in the water. "And you know what?" She looked up at him. "I don't blame you, given our history. So, I will admit I am working on a story. Beyond that, I do not owe you any explanation."

"But you do," he said. "I owe an allegiance to the woman who lives in that home."

Madeline's fingers stilled. "Why? And why are you here in Galveston? Are you investigating her too or just me and my family?"

"I cannot say who or what I am investigating, except that I assure you it's neither you nor your family. Have you considered that I might be visiting *my* family?"

She gave him a look that told him exactly what she thought of that statement. "Someone is investigating."

"Someone from the Pinkertons?"

Madeline nodded. "That is what my father was told."

Given the secretive nature of the company, Jonah wasn't surprised that they were being investigated. Though he was never certain exactly what sort of business activities were conducted by Latour & Sons, he'd done his own investigation and found nothing untoward. For more than one hundred years, they helped those who could afford help, adhered to the laws of the land, and refused to betray any of the secrets they were charged with keeping.

Jonah lowered himself to sit beside her on the ledge of the fountain. "I'm sorry, Madeline. I can tell you that is not my assignment."

"Thank you." Madeline peered over at him with those beautiful brown eyes. "I could help with your investigation."

"Not if I cannot tell you what I am investigating."

"Then tell me about your family. How are Susanna and your mother?"

Her question caught Jonah off guard. "You stay away from my family, understand?"

"I mean no harm." She paused. "Off the record, I promise."

"Nothing is ever off the record with you," he said. "You've proved that."

"When are you going to accept my apology over the McRee case?"

His temper sparked. "I accepted your apology a long time ago, Madeline."

She shook her head. "I never meant for any of that to happen. When I found out the judge blamed you that the witness was identified in the press, I—"

"You got that witness's name from me, so it was my fault for trusting you," he said evenly. "That will not happen again. You don't think of the consequences."

"That isn't fair," she said. "I do."

"Okay, let's talk about what just happened. When you did whatever you did to end up in that palm tree, did you consider what might happen?"

She looked away. "No," she said softly.

"That's what I mean, Madeline. You are relentless when you're working on a story, but you do not stop to think what you're doing to other people in the process."

When she did not respond, Jonah continued. "Tell me what your connection is to Mrs. Smith."

"I can't," she said.

"You won't," he countered.

She stood abruptly. "I'm not going to argue with you. For once I am thinking of the consequences. Goodbye, Jonah."

"Madeline, one question before you go?"

"And what is that?" she asked as she barely paused.

"When did you arrive on the island?"

She shook her head. "Why?"

"Humor me," he responded as casually as he could manage.

"It will be one week ago tomorrow."

"Thank you," he said as he decided she would be added to the list of people with a reason and the opportunity to dig holes on Cahill property.

From the moment she discovered his family home was built on the ashes of the old Lafitte residence, Madeline had professed a curiosity about the pirate. She'd worked through elaborate theories by which the man hadn't died young but rather lived to a ripe old age. Jonah had been supportive of her claims but never thought much would come of her investigations into the facts.

He watched Madeline make her exit, her back straight and her pace brisk. Under other circumstances, a woman with her combination of beauty and intelligence would have caught his attention and made him want to spend more time getting to know her.

But this was Madeline Latour. She had long ago caught his attention and had not yet let it go.

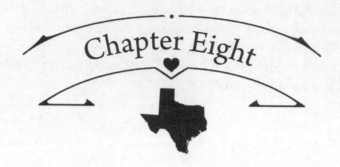

Chapter Eight

Madeline picked up her pace as the iron gate slammed shut behind her. When she reached the sidewalk, she found Jonah's friend there.

"Leaving so soon?" he asked. "I'm Detective Donovan."

"Another Pinkerton?" she said with a sigh.

"Guilty." He offered a smile. "I tried not to listen, but I could tell you weren't happy with my colleague. Cahill is good at what he does, but he can be a little rough around the edges. I hope you'll accept my apology on his behalf."

"I hope he doesn't hear you saying that," she said. "I doubt Jonah would agree."

"That he's rough around the edges?" he said as he leaned against the fence.

"No, that an apology is deserved."

Madeline offered a smile and a wave and then hurried down the street. At the corner she turned, daring to look back to see if Jonah was following. He wasn't, although he had once again stopped beside Detective Donovan in front of the Brown home.

Madeline turned down the alley and quickly found the back gate to Madame's rented property. Casting a quick glance at the palm tree, she cringed and then hurried inside. Gretchen was waiting for her in the kitchen.

"Madame has asked for you more than once. Where did you go?" she demanded.

"You closed the window, Gretchen," she said. "How did you expect me to get back inside?"

The maid gave her a half grin. "It must have slipped," she said.

"Of course," Madeline said with a heavy measure of sarcasm. "Please let Madame know I will be waiting for her in the parlor."

"She's already there," Gretchen said as she turned and walked away.

Madeline hurried up the back steps to her room and retrieved her writing materials and then pulled the topmost journal off the stack. A few minutes later, she stood outside the parlor door.

"Do come in, child," Madame said sweetly.

Pasting on a smile, Madeline stepped inside. She found Madame Smith seated in her favorite chair beside the window that faced Broadway Avenue. Her hair had been freshly coiled into an iron-gray bun on the back of her head, and she was dressed in an afternoon gown of pale green.

Once again, Madeline was struck by the older woman's beauty. It was easy to see how she had once been the toast of New Orleans. Easier still to understand why the enigmatic pirate Lafitte would fall in love with her.

If only Madeline could find evidence of that love. She was determined to investigate further, and yet she knew Madame would reveal her secrets in her own way, in her own time.

A fresh bouquet of pink roses sat on the table beside her. Madeline focused on them instead of her employer as she took a seat. With care, she laid out the tools of her work: first the notebook and then the ink and pen.

"Gretchen said you wished to see me, Madame?"

The older woman regarded her impassively. Slowly a smile arose. "She also said you had returned, but that was some twenty minutes or more ago."

"Yes, I had returned, but I had to go out again," Madeline said. "I'm terribly sorry for causing you to wait. What is it you need? Perhaps another story recorded for the journals?"

"Where did you go, Miss Winston?"

"Go?" Madeline said, stalling for time. "Well, I went out to have a quick meeting with a friend."

"I see." She studied her bejeweled hand and then returned her attention to Madeline. "I did not realize you had friends in Galveston."

"Nor did I, but I saw my friend this morning while I was shopping. Apparently, my friend is in Galveston on business."

Madeline hated being so evasive. Her employer did not deserve half truths, and yet there was no reason for her to be concerned. Unlike the charge the Pinkerton made about her, Madeline was indeed thinking of the consequences of her actions this time.

Madame's eyes were bright, and her expression appeared curious. "Was your meeting successful, then?"

"I am not sure," she said. "I hope so, but one never knows."

"That is true," she said. "But the setting for the meeting must have been lovely."

Madeline frowned. "It was. How did you know?"

She motioned for Madeline to approach and then reached over to pluck something from her hair. "This was my clue," she said as she held out a deep red rose petal. "And since the only place in the city where this type of red rose is blooming right now is in my neighbor Mrs. Brown's garden, I must assume you found the setting quite pleasing."

"Oh yes," she said. "It was truly magical."

"As I recall, it is," she said. "So please be seated again. I've a bit of my own business to discuss with you."

"Of course," she said as she complied.

"Do you recall that I told you I had hired some assistance in our hunt?" At Madeline's nod, she continued. "I've had a preliminary discussion with my expert today. He has requested to view the journals we have been working on."

"Oh," she said. "Of course. May I ask what he thinks he will find in the journals?"

"Well, I don't know," Madame said. "He did not tell me other than to say that perhaps there is some insight to be gained in them. Thus, if you could please make them ready for him to view tomorrow. I told him to call here after ten."

"Of course," she said. "Would you like to add anything to them today?"

"Yes," she said slowly. "I believe I would. Have I ever told you the story of how my son settled right here on this island and fell in love with a local girl?"

Madeline shook her head. "No, you have not."

"Oh my," she said with a chuckle. "I suppose I should tell that story before I get to the other one, shouldn't I?"

"Yes, I think so." Madeline prepared to begin. "Whenever you are ready," she told her. "I am ready to write your memories down."

"But oh, Miss Winston, am I ready to remember them? That is the question. You see, it was a very long time ago when I learned I was to be a mother. In spite of the happiness of this news, it was a very sad time. A time when I had not expected to be the bearer of new life."

She listened in silence as Madame told her the story of having been a young bride, her groom much older and of a different social group than her own. "My parents, they were particular as to whom I could be seen with. To spend time in the company of a gentleman who was not approved by them was considered most improper."

Madeline wondered again if Madame ever knew that her father had paid for an investigation to be done on this man she loved. There had certainly been no mention of the lengths Madame's papa had gone to in order to prevent this union. Obviously, he had not been successful.

She decided to risk a question. "Did your father do anything to come between you and Monsieur Smith?"

"Oh, indeed he did. In fact, I knew he would stop at nothing to see us permanently apart."

"I am sorry," Madeline said. "It does sound like his efforts failed."

"Indeed they did." Madame paused to look out the window for what seemed to be a very long time. Finally she returned her attention to Madeline. "Perhaps that is not something you can understand, but in my time a father and mother, they chose for you when it came to things such as marriages. It was considered an act of love from a father to a daughter and a mother to a daughter when that daughter's future was carefully planned for her. What do you think about that?"

Madeline tried to imagine her parents planning the rest of her life and failed miserably. Rather, they had raised her to be strong and independent, a woman capable to make good decisions and follow through with them.

Very much the opposite of what Jonah Cahill thought of her.

"Miss Winston?"

"Oh," she said as Madame's voice drew her back from her thoughts. "I'm sorry. Honestly, I think that sounds awful."

Madame laughed. "So did I," she said. "So I rebelled. Only later did I realize that, at least in part, my parents were right. Marrying a man who is unlike anyone you've ever met will take you down a path you may not be expecting." She paused to smile as if thinking of some particular but private memory. "Oh, but what an adventure it can be."

Her heart lurched. Was this the connection to the Lafitte family that she had been hoping to find? Jean Lafitte had certainly been much older than Madame.

"Madame," she said gently. "You have provided few details regarding your husband."

"Oh, but I have," she said sweetly. "He has been with me on every adventure I've had. In a way, he is still with me today."

This was not the answer she expected. In fact, it answered nothing she'd asked.

"You think I've gone daft."

"I think you have precious memories as yet unrecorded," she said to cover her surprise. "Perhaps we should start with that premise and begin our session with more information about your husband."

"Miss Winston," she said slowly. "Have you ever been in love?"

Another unexpected response. "I thought so once, but I was wrong."

"Oh, my dear, I do highly recommend it."

An uncomfortable silence fell between them. Eventually, Madame sighed. "I do believe I will put this off until another time. I find myself suddenly tired. Are you terribly disappointed that you will not find out the answers to your questions?"

She was, of course, but there was nothing to be done for it. "I will ring for Gretchen," she told Madame. "When you've rested we can start again with this topic."

But as Madeline packed up her writing materials, she couldn't help but feel disappointed. The information she was looking for—the link to Lafitte—felt so close.

And yet so far away.

❤

The next day, Jonah knocked on the door of Mrs. Smith's home at precisely ten o'clock in the morning. A maid let him in and guided him to a library where a stack of leather-bound black books had been laid out. He also found writing paper, pens, and ink.

"Will there be anything else?" the maid asked.

He glanced around the room and then shook his head. "No, I believe Mrs. Smith has provided me with all I need."

"Very well, then," she said as she turned to leave. "Should you change your mind, please use the bellpull and someone will assist you."

Sorting through the books, Jonah soon realized there was no rhyme or reason to the stories. It appeared Mrs. Smith told her tales to the writer and the writer recorded them as they were told. Putting a date to these tales or a time line to her memories would never be possible.

He reached for the top book on the stack and began to make notes regarding names and locations. When he completed his reading of the first book, he had a half page of names but only one location: New Orleans. The second and third books yielded a similar result.

By the time Jonah got to the third book, he was almost ready to decide that taking the time to read all of these journals would be a wasted effort. Then he arrived upon a story of a storm and a ship lost at sea along with a family and their child.

Jonah sat up straighter in his chair and went back to reading. Unfortunately, there was no indication that this lost child had any relation to Mrs. Smith. Nor was there anything to indicate the date or location of the tragedy.

Frustrated, Jonah continued to turn the pages even as his stomach began to growl. The clock over the mantel struck half past eleven and then, seemingly only a few minutes later, struck noon.

Gradually, Jonah became aware of the smell of something delicious. Something that smelled very much like fried chicken.

He set the book aside and reviewed his notes once more. He had read every one of these journals once and had gone back to look at sections he had marked. There was nothing else to be done here.

Jonah rose and pulled the bell then returned to the table to put away the writing tools. A moment later, rather than a maid, in walked Mrs. Smith.

"I do hope you'll join us for lunch, Detective Cahill."

Again his stomach growled, and he hoped his host's hearing was poor enough to miss the sound of it. "I couldn't really."

"I insist," she said as she stepped away from the doorway and indicated he should follow her. "I believe you'll enjoy the company today."

"I do not want to intrude on guests," he said. "Just let me take my notes and be on my way."

"Nonsense. You leave those notes right there," she said as she linked arms with him.

Without another word, she urged him toward what he figured was the dining room. Just outside the door she paused once again. "Remember, you can leave the service of your duties here at any time."

He shook his head. "Why would I want to do that?"

"I don't expect you will, though I do not wish to keep you in my employ under duress. I am well aware of the fact that you have serious doubts as to whether you are able to complete the task I have hired you for."

"That is not true," he said. "I will complete the task. What I have doubts about is whether you will like what I discover."

"Well now," she said with a chuckle, "that is an entirely different matter, isn't it? Yet I will give you one last chance to escape this with your reputation intact and no hard feelings from me."

"Thank you, Mrs. Smith," he said. "But I believe I will stay and see how all of this turns out."

"Excellent," she said with a broad smile. "Then come in and meet your partner in this search."

"I don't understand," he said. "I was not under the impression I would be working with a partner."

She paused for just a moment, her smile radiant. "That is because I am only just telling you now."

Jonah followed Mrs. Smith into the dining room and helped her to her seat at the head of the table. Unlike the book-filled library or the rose-filled parlor, this room held all the grandeur of a formal dining room.

From the deep-burgundy-papered walls and golden curtains that held back the noonday sun to the massive chandelier that cast a brilliant light over the crystal and china on the table, they might well have been in a castle somewhere in Europe.

"Do please sit down," she said and then cast her gaze around the room with a frown. "I wonder where your new partner has gotten off to."

Mrs. Smith rang a bell, and the maid appeared. "Gretchen, please tell Miss Winston we are waiting."

"Yes, ma'am," she said.

"And who is Miss Winston?"

"Miss Winston is my assistant. She is the author of the journals you read this morning, and she is a very knowledgeable woman. I do believe you two will make quite a team."

"Don't get me wrong, Mrs. Smith. I don't mind working with a woman. In fact, I sometimes prefer it as females tend to be able to get things done in a situation when a male might fail." He paused. "However, unless your Miss Winston has training equivalent to a Pinkerton detective or police officer, I fail to see how she and I will work well together."

"Oh," she said sweetly, "I know the answer to that. You two will work well together because that is what I am paying you both to do." She paused, her expression just as congenial as it had been since she intercepted him in the library. "I do hope I make myself clear."

"Crystal clear," he said, slightly in awe of the elderly lady's spunk.

"Excellent. Oh, look, here's Gretchen with our lunch."

The maid set a silver tray laden with food, chief among the dishes being a platter of fried chicken, on the table in front of them. She offered Mrs. Smith a smile and Jonah a look of undisguised curiosity.

"Gretchen, were you able to find Miss Winston?"

"I'm sorry, Mrs. Smith," she said as she kept her attention focused on

Jonah. "Miss Winston was not upstairs, but no one has seen her leave, so I am sure she must be on the grounds somewhere. Or perhaps outside. I will have the stable boy hunt for her."

"Thank you, dear," Mrs. Smith said as she moved her attention to Jonah. "So in the meantime, would you like to bless the meal, Detective Cahill?"

Jonah obliged and then his host joined him in saying, "Amen."

Once their plates were filled, Jonah decided to plunge forward with the question foremost on his mind. "So, Mrs. Smith, what can you tell me about my new partner, Miss Winston?"

"Well now," she said slowly, "Miss Winston has been in my employ since February. She responded to an advertisement in the *Picayune* for an assistant to record my memoirs and serve as a companion of sorts."

"And in that role, she has been a satisfactory employee?"

Madame took a sip of iced tea and then returned her glass to the table. "Indeed she has. You appear to be enjoying the chicken."

"It is delicious, and I am thankful to be enjoying such a grand meal." He paused, unwilling to let go of the topic of the mysterious Miss Winston. "What do you know about Miss Winston's background?"

"Goodness, Detective Cahill. You have a curious nature, don't you?" she said with a smile.

"Yes, ma'am," he said. "You are paying well for my curious nature. So humor me, if you please. I would like to know more about this assistant of yours."

"I suppose I am." She gave him an amused look. "As I said, I met her through an advertisement. If you were to bother to check, and I suppose you just might, you would find that I posted several advertisements over the past few years until the right person for the job finally applied. Miss Winston has become a valued employee."

She was hiding something. But what? "And that is all you're willing to tell me?"

"That is all I *will* tell you," she corrected. "Although you are more than welcome to quiz my assistant at length regarding this topic and any others you might think relevant to your assignment."

"I will."

Mrs. Smith offered a broad grin. "I have no doubt. Now do try those mashed potatoes. My cook makes the best I've ever tasted, and at my age I have tasted plenty."

The front door opened and then shut again. Jonah heard footsteps in the hall behind him. Before he could turn around, Mrs. Smith called out.

"There you are, Miss Winston. Do join us for lunch and say hello to Detective Cahill of the Pinkerton Detective Agency."

Jonah turned then and came face-to-face with Madeline Latour. He pasted on his most welcoming smile and aimed it at the nosy reporter. "Hello, Miss Winston."

Chapter Nine

Madeline froze. What was Jonah Cahill doing feasting on fried chicken and mashed potatoes at Madame Smith's dining table?

The Pinkerton agent slid her a look that made Madeline's blood run cold. Either he was about to unmask her or he planned to play along—for a price.

Madeline stood her ground, thankful that her skirts hid her shaking knees. "Hello," she responded as calmly as she could manage before turning her attention to Madame. "It appears you and your guest have already started your meal, so I won't bother you."

"It is no bother," Madame said.

"Well, I do appreciate that, but I have errands to run, so I'll just have Gretchen fix up a plate of something later. When I get back. From where I was about to be going."

Madame chuckled. "My dear, you just came back. We do not mind at all if you join us, do we, Detective Cahill?"

"Oh no. We don't mind at all," he said with the most infuriating grin. "In fact, I have been looking forward to meeting the mysterious Miss Winston that Mrs. Smith has been telling me so much about. However, I must say I was not prepared for meeting you in person."

"Please do sit, Miss Winston," Madame said, her smile now gone. "You're keeping Detective Cahill from his lunch."

"Yes, of course," she said. "Just let me drop off my bag—"

"Not necessary." Madame rang for Gretchen, who of course appeared immediately, likely because she was eavesdropping on the other side of the door. "Take Miss Winston's bag up to her room, please."

"Yes, Madame."

As soon as Gretchen's back was turned to Madame and the Pinkerton, she gave Madeline an I-hope-you-are-in-trouble look. Madeline handed the maid the bag but held her gaze just long enough to let Gretchen know she didn't care whether the maid liked her or not.

"Thank you, Gretchen," Madame said. "That will do. Sit here, Miss Winston."

Of course she chose a seat across from the Pinkerton. Madeline moved toward the chair Madame indicated only to realize once she'd arrived that Detective Cahill was already holding the chair out for her to sit.

His expression gave nothing away of his thoughts, but Madeline could guess. She tried to keep her face just as neutral, but whether she succeeded was debatable.

"Thank you, Detective Cahill," she said once she'd been seated.

"Not at all, Miss Winston," was his far-too-sweet response as he returned to his chair.

"Well now," Madame said as she looked first at Madeline and then at Jonah. "The two of you finally meet. This is a momentous occasion." She looked beyond them to where Gretchen had returned.

"I'm sorry for the interruption, Madame," Gretchen said as she glanced over at Madeline. "There's a situation in the kitchen that needs your attention."

"Please excuse me. Do go on with your meal in my absence. And get to know one another." Madame rose and left the room with Gretchen.

Their hostess had barely disappeared down the hall when Jonah's eyes locked with hers. "Give me one good reason why I shouldn't tell that nice old lady that you are lying to her."

"Because there is no good reason to. I am writing down her memories. And yes, I did take an alias. I thought it prudent."

Even as she spoke the words, words that were true, her conscience twinged. Madeline had been ignoring this twinge ever since she concocted this plan. Perhaps it was time to stop ignoring and to do something about it.

Jonah's eyes narrowed. "You thought it prudent? Why?"

"All right," she said on an exhale of breath. "I meant no harm to Madame Smith, but when I take on an assignment, I never do my research under the name that I use to publish my stories."

"So you admit you're writing about that kind lady?"

"I admit nothing of the kind," she snapped. "My editor knows I am working on a story, but I have made no promises as to what I will be writing about. Or, for that matter, *if* I will be writing a story at all."

Jonah fixed her with a smug look. "You mean in case you feel guilty?"

"I mean in case I am wrong about what I believe the facts of the story to be."

"You're talking in riddles, Madeline," he said as he shook his head.

"I am answering your question," she said. "It will serve no purpose to tell her I am a reporter because it has nothing to do with what I am doing here. First and foremost, I am the assistant recording her memories. And second, I am apparently helping you."

There went that twinge again. Her mother would ask if she would be able to offer that excuse to the Lord and feel good about it. At this moment, Madeline knew the answer was a most uncomfortable no.

"If there's a story somewhere in those memories, then you are the reporter who isn't above profiting from that story."

The truth of that statement stung even further. "Yes, I am looking for a story, but I don't care to profit," she said. "This is personal. And it will not harm Madame, this I can promise."

Jonah studied her face. "I still don't believe you."

"It's the truth whether you believe me or not."

Madame returned before Jonah had a chance to respond. As Madame took her seat at the head of the table, Madeline took a deep breath and let it out slowly. Much as she hated it, Jonah was right. She needed to tell Madame the truth regarding her identity.

If this was the end of her employment with Madame Smith, so be it. She would get her information on Lafitte and the story she hoped to discover another way. There was no blessing from the Lord on a project

He hadn't approved of. And He certainly did not approve of deception.

Not having to hide her identity from the sweet widow would be a relief. Explaining to Madame why she had chosen to hide it, not so much.

"My team has assembled and now the hunt can begin," Madame said with a smile before Madeline could speak. "Miss Winston, you and Detective Cahill will be working together to find my treasure."

"Excuse me, Mrs. Smith," Jonah said. "You hired me to find your granddaughter, not a treasure."

"Treasure. Trésor. It is all the same," Madame said with a wave of her hand.

"I don't understand," Madeline said.

"Treasure in English. Trésor in French," she said. "My granddaughter Trésor is my lost treasure. That is what—and who—you search for. So, in essence, you are correct."

"I thought for a minute we were going to have to dig for actual buried treasure," Madeline said. "Not that I mind, of course."

"Well of course you wouldn't mind, Madeline," Jonah said. "You always were interested in treasure hunting."

"What does that mean?"

Jonah stared at her across the table, anger flashing in those silver eyes. "There would be quite a story in finding buried treasure here in Galveston, don't you think?"

Madeline straightened her spine. "You are making no sense, Jonah."

"Oh dear," Madame said as she rose. "It appears my team is having its first disagreement. It was not unexpected given the circumstances, of course. Please do not speak but rather nod when I ask you a question, do you understand?"

For a small woman, Madame certainly could take command of a room. Madeline nodded and watched Jonah do the same. Madame looked at Jonah. "Do you wish to resign this assignment?"

Jonah slid Madeline a quick look and then shook his head to indicate he did not. Madame then turned her attention to Madeline. "Do you?" Madeline responded in the same way.

"All right, then. If you have something to say, then speak."

"With respect, Mrs. Smith," Jonah said before Madeline could speak. "I do offer my deepest apologies that I have abused your hospitality."

"Nonsense," Madame said. "I quite expected this sort of reaction when the two of you finally met. Is that all?"

Jonah seemed to be considering the question. "No, that is all for now."

"Very well. You may not understand today why I have chosen you to work together, but I hope someday you will."

"Madame, I do have a question. You said Detective Cahill and I are a team. Might I ask what your instructions are to the team?"

She smiled. "Of course, dear. You are to be as invaluable to Detective Cahill as you are to me."

"So I am in charge of this investigation?" Jonah asked, his tone smug and his smile broad.

"No, Detective Cahill, you are responsible for it." She turned to Madeline. "And you are responsible for following the detective's instructions in regard to the investigation. Do you anticipate any problem doing that?"

"In regard to the investigation, I do not," she said. "However, I need to be honest about something. And once I do, I will leave it to you to decide if you still trust me enough to continue with me in your employ."

"Go ahead," Madame said gently.

Madeline glanced quickly at Jonah before returning her attention to Madame Smith. "I have not been truthful with you. My name is not Maggie Winston. I am Madeline Latour, and I am a reporter for the *New Orleans Picayune*. I chose to apply for the job under the name of Maggie Winston because I did not want you to form your opinion of me and my ability to work for you based on anything you might have heard about me or my family."

"Is that all?"

Madeline paused. "No. I was wrong. I have no excuse for my behavior. I did not think of the consequences." She slid a covert glance at Jonah and then returned her attention to Madame. "I do, however, want to assure you that I am under no assignment from the paper but rather investigating on my own time."

"I know, Madeline," she said, her voice holding no sign of anger. "I have known from the beginning."

"You did?"

"Yes, I did. The question of the pirates, it is intriguing to you, as it is to me. I understood."

"I'm sorry to jump in here," Jonah said. "If you knew she wasn't telling the truth, why would you hire her?"

Madame seemed to consider the question for a moment. Then she offered Jonah a smile. "Because she is the right one for the job. What name she gives herself has never been important."

"Madame," Madeline said softly, "might I be excused now. I find I no longer have an appetite."

"Running away will not repair what has been broken here," Madame said.

Jonah looked up from his meal but said nothing. Madeline nodded and turned her attention to her plate, where she pushed food around until Madame finally rang for Gretchen.

"Has the family Bible been found yet?" she asked the maid.

"Not yet, but we are still looking," she said.

Madame dismissed Gretchen. Not long after, she declared the meal at an end and dismissed Madeline and Jonah as well. She crept away while Jonah was saying his goodbyes to Madame and hid herself upstairs, even turning down the evening meal.

Later that evening, when Madeline was unable to rest, she crept downstairs with a letter of apology she'd written. Meaning to leave the letter on Madame's chair, she was surprised to find the widow seated there, her gaze lifted to the heavens outside the open window.

Had the floorboard not creaked just at the moment Madeline attempted to make her escape, she might have gone back upstairs unnoticed and delivered the letter in the morning. Instead, the home and her conscience had conspired to put her right there in front of the one woman to whom she owed more than just a written apology.

"Come in, child," Madame said softly. "I have been expecting you."

Madeline crossed the distance between them to kneel in front of Madame. Holding the letter in her hand, she lifted her gaze to find her employer smiling.

"Words are so inadequate," Madeline said as she handed the note to Madame and then bowed her head. "You trusted me. For that I am grateful, but for what I have done in deceiving you. . ."

Tears shimmered as Madame reached to lift her head and then placed her old and gnarled hands over Madeline's. "You only thought to deceive me, Madeline, for I already knew who you were."

"Blessed are the peacemakers: for they shall be called the children of God." In that moment with the covering of the old fitted sweetly and softly over the hands of the new, Madeline smiled. And then she rested her head on Madame's hands and cried.

Two days later

Jonah reluctantly slowed his pace to match Madeline's as they walked down the Morgan's Steamship Company dock toward the steamship *Haven* for their trip south down the coast to Indianola, a distance of just over one hundred fifty miles.

He gave his partner in this endeavor a sideways look. "Mrs. Smith might not think your lack of honesty is important, but I do."

"My apology has been accepted. That's all you need to know."

Of course she would have convinced that nice old lady to forgive her. Madeline Latour could be quite convincing when she set her mind to it.

"I just want you to understand that I will have nothing but the truth from you as long as we are forced to work together," he said.

"And had I any say in the matter, we would not be working together." She looked away. "But part of my job with Madame is to do what she asks of me. This is what she has asked."

"And in exchange, you get access to whatever information you're looking for." He shook his head. "Madeline, you never cease to amaze me. How did you decide she was the one who would give you your answers on Lafitte? That is what this story you're working on is about, isn't it?"

"No comment."

"Fine." He let silence fall between them, preferring to end the discussion rather than listen to excuses or evasiveness. Two days had gone by and he still had not decided where the truth was in Madeline's claims. If Mrs. Smith hadn't insisted he make this trip immediately, Jonah might have put it off until he could better decide how to handle the nosy reporter.

He also disliked being away from his mother and sister while the person who dug holes on Cahill property remained at large. With Officer Pearson agreeing to stand guard in Jonah's absence, he had reluctantly left the Cahill ladies in the police officer's capable hands.

There had been no other holes dug, either on the property or in the cellar, since Jonah's arrival on the island. He intended to keep it that way.

At the end of the dock, a representative of Morgan's met them and took their bags. Another representative of the company escorted them to their staterooms. With a fine meal packed into a hamper by Mrs. Smith's cook and his case notes to read, Jonah settled in for the overnight journey to Indianola.

After a few minutes, someone knocked on the door. Jonah opened the door to find Madeline standing there. He suppressed a groan. "Yes?"

She presented Jonah with a note. "This was in my hamper."

Jonah opened it and read, "Please see Detective Cahill for your evening meal. Cook packed the dinner meal in his hamper and the breakfast meal in yours. Both are for you to share."

He looked up at Madeline and then went over to the hamper and opened it. Inside was a selection of meats, several sealed bowls of side dishes, and a basket containing not only fluffy rolls and butter but also several wedges of corn bread. Stacked beneath it all in a container meant to keep the delicacy from being flattened was a pie.

"Apple," Madeline said as she peered inside the basket.

"How can you tell?"

"Cook always leaves a clue there in the center of the piecrust."

Jonah looked closely and found a small piece of dough carved into the shape of an apple and placed atop the crust. A dusting of sugar and cinnamon coated it all.

"Will it be an intrusion if I just prepare a plate and take it back to my cabin? I can return the plate with your half of tomorrow's breakfast on it." She paused. "After I wash it, of course."

Jonah suppressed a smile. Madeline was nervous around him. Good. That gave him an advantage.

"Fine." He returned to his chair and retrieved the case file, covertly observing the reporter as she went about the business of preparing her meal.

Though he tried, Jonah couldn't see her standing over there and not think of what might have been. If he allowed himself, he could fall in love with her all over again.

But he couldn't allow that to happen. He wouldn't.

Madeline caught him watching and set her plate down. "I know you still don't trust me, but you know what? There are things I do not trust about you either."

"Brutal honesty, is it?" He lifted a brow and set the case file aside. "All right. Like what?"

The vessel shuddered, and she paused to brace herself against the wall beside her. "Detective Donovan is across the street from where I am staying when there is already one Pinkerton in town." She paused. "I am taking you at your word that you aren't investigating me or my family, but is he?"

Jonah gave the question a moment's thought. Donovan's explanation was plausible but could easily be a cover. "I honestly don't know."

"I believe you," she said. "But again, I am not sure I believe him. Two Pinkerton agents working cases across the street from each other?"

He agreed. Still, he wouldn't betray a fellow detective. "No comment," he said instead. "So what has your papa done to warrant an investigation?"

"He claims there is nothing," she was quick to say, although he thought he noted a slight quiver in her voice. "But in the course of helping his clients, I am sure he's made a few enemies."

Though Jonah had been ready to marry Madeline, her father had not seen fit to trust him with the secret of exactly what Latour & Sons did in their offices above the apothecary on Royal Street. With no sign on the door, anyone who walked past could miss the fact that three generations of Latours had toiled inside.

Being a careful man, Jonah had done his best to discover what went on there. All he could learn was that a century's worth of goodwill earned by treating very high-placed clients well had given the company a sterling reputation.

"Have you thought of making a list of those enemies and investigating that angle?"

She looked surprised. "It would be helpful if my father would be forthcoming with that information. He is not."

"That is the nature of the business, I guess," Jonah said.

Madeline seemed to consider the statement. "It is, and that is why it could be anyone behind that investigation. I suppose my father will handle this without my help."

"The company has been in business for a very long time without your help," Jonah said. "So yes, I agree."

Madeline smiled. "You know my father always liked you."

"No," he said truthfully, "I did not."

"All right, maybe *liked* isn't the right word," she said with a grin. "He respected you. So, you made some veiled references in front of Madame. What was that about?"

He let out a long breath. Bad behavior on his part was inexcusable, but to have acted in such a way in front of a client was even worse.

"That," Jonah said, "was a statement made in anger. I apologize."

Again the vessel shuddered, and thunder rumbled outside.

"Oh, something has happened."

"Oh no. I won't be giving you fodder for one of your newspaper articles." The expression on Madeline's face told him he had said the wrong thing again. "Look, I'm sorry. Something did happen while I was away from my family that has me concerned."

"Something related to treasure? You knew I've been interested in the Lafitte legacy for a long time."

"Yes," he said, again feeling ashamed of his assumption.

"Whether you believe me or not, it isn't Lafitte's treasure I am looking for or writing about. It's something else, and I assure you it isn't found in any hole in anyone's yard."

Madeline gathered up a set of utensils wrapped in a checked linen cloth and dropped them into her pocket. "Good night, Detective Cahill."

"Good night, Madeline."

She walked toward the door just in time for the vessel to lurch again, causing her to trip and fall against the wall. In the process, her plate went sliding in Jonah's direction, splattering food everywhere.

"Oh!" she said as she landed on the floor beside a chicken leg and a slice of mutton that were somehow still situated on the plate. Madeline looked down in dismay at her skirts, now decorated with streaks of mashed potatoes, cranberry preserves, and a half slice of corn bread.

Her gaze swung over to where Jonah sat, her face unreadable. A sweet potato detached itself from the ceiling and landed in Madeline's lap. She looked down at it and then back up at Jonah.

And then she began to laugh.

In that moment, it didn't matter that there was a broken engagement and no trust between them. It mattered not that nothing bound them except their obligation to an assignment each had agreed to continue despite the other.

Until the *Haven* docked tomorrow at Indianola, they were just two hungry travelers on a steamship skirting the Texas coast. His stomach growled in response.

Jonah rose and picked his way across a floor dotted with once edible food to reach the hamper. Serving himself a plate that included some of everything Cook had included, he retrieved his utensils and walked over to where Madeline still sat making the best of the remains of her meal.

And then he joined her on the floor.

Chapter Ten

Why Indianola?" Madeline asked as she accepted Jonah's offer of a slice of buttered corn bread. "From what Madame has told me, her granddaughter is thought to be in Galveston."

They had remained on the floor of the cabin, the better to dine without falling on a vessel that seemed to have arrived in choppy waters. While Jonah had been kind enough to overlook her awkward tumble and subsequent loss of her meal on his cabin floor, his face still bore a look of reluctance when she spoke.

"Because Indianola is where she was born. We're starting at the beginning and following the trail of her life." He paused. "So has she told you more stories since I read through the journals?"

"Only a few. Nothing of value as far as I can tell."

Jonah regarded her across his plate. Outside, rain beat a heavy cadence on the deck above them, and the floor rolled beneath them. "I would like to see those new journal entries. I'm also waiting on the family Bible to be found."

"I will check into both," she said. "But I will warn you that it sounds more like a grandmother who believes her granddaughter can do no wrong rather than anything of use to our search."

"Interesting that she would only now dictate a story on the granddaughter she has been so keen to find." Jonah speared a slice of ham. "Exactly what kind of information on Lafitte were you seeking when you took the job with Mrs. Smith?"

"I cannot tell you that."

"Will not," he corrected.

She shrugged. "All right. Will not. I assure you I mean her no harm. That is really all you need to know."

"I prefer to think that is merely all you plan to tell me right now." He paused. "So let me guess. You've probably found some obscure story about Lafitte that you're convinced that nice Smith lady can corroborate. Am I right?"

"No comment," she said sweetly, unwilling to let him know how close he was to the truth.

The vessel shuddered while the sound of thunder echoed in the tiny cabin. "When you're working on a story, where do you get your research, Madeline?"

The question startled her. Madeline swung her attention from the plate in front of her to the Pinkerton detective. "What an odd question, Jonah."

"I'm just curious." Jonah shifted positions and pushed his plate away. "As a Pinkerton agent, I am trained in investigative technique. I have been taught to deduce and to look beyond the obvious to uncover the facts. I learned this from my training. I've seen you work but I never asked, 'Where did you learn it?'"

The full answer would have been that she learned at her father's knee. She learned by following her father and brother, and not always with their permission. She read case files by candlelight when all the other family members were fast asleep, and then she practiced her skills on cases her family turned down. She hounded her brother relentlessly until he would share the details of whatever matter he'd been assigned to handle. Finally, she used those same relentless arguments to convince Papa that she too could work just fine in the family business.

"Madeline?"

She shook her head and reached to touch the chain at her neck. "Anything I have learned since convent school was simply absorbed by watching others or asking questions."

Jonah chuckled. She had always been curious, and he'd been on the receiving end of those persistent questions for as long as he had known her. "Those are the basis of the Pinkerton's observation skills as well."

"Well, there you have it," she said as she forced a smile. "I suppose I should have become a Pinkerton detective instead of a reporter."

Jonah chuckled. "Now there's a good idea. It is never too late to change your ways. The agency is always looking for women to join our ranks."

"I would think so," she said. "Considering it was a woman who saved President-elect Lincoln from assassination in Baltimore before his inauguration."

"That is true," he said. "I have found when I partner with a female agent, I can send her into a situation and get a successful result when a man going into that same situation would likely not succeed." He paused to lean against a trunk. "I suppose that the Lord created men and women distinctly different for a good reason."

Madeline allowed her smile to show him she agreed. "Is that why you asked Madame to send me on this trip?"

"No," he said quickly. "In fact, I argued against bringing you along. The last thing I need on a fact-finding mission is a woman without training following me around and ruining my investigation."

"I see." She paused, her feelings a little hurt. "And yet you've just complimented my skills as an investigator."

"While I said you might make a good Pinkerton detective, I did not mean you were ready for the work just yet."

She shrugged. "I fail to see what preparation I need. We're going to Indianola to look for clues to help Madame find her granddaughter's current whereabouts. I know how I would handle this as a reporter, and it likely isn't any different than how you plan to handle it."

"All right," he said slowly. "Tell me your plan, Madeline."

"I would begin by looking for any public records that might exist."

"The city was nearly wiped out by a hurricane five years ago," he said with a shrug. "There are no records prior to then, at least none that are legible."

"All right," she said slowly, "then I would start by asking questions of anyone who might have known her."

"What about a description?"

"In the story I recorded yesterday, Madame comments on her

granddaughter's dark hair. Unlike fair-haired children whose hair darkens with age, a woman who started life with black hair will very likely still have black hair as she ages."

"Agreed," he said. "And owing to the fact of Mrs. Smith's Louisiana background, there is probably a strong French influence in her features. At least that is what I was assuming. As a Pinkerton, that is."

"And as a reporter, I would agree." She shook her head. "So what do you suggest? We find all the dark-haired women and interrogate them for their names and backgrounds?"

He laughed at her suggestion. "Hardly. We start with the town doctor in the hopes he's been there long enough to deliver a child the age of the woman we are looking for. Then we find out who else has been in town that long and speak to them."

"Then we interrogate the dark-haired women?" she added with a smile.

"Exactly. So, your necklace," he said as he nodded toward her. "What is the meaning of the key?"

She grasped for the chain that had obviously been exposed when she took her tumble and tucked it back into her bodice. "It was a gift from my father," she told him truthfully. "It has no meaning beyond a kind remembrance from parent to child."

"I see," Jonah said, although his tone gave Madeline reason to suspect he did not.

Climbing to her feet, Madeline surveyed the damage her clumsiness had caused. "I have a length of toweling in my cabin. I'll just go get it and clean up this mess."

"Leave it," he said. "I'll alert the porter and have him take care of it."

She collected her plate and utensils and put them away then used her napkin to dab at the remains of the mess she made of her skirt. "If you're certain, then, I will say good night."

"I am certain," he said, bidding her good night.

Madeline hurried back to the seclusion of her cabin. What was it about Jonah Cahill that never failed to put her on her guard? Perhaps because he could be kind and he could be ruthless, often in the same conversation.

Realizing she would have to share yet another meal with the Pinkerton agent before the steamship arrived at Indianola, she opened the crate and filled a plate with enough food for her own breakfast. Closing the hamper once more, she carried it to Jonah's cabin door and knocked.

He opened the door and looked down at her, a bemused expression on his face as he glanced at the hamper in her hand. "Still hungry?"

Madeline thrust the hamper toward him. "I thought it would be easier for both of us if I brought this to you tonight. That way you can have your breakfast whenever you wish."

"And you?" he asked with a quirk of his dark brow.

"I've set my portion aside," she said. "So this is all yours."

She hurried back to her room before he could respond. With the door latched behind her and the possibility of sharing a breakfast with Jonah Cahill now gone, Madeline breathed a sigh of relief.

As she undressed and donned her nightgown, Madeline thought back over their conversation. She retrieved her notebook and writing materials and padded over to the desk to make notes.

When she was done, Madeline sat back and looked over the information. That task accomplished, she climbed into her bunk and curled beneath the blankets.

On the other side of the wall was the most frustrating Pinkerton detective in the employ of the agency. Why then did she dream of the two of them in a garden somewhere, Jonah digging holes and her covering them up? Stranger still, Madame sat in a garden chair covered in roses supervising the entire hopeless endeavor.

Madeline sat bolt upright, trying to decide whether to laugh or hurry to record the silly dream in her notebook. A knock at her cabin door interrupted her debate.

She wrapped the blanket over her nightclothes and hurried to the door. "Yes?" she called.

"We're docking soon," Jonah said. "Were you sleeping?"

"No," she said as she shifted her blanket. "But thank you for letting me know."

She hurried to dress and perform her morning tasks, taking bites of the delicious breakfast Cook had prepared in between attempts at taming her hair and tying the ribbons on her dress. Finally, as the steam engines shuddered to silence, Madeline was ready to depart.

While Jonah made arrangements to store their things for their return trip, Madeline wandered out on the deck to take a look around. Indianola appeared to be much more of a bustling port city than she expected.

More than a dozen ships—among them several from the Morgan line—lay at anchor near the two massive wharves that stretched out almost as far as she could see. A smaller wharf, populated this morning by a fishing boat and a small craft of some sort, had been situated some distance away down the beach.

Madeline turned her attention to the city itself, a jumble of buildings hugging the coastline and sprawling off both to the east and to the west of where she stood. A salt-scented breeze kicked up, and Madeline held tight to the rail beside her. The morning was warm, and yet many of the men and women who pressed past her, recent arrivals from a vessel of Bremen registry, wore several layers of garments.

Other travelers milled about, speaking what sounded like German or Czech. Owing to the vast amount of laughter and animated embraces, some seemed to be meeting long-lost friends or family.

Jonah appeared beside her and nodded toward the city. "Shall we?" he said as he led her down the wharf.

Their first stop was the doctor's office, where they discovered that the current physician, a Dr. Hardy, had only been practicing in the city since the previous fall. His slight stature, obvious youth, and pimpled complexion gave away the fact before he admitted it.

"I have the address of the former resident of my office. Please just wait one moment, Detective Cahill," he told Jonah as he went back to get the information.

"This appears to be a dead end," Madeline said while they were left alone. "So I suppose we're off to the preacher next?"

"We are," Jonah said. "Unless you have another idea."

"Off to the preacher it is," she said as she watched the bustle of traffic out the doctor's front window.

"Well, isn't that nice?" Dr. Hardy said as he handed Jonah a slip of paper. "You two off to the preacher. I do hope you'll be staying in the city. Perhaps your wife might want to trust me with whatever ails her," he said as he eyed Madeline with a less than medical interest. "Should the time come that I am needed, that is."

"I assure you it will not," Madeline said as she thrust the door open and departed, leaving Jonah and the disgusting doctor in her wake. Two steps onto the porch, Madeline heard a bullet zing past.

Jonah hauled her against him and ducked back inside. "Is there another exit?" he asked the doctor.

Dr. Hardy seemed befuddled for a moment. "Is she hurt?"

"I'm fine," Madeline said.

"An exit," Jonah repeated. "Is this door the only one?"

"Oh," he said as he recovered. "No, there's another back in the exam room." He cast a furtive glance at Madeline then hurried to show them the way out.

Jonah stepped out first, his gun drawn. At his nod, Madeline followed. A moment later, the doctor slammed the door shut and the lock sounded as he barred the door.

"Did you see who fired the shot?" Jonah asked as they crept around the side of the building.

Madeline tried her best to recall anything—or anyone—suspicious. "No," she finally said. "But there were plenty of people out there who might have taken aim at us." She paused. "Or maybe the shot was meant for that doctor. He's not exactly a man I would trust whatever ails me to."

Despite the gravity of the situation, Jonah smiled. "That's certainly possible. It's also possible the shot was accidental."

"True," Madeline said just as another shot sounded.

Chapter Eleven

The idiot shooting at them had best be wishing today was his last day, because once Jonah found him, it would be. He looked over at Madeline, obediently waiting in her hiding place behind a water barrel, and then took another step forward.

He was now able to see into the alley, the only place the shooter could have ducked into after firing. Though there were several cats yowling and a child peering at him from behind a washtub, he found no one who could have fired the shot.

"Did you see a man with a gun?" he called to the child, who nodded. "Where did he go, then?"

The little one calmly pointed directly at Jonah. "Me? You mean you only saw me?"

The child nodded as Jonah stifled a grumble. The shooter was likely long gone now. Still, he called to the child. "Go inside, now. It's not safe out."

"What are you hollering for?" a woman said as she stepped out onto the porch.

"Someone is firing shots," Jonah said to her. "It's not a place I would want my child to be playing."

She was young, almost too young to be the mother of this imp, and yet the woman's face wore the aged look of someone who had seen more than her years should have allowed. She focused weary brown eyes in Jonah's direction.

"They shooting at you?" she asked as she hauled the child up onto her hip.

"It's possible," Jonah said. "Me and my companion, that is."

"Then you'll be needing a way out of that alley. It don't go much farther before it turns and dumps you off at the water. Ain't nobody going to get out that way if someone's shooting at you."

She disappeared inside, and Jonah thought he had seen the last of her. Then she reappeared and waved to him. "Come on in here, you and your companion," she said. "But if you get shot at, don't blame me."

"Well, that is comforting," he muttered as he turned to indicate to Madeline that she should follow him.

Wonder of all wonders, the frustrating female once again did as she was told and hurried to join him. He offered her a firm look.

"See that porch over there?" At her nod, he continued. "I want you to follow me as close as you can, so close your hands are on my waist. We're going to walk over there and go inside that door. If the idiot who has been firing shots goes at it again, I want you to get down on the ground then make for that alley again as fast as you can."

She shook her head. "You want me to lie down and crawl to the alley?" Madeline looked down at the silly white confection of ribbons and bows she'd chosen as her attire for this trip and then back up at him. "In this dress?"

"You do have a choice," he told her. "You could preserve your dress by keeping it off the ground but ruin it with blood when the bullet hits you."

"Oh," she said, her eyes widening. "You do know how to draw a word picture. Maybe you ought to be writing Madame's memories down instead of me."

"Madeline," he said, his jaw clenched. "Stay focused. I am going on three. One. Two. Three."

Jonah stepped into the clearing, his gun drawn and his senses on high alert. Madeline once again did as she was told and grasped his waist as they walked down the alley. He kept his body between her and the direction the bullet had come until they reached the porch. Then he put her in front of him and sent her up the rickety back steps and inside.

Spending another minute looking around for evidence, he located a bullet near the porch. Slipping the .45 caliber shell into his pocket, Jonah stepped inside with his weapon still handy.

There he found Madeline waiting for him, the young woman and child now gone. "Out here," the girl called, and Jonah followed the sound of her voice through the dark hallway and out into what appeared to be the first floor of a boardinghouse.

The woman stood in the center of a small entry area. To her right was a room with a long table made of boards and a mismatched set of a dozen chairs and benches. To the left a door led to an interior room, possibly a kitchen. Behind them was a staircase, and straight ahead the door to the front of the building.

"Annabelle," she told them. "I'm Annabelle Lee, and this is Jordy."

Madeline tickled the little one under the chin and smiled. "Thank you, Annabelle," she said. "And hello, Jordy."

The child giggled and kicked his feet, but his mother ignored him. Instead, she appeared to be preoccupied with the staircase behind Jonah and Madeline.

"Yes," Jonah said. "I do appreciate your kindness." He reached for Madeline's elbow and moved her toward the closed front door then paused to pull one of his cards out of his pocket and thrust it into Annabelle's palm. "If you are ever in Galveston and need help, go to the Galveston Police Station and ask for Officer Pearson. Can you remember that? Officer Pearson. He will know how to reach me."

"Office Pearson. Sure." She looked down at the card and then back up at Jonah. "A Pinkerton man, are you? Well now, how about that, Jordy?"

Jordy gave Jonah a toothless grin. His gaze then went up to the stairs as well.

"Let's go," he said to Madeline and then hurried her out onto the sidewalk.

Keeping a tight grip on the reporter's elbow, Jonah headed down the street, not slowing until he reached the sheriff's office. He found the sheriff behind his desk, his feet resting atop a stack of wanted posters on the table behind him.

"Somebody shot at you?" the sheriff demanded. "Did you shoot him back?"

Jonah gripped the door frame. "No, but I know where he is."

Madeline gaped. "You do?"

He nodded and turned his attention to the sheriff, a portly man of advanced years who had introduced himself as Pake Simmons. "You know the boardinghouse just down the road? The one where a young lady named Annabelle stays?"

"She don't just stay there," the sheriff said. "Her mama owned the place. What about it?"

"I have reason to believe whoever fired this shot is up on the second floor of that building right now." He pulled the shell casing out of his pocket and handed it to the lawman. "If there hadn't been women and a child with me down in that lobby, I would have gone up there and looked for myself."

Madeline tugged on his sleeve. "Is that why Annabelle kept looking up the stairs?"

"I believe so." He turned his attention back to the sheriff. "I'd be obliged if I could leave Miss Latour here and go back with you." He pulled another of his cards out and offered it to the sheriff.

"Pinkerton man, are you? Well now," he said. "Seems like the Pinkertons have quite an interest in this town of late."

"Is that so?" Jonah asked. "Who else has been here?"

"Can't quite remember the name but he was a fella. Average height. Talked like he wasn't from around here. Seems to me that's right."

"Was his name Donovan?"

"Might be." He pulled off his hat and scratched his bald head. "Don't really matter, though, does it? If we got a shooter over at Mrs. Francine's Boardinghouse, then that needs to be handled." He whistled, and a man even older than him came shuffling out from the back of the building. "Elmer, take care that this lady is safe, would you?"

Elmer nodded and then offered Madeline a smile. "She'll be just fine here. What's happening I need to know about?"

"Offer the lady a cup of tea, Elmer," the lawman said. "And stay away from open windows. That ought to be all you need to know."

With that, Jonah left Madeline in the questionable care of Elmer and stepped out onto the sidewalk. Though there was the usual traffic a town of this size might have, no one looked or seemed suspicious. In Jonah's experience, that was the worst scenario.

Because every single one of them from the old man on the wagon to the young girl flirting with the stable hand was suspicious until the shooter had been caught.

"I figure a direct approach to be best. What say you, Pinkerton man?"

"Agreed," Jonah said, taking the lead as they closed the distance between the sheriff's office and Mrs. Francine's Boardinghouse.

Opening the front door with their guns drawn, Jonah stepped inside first with the sheriff a step behind. The place was quiet. Too quiet for a home that had a child in it.

Jonah nodded toward the staircase. "Annabelle kept looking up there," he said as quietly as he could. "How many rooms are there?"

"Five, best I remember. Where did those shots come from, or can you tell?"

He thought a minute. "Northeast corner." He paused. "I'll go first and you follow. That work for you?"

"Son, that's how I managed to keep doing this so long. You go on ahead and I will stand watch behind you."

At Jonah's nod, they proceeded up the staircase, pausing occasionally to listen for any sound on the upper floor. Finally they reached the landing. All the doors were shut, leaving the space in only the dimmest of light.

The corridor had that musty smell familiar to coastal dwellings that were not exposed to fresh air, and the floors were stained and uneven. Boards were missing in several places, and it looked as if something had chewed on the door frame nearest him. If Annabelle took in boarders, they obviously did not pay well enough to cause her to put any money toward repairs.

Jonah nodded toward the room in the northeast corner and then inched his way there as quietly as he could manage. He tried the knob and found it either locked or stuck. Either way, the door would not budge.

Holding up his index finger, he began to count off one, two, and then three. On three, he turned sharply and kicked the door.

The door flew open and slammed against the wall. Jonah stepped inside and found it completely empty, with neither a bed nor wardrobe in sight. And definitely no one who could have aimed a gun at Madeline.

Jonah went to the window and raised it. From where he stood, there was no ledge, but rather just a drop-off that fell two stories to the ground.

The sheriff gave him a doubtful look that quickly turned disgusted. "Either you're wasting my time or whoever fired that shot at you was awful quick in vacating the place."

A board creaked in the hall, and Jonah lifted his finger to his lips.

His gun aimed and ready, Jonah whirled around the corner and out into the corridor ready to shoot whoever was out there. Until he saw it was a cat.

The fat orange tabby threaded itself around his legs as Jonah reassessed his next move. With four more rooms upstairs, he determined to search them all.

Extricating himself from the cat, he crept down the hall only to find the sheriff had stayed behind to give his attention to the feline. The first door opened easily, and the room proved empty. The search of the remaining three rooms had similar results.

"If anyone was up here, they're gone now, ain't they?" Sheriff Simmons said as he knelt down and scratched the cat behind the ears.

"It looks that way," Jonah admitted, although he was certain someone had been here. His gut told him so, as did the strange looks upstairs by Annabelle and her child. Just to be certain, he would search the downstairs rooms as well.

There he found a kitchen that, while in less than desirable condition, had been recently used for meal preparation. A child's cup sat on a cluttered table beside a copy of last week's *Galveston Daily News*.

Jonah walked back into the front hall and saw the sheriff walking down the stairs with the cat following close behind. He completed the search of the first floor, finding a room in the back of the house that appeared to be the place where Annabelle and her child were living.

The sheriff joined him there. "Looks like Mrs. Francine's

Boardinghouse has fallen on hard times."

"It appears so. What do you think happened to Mrs. Francine?"

The lawman shrugged. "Buried her last fall. Place belongs to Annabelle now."

"And she lives here alone?"

"I believe so. Her man ships out, so he ain't here much." He lifted his hat to scratch his bare head again. "Pinkerton man, I won't be saying my expertise is greater than yours, but I have to wonder if that shell you found didn't come from a gun accidentally fired."

"But accidentally fired twice?"

"Well, you do have a point, but—"

The front door opened, and Jonah once again reached for his gun. He stepped out of the room and slowly moved around the staircase with his gun drawn.

"Elmer?" Jonah said as he put away his weapon. "Where is Madeline?"

"One minute we were playing cards and the next she was gone," he said, eyes wide.

"Hold on now," Sheriff Simmons said. "She couldn't have disappeared right there in front of you. Either you left or she did. Which was it?"

"She did, Pake," he said as he snapped his fingers. "Just up and gone."

Jonah took a deep breath and let it out slowly. "Think, man," he said, his jaw clenched. "Where did you see her go? Did someone take her?"

"No, sir," he said, shaking his head so hard he almost fell over. "She took herself. Just up and went right out of the room in the middle of a hand of Go Fish, and it being her turn too. I blame it on that preacher man."

As Jonah headed for the door, he heard the sheriff ask, "What in the world did the preacher do to cause that Pinkerton man's woman to up and disappear?"

Jonah paused to turn around. The orange cat had found Elmer and was now weaving itself around his legs.

"Well, he walked by with one of those fellers from the wharf, like I said. And we were just sitting here playing cards, again like I said, and I pointed out the preacher man, and she said well, if all she was doing was playing cards she would at least pass the time doing something worthwhile."

Jonah shook his head. "And what was that?"

He shrugged. "Talking to the preacher man, I guess."

"Sheriff," Jonah asked. "Which way is the church?"

Shaking his head, the sheriff laughed. "Practically one on every corner here, thank the Lord. Which one do you want?"

"I think he means the preacher man's church," Elmer offered. "I can take you there."

Jonah and the sheriff followed the old man down the street and around the corner until they stood in front of the church pastored by the fellow Elmer called the preacher man. Out of the corner of his eye, Jonah saw the orange cat ambling toward them.

"Great," he muttered.

Then a woman's scream erupted from somewhere inside the church. Jonah ran inside and followed the sound until he located its source in a small library next to the sanctuary.

He found Madeline atop a table in the center of the room. An older fellow who he assumed was the preacher was chasing a rat with a fisherman's net.

"What are you doing here?" Jonah shouted over the din, his heart racing.

"Jonah!" she managed. "I was just speaking with Reverend Wyatt when that rat jumped out of the box over there and right into my lap."

The rat skittered past Jonah only to run straight into the waiting jaws of the orange tabby cat. "I don't think you'll be pestered by that rat again," the sheriff said with a chuckle.

Madeline carefully climbed down from the table and nodded toward the preacher. "Before we were set upon by the vermin, Reverend Wyatt was about to show me the church records going back to well before the war."

"I thought they were destroyed in the '75 hurricane."

"This building survived the storm, and because the registries were in this waterproof box that one of our parishioners made, they were hardly touched by all that water. Just a spot or two. Oh yes, I've got them right here," he said as he reached deeper into the box where Madeline claimed the rat had come from and pulled out two large books then placed them on the table. Madeline reached for one and Jonah took the other.

"What are we looking for?" she asked him.

"Baby girl born on the 18th or 19th of September in 1855. Father is Samuel Smith and mother is Eliza Smith," he said.

"Did you say Samuel Smith?" Sheriff Simmons said. "We knew him, didn't we, Elmer?"

"Sure did. Good man, he was, and a fine sailor, but I don't remember any child of his being born here, do you, Reverend?"

The preacher pointed to the books. "Ought to be in there somewhere if he did."

"All right," Jonah said to Madeline. "You know what we're looking for."

She nodded and turned to the first page of the book in front of her as the three other men sat down to chat. Though Jonah was trying to be diligent in his reading of the old and spidery handwriting in the registry, it was obvious that Madeline was more interested in listening carefully to the old-timers' conversation.

"Wasn't it rumored that old Smith had another name he wasn't so proud of?" Elmer said.

"Aw now," the sheriff said. "Ain't nobody credits those crazy tales any more than they do the stories of pirate treasure."

"What's this about pirate treasure?" Madeline said as Jonah stifled a groan.

"Just nonsense," the sheriff said. "Ain't that so, preacher?"

Reverend Wyatt shook his head. "You know I can't talk about things people tell me in confidence, especially when they aren't here to defend themselves."

Madeline set her work aside and offered the preacher a smile. "I am not asking you to tell me what people said, only just to tell whether it was a certain person who said it. Would that be all right?"

"I suppose so," Reverend Wyatt said.

"This treasure they're talking about, did it belong to Samuel Smith?"

"Oh no," the reverend said. "It wasn't his at all."

"I see," she said, disappointment evident in her voice as she turned to the table and began thumbing through the pages of the register again.

"You couldn't miss the opportunity to dig for pirate treasure, could you?" he whispered.

Her only response was to ignore him. That didn't bother Jonah at all, for at least she was back at work doing what needed to be done. Between dodging bullets and roaming through a run-down boardinghouse, they were already way behind schedule.

"That's the truth," the sheriff said. "Wasn't old Samuel's treasure at all."

"No, Samuel, he got put in the churchyard long before there was any question of treasure." Elmer coughed then regained his voice. "Was that before the war?"

"Yep," the sheriff said. "Samuel went to his reward in '58 or '59, I do believe. Or maybe it was earlier than that. I don't rightly recall, now that I think of it."

Jonah looked up to see if Madeline was paying attention. Of course she was.

"Yes sir," Elmer said. "That treasure belonged to ole what's his name."

Madeline turned around to face the men. "Jean Lafitte?"

The preacher turned red as a beet and began to cough. When he caught his breath, he turned to face Madeline. "Why would you say that?"

Chapter Twelve

"I hope you've learned your lesson," Jonah said as they walked together down the wharf toward the *Haven*.

"I have no idea what you're talking about," she said as she picked up her pace in order to shorten the time she had to spend with the infuriating Pinkerton detective.

"Even I have not interrogated a man of the cloth until he wept!"

"You're being ridiculous. He did not weep," she countered as she stepped around a fat orange cat preening in the evening sun. "And I was not interrogating. I was merely asking."

His laughter chased her up the wharf. "Asking stopped about ten minutes in. When we get back to Galveston, I plan to send a telegram to the captain to let him know I have a candidate for the next open position at the agency."

She whirled around to face him, and Jonah had to sidestep to keep from running into her. "All right," she admitted. "I may have gotten a little overzealous in my questioning of the preacher, but you know I was right. He knows something and won't tell us."

"Cannot tell us," Jonah corrected. "He is a preacher. He's taken a vow, Madeline. It would go against his oath to give up a confidence."

"Then there must be another way." She looked down and then back up at Jonah, ignoring the way his silver eyes reflected the color of the water around them. "Why is that cat following you?"

Jonah looked down at the cat that was now threading itself around his ankles. "I have no idea," he said, "but you are not going to change the subject. The purpose of our trip to Indianola was to find out all we could about Mrs. Smith's granddaughter."

"Which we did," she reminded him. "Not only did Sheriff Simmons, Elmer, and Reverend Wyatt agree that Samuel Smith lived in Indianola, but they also sent us to the courthouse where deed records showed where his home used to be and death records indicated his date and cause of death."

"I believe that was me who went to the courthouse," he said as he ignored the fat orange cat. "You remained back at the church to torture the reverend."

"Truly, you are so dramatic, Jonah."

She turned and walked toward the steamship, not caring whether Jonah followed. Once on board, she found a porter and located her cabin. By the time she'd been settled inside and discovered that yet another hamper of food had appeared, she did not care whether the Pinkerton agent got on the ship or not.

Unfortunately, he did. This she discovered when he came pounding on her door a few minutes later.

"Have you opened your hamper?" he demanded.

"Come in, Jonah," was her bland response.

He stepped inside and nodded to the hamper. "Go ahead. Open it."

She did as he asked and then looked over at him. "All right, I opened it."

"And what do you see?"

"Food," she said. "Lots of food, actually. Much more than I could possibly want."

The Pinkerton agent crossed the distance between them and looked down into the hamper. "That's interesting," he said.

"Why? What was in yours?"

He met her gaze, his expression serious as he pulled something out of his pocket and cradled it in his palm. "Nothing but this spent .45 caliber shell."

"Oh," she said. And then again, "Oh."

Jonah stuffed the bullet back into his pocket. "It is the same caliber as the one I got out of the alley behind the boardinghouse and left with the sheriff."

"I see." Madeline sat in the nearest chair and tried to make sense of it all. Finally, she gave up. "What does all of this mean, Jonah?"

He sat beside her. "I don't know. After we hit those dead ends at the boardinghouse, I thought for sure that those two shots, while coming too close for comfort, were just random shots. I know that's what the sheriff believes."

"Understandable considering there was no obvious culprit. And weapons do get discharged by accident."

"They do, but nearly missing you?" He shook his head. "And more than once? No, accidental doesn't add up."

"But what does?"

He shook his head. "Nothing. Having said that, there isn't anything we can do about it until we get back to Galveston. In light of that, and in light of the fact I'm starving, I propose we divide the bounty in your hamper and have dinner."

Much as she wanted him out of her cabin, it seemed simpler to agree. Let the Pinkerton agent have his supper and then perhaps he would leave her in peace.

"I also propose we use the table for our meal this time." He paused in his rummaging through the contents of the hamper to give her a mischievous grin. "Unless you prefer another picnic."

"You are truly impossible, Jonah Cahill," she said as she grudgingly laughed.

"I thought I was dramatic," he countered.

"You are both," she said as she shook her head and joined him at the hamper.

"I am neither," he said.

Madeline looked up into those impossible eyes, and her heart lurched. For a moment she let herself remember why she had fallen in love with this man. Then, just as quickly, she pushed all those reasons away.

"Then we shall agree to disagree," she managed.

Hours later, when Jonah had long ago gone to his cabin and she was alone and trying to sleep in spite of the sounds of the steam engines, Madeline could only lie on her back and wish she was looking up at the stars.

Silly as it seemed, she needed to see those stars tonight. So she dressed quickly, braided her hair, and then hurried up onto the deck.

The noise of the steam engines was much louder here, so she moved as far away from them as she could. Up front with the wind blowing and the seas lightly chopping, she felt miles away from the cramped and dark cabin below the deck. And though the deck was full of men in the employ of Morgan's Steamship Company going about their work, in this darkened corner she felt blissfully alone.

The moon had just passed its first quarter a few days ago, and the full moon would not come until next week. Thus, the silver moonlight that danced over the waves was muted and pale.

Madeline gripped the rail and let the salt breeze and sea spray wash over her face as she looked up into the night sky to count the constellations. Times like this always brought Papa to mind, for he was the source of her first interest in studying the stars.

Papa had an encyclopedic knowledge of the constellations and stars, and he could answer almost any question the young Madeline had posed. Later she took up the amateur study of astronomy as a way to learn even more about the fathomless creation the Lord placed overhead.

"The Lord, He makes plans that we do not always understand, you know."

Papa's words, and yet as she felt the roll of the waves beneath her feet they became her words as well. Then came the verse from 2 Samuel that she had committed to memory so long ago, she had lost the number of years since she'd first learned it:

"For we must needs die, and are as water spilt on the ground, which cannot be gathered up again; neither doth God respect any person: yet doth he devise means, that his banished be not expelled from him."

How easy it was to stand here on this vessel headed for Galveston and forget that there were higher purposes and bigger plans than her simple goal of finding the facts behind the myth of Lafitte the pirate.

Jonah was right in saying she had gone too far in questioning the reverend. And while she was not ready to admit she had made him cry, she did cringe when she thought of the relentless way she went about her questioning of him.

Even as she was uncomfortable thinking about the conversation, Madeline knew she would do it the same way if the same situation arose.

The facts were the facts, and facts were meant to be discovered.

This was why she excelled as a reporter. It would be why she excelled at completing this investigation.

Something bumped against her leg, and she jolted. A plaintive yowl arose over the sound of the waves.

Madeline looked down to see a fat orange tabby cat that looked very much like the one that had been sunning itself on the dock at Indianola. "What are you doing here, little fellow?" she murmured as she knelt down to scratch the feline behind its ear.

"First you torture a preacher in his own church, and now you bring contraband aboard an oceangoing vessel. Where will it all end?"

Madeline looked up to see Jonah walking toward her, a broad smile on his face. She rose and swiped the backs of her hands on her skirt as the Pinkerton detective came to stand beside her at the rail.

"Hello, Madeline," he said as he slid her a sideways look. "Shouldn't you be sleeping?"

"Not when the skies are this beautiful," she said as she looked back up into the heavens.

"When I was a boy, I would wait until my parents and sister were asleep then I would climb up to the roof and lie on my back to look at the stars. One morning I woke up with the sun shining on my face and the entire household in an uproar because I was missing from my bed."

"You never told me this story, Jonah," she said as she imagined her former fiancé as a child.

He paused to chuckle. "After doling out the punishment I deserved, my father bought me a book on astronomy and made me promise not to fall off the roof."

Madeline smiled. "And did you keep that promise, or is that why you are so hardheaded?"

Jonah laughed again. "I did keep that promise, except for one memorable occasion that involved a bee."

She thought of the bee that had caused her downfall—literally—while trying to decide how to best escape the palm tree and joined him in his laughter. "Bees are devious creatures sometimes," she said.

"As are some females." At her scowl, Jonah held up both hands as if attempting to fend her off. "I am making a joke, Madeline."

"I know," she said slowly as her smile faded. "Neither of us took our jobs expecting to work with each other."

He reached down to pet the cat that was now weaving around his ankles. "I am beginning to wonder what her real reason is in hiring both of us."

"I doubt you'll ever get that information out of her."

Jonah stood to return to his place beside her. "Much as I hate to admit it, you have been a decent partner on this trip, Madeline. You were shot at—twice—and you never once acted like it scared you."

"Oh, I was terrified," she admitted. "But I have learned that being afraid isn't a bad thing. Acting afraid, now that's another thing altogether."

"For a nosy reporter, you've got some good advice," he said as he slid her a grin.

"And for an irritating Pinkerton detective, you've got some good sense."

"Touché," he said with a grin.

They fell into a companionable silence until the watch bell rang and Madeline jumped. Jonah placed his hand atop hers to steady her, and instantly that connection tossed her back in time to a place where neither of them distrusted the other.

Where all they wanted was a future together.

For just this moment, that possibility did not seem as though it was a lifetime ago. Then Jonah lifted his hand.

"We ought to get out of their way and get some sleep," he told her.

"I suppose." Madeline took one last long look at the heavens and then followed Jonah back to the corridor below deck. "Good night, Jonah," she said as she stepped inside.

"Good night, Madeline," she heard him say as he opened his door down the hall. Just as she was shutting her door, she heard him add, "Oh come on in, then."

Peering out into the corridor, she spied the fat orange cat's tail as it slipped into Jonah's room just before the door closed. "Contraband indeed," she whispered with a smile as she bolted her door and climbed into bed fully dressed and ready to sleep.

That night she didn't dream of digging holes and filling them. Instead, she dreamed of falling stars and fat orange cats.

And of Jonah Cahill.

❤

The next afternoon, Jonah banished the thought of Madeline Latour standing in the moonlight beneath the stars and focused on the stack of telegrams and mail that had arrived in his absence. Unfortunately, that thought kept occurring, along with the feel of her hand beneath his.

"There you are," his sister called from the doorway before joining him at his desk. "I thought you might want to see this."

Jonah sat back and pushed away all thoughts of the nosy reporter. "What is it?"

She plopped a copy of the *Galveston Daily News* on his desk, sending the letters and telegrams flying in all directions. The fat orange cat that had followed him home from the docks yesterday, now aptly named Stowaway, chased after them.

"Hey watch out," he said as he leaned down to retrieve the captain's letter before Stowaway destroyed it.

Then he saw the headline: Local Home Hides Possible Treasure.

Jonah dropped the letter and snatched up the newspaper to read the article, which was thankfully brief and buried in the middle of the third page under an ad for Labadie's Ten Cent Table. There was no byline, but he had a good idea of who might have written it.

Reaching for his hat, Jonah left the mess and his sister behind in the library and headed off to visit the first of the two possible suspects, that idiot Townsend. He found Townsend hurrying out of the *Daily News* building at 113 and 115 Market Street.

Madeline was walking by the reporter's side.

Chapter Thirteen

"Hello, Madeline." Jonah stepped in front of the pair. "Townsend," he added as he gave the reporter a look that let him know how difficult it was to choose to talk to him rather than throttle him.

"What are you doing here?" Madeline asked.

"Hold on here," the *Daily News* reporter said as he stopped short to avoid a collision with Jonah. "First her and now you."

"That's right," Madeline said to Jonah. "I got here first."

"So I see."

Townsend shook his head. "This woman believes some kind of nonsense about an article she claims I wrote. If that's why you're here, then you're both wasting your time."

"Because you don't think you have to answer my questions?" Jonah asked.

"Well, I don't," he said. "I am a reporter and as such I am protected by freedom of the press, so that much is true."

"I have no problem taking you down to the police station and allowing Officer Pearson to ask them. Is that what you want, or do you think maybe you can change your mind and speak to me first?"

"No, he will be speaking to me first," Madeline said.

Jonah glared at her, but Madeline ignored him. He turned his attention to Townsend.

"I'm not talking to either of you out here on Market Street,"

Townsend said. "Look around you. Do you think I want to say anything that could be overheard?"

"Then I suppose you need to make your choice," Jonah said. "We can go back inside, we can go over to the police station, or we can walk around the corner to my house and talk there. No matter which of these options you pick, you and I will be having a conversation today."

"You will be talking to me too," Madeline said. "First," she added.

He offered her a sideways look that told her to keep quiet. Again she ignored him.

"I suggest you choose the Cahill property," she said. "Especially since you think you know so much about buried treasure. While you're there, you can prove the article you wrote is true and dig some up to show us."

"Oh you would like that, wouldn't you, Madeline?" Jonah said, turning toward her. "Then you could have your story about Lafitte gold handed to you by this guy."

"Not just gold, Jonah," she snapped. "There could be silver, precious gems, and all sorts of other things. However, if I was going to get any information out of this man regarding Lafitte treasure or anything else, do you really think this is how I would choose to do it?"

The truth of that statement was hard to ignore. For all her irritating qualities, Madeline Latour was an intelligent woman. And an intelligent woman would know better than to draw attention to an investigation she wanted to keep secret.

Still, she was here. With Townsend. And she had gotten to him first.

Jonah glared at her and then returned his attention to the reporter. "Time's up. Where is this interview going to happen, Townsend?"

"Shortest distance is to your place, Cahill," he said as he started walking that way. "And for the record, when I followed you from the train station that day, I had no idea that was your family home."

"Didn't seem to matter." Jonah fell into step beside him.

"Hey, all I knew was that a Pinkerton man was in town, and I figured he might be wanting to follow up on those reports of criminal mischief."

They turned the corner, and the Cahill property came into view. A few minutes later, they had arrived.

"Can't we wait until we get inside?" Townsend said, looking miserable.

"We aren't going inside," Jonah snapped. "You're not fit to meet my family until I decide you are."

Jonah paused to open the gate and then directed them all around to the back of the house where an outdoor table and chairs awaited. Townsend did as he was told and followed them.

He took the seat nearest Townsend. If the *Daily News* reporter decided to make a run for it, Jonah didn't want anything—or anyone—to impede his ability to catch the man.

The fat orange cat hurried over from its perch beneath the fig tree to thread itself around his ankles. Jonah reached down and scratched its ears.

"All right, Townsend," he said. "Spill your guts. Why did you write that article?"

"I already told you," the reporter protested, "I do not know what you are talking about."

Jonah held his temper in check as he responded. "We are talking about the article regarding the property where you are now located, Mr. Townsend. Why did you write it and on what is your information based? And I warn you that while Miss Latour got to you first this morning, I assure you I am the one you need to be answering first."

Madeline shook her head. "I believe Detective Cahill and I have similar questions. I propose that I will be asking them much more nicely than he will."

Jonah let out a long breath. "All right. I am sorry, Miss Latour, for the slight. Mr. Townsend, do not ignore your esteemed colleague from the *Picayune*, but also do not forget you are here to answer to me."

"Wait." He turned to Madeline. "You work at the *Picayune*?"

"I do."

"Well, how about that? I always wanted to work at the *Picayune*. Do you think you might put a word in for me? I've done some serious journalist work since I got here, most recently—"

"Most recently the piece on the Lafitte treasure that lies beneath Cahill soil," Jonah interjected. "Let's get right to it, Townsend. Where did you get your information for that article, and are you missing a shovel?"

Townsend opened his mouth to speak. Jonah held up his hand to silence him.

"And before you answer, I want you to think about this carefully. Remember, you have just sold yourself to us as a reporter of some considerable skills, have you not?"

At Townsend's nod, Jonah continued. "And a reporter of some considerable skills ought to be able to give me the answer to that question, especially given the fact that you are employed by that paper, wouldn't you think?"

Townsend sighed. "One would think," he agreed. "Look, you can ask me as many times as you want, and all I can say to you is that I do not know who put that article into the paper today."

"Do you know who wrote it, then?" Madeline asked.

"I can find out," Townsend told her. "I just need to do some digging."

"And speaking of digging," he and Madeline said together as the cat jumped up into Jonah's lap.

Jonah set Stowaway back on the ground and then fixed Madeline with a look before turning his attention to the man he'd brought here to question. "As you know, someone has been digging holes on this property. Who was it?"

Townsend leaned back in his chair and held out his hands as if physically fending off the question. "Hey now, I am the one who told you about that, and I am also the one who asked you if you knew who it was."

"Well, I don't," Jonah said. "So who was it?"

He looked around, first at Madeline and then back at Jonah. "Why would I ask if I knew?"

"To throw one of us off?" He glanced at Madeline. "Miss Latour is somewhat of an amateur treasure hunter. Do you think she dug those holes?"

"Of course not," Townsend said.

"You said that awfully quickly." Ignoring Madeline's look of outrage, he focused on Townsend. "How do you know?"

"Because if she had, she would have covered them back up."

Jonah shook his head. "Why do you say that?"

Townsend's laugh held no humor. "Reporters are trained to be as unobtrusive as possible. We blend in and we do our jobs. Now maybe I'm still learning how to do that, but I would bet Miss Latour is pretty good at it. So given that, if she's investigating treasure, maybe she would dig holes to see what she could find, but wouldn't she cover them back up afterward to keep anyone else from knowing she'd been there?"

The truth of that statement hit Jonah in the gut. All this time he had been so focused on Madeline as a possible suspect, he'd missed the clues that told him it could not be her.

"Thank you, Mr. Townsend," Madeline said gently, picking up the thread of the questioning. "As a fellow reporter, I understand the need to protect a source. I also understand that it is a matter of journalistic integrity to verify the information we receive. Would you agree?"

"Oh, I definitely would, Miss Latour," he said eagerly. "Why, all it takes is for some folks to find out you're a reporter and the next thing you know they're giving you all sorts of information that may or may not be the truth."

"And how do you decide what is true from what is not true?" Jonah interjected.

Townsend seemed happy to be asked a question not directly related to the matter at hand. He grinned and leaned forward in his chair, resting his elbows on his knees.

"Well, you see," he began, "first and foremost a reporter has to develop a gut sense for when someone's telling him the truth. He's got to know that what he is writing and putting out there in the paper for the world to read is the facts as they truly exist. That's the kind of reporter I am, Miss Latour."

Madeline looked at Jonah and rolled her eyes. Keeping his expression neutral, Jonah continued.

"So who dug the holes, Townsend?"

"I told you I don't know," he shouted as he stood.

"Sit down," Jonah told him.

"Something going on back here?" Officer Pearson called as he walked around the house.

"We were just having a conversation with Mr. Townsend of the

Daily News regarding these holes that have been dug on the property."

"Is that so?" the policeman said as he joined them.

Jonah turned to Madeline. "Miss Latour, this is Officer Pearson of the Galveston Police Department. He is the gentleman who was kind enough to watch over my mother and sister while we were away being shot at."

At Jonah's statement, the police officer's brows went up. "You didn't mention anything about being shot at, Jonah."

"That's because they missed. Both times. And honestly, I'm pretty sure they were after Miss Latour. So, Thomas Pearson, please meet Miss Madeline Latour."

Madeline and the officer exchanged pleasantries, and then Pearson took the last empty chair on the patio, directly across from the *Daily News* reporter. "So what did you tell them, Mr. Townsend?"

"I told them I don't know," he said. "Don't know who dug those holes and don't know who put that article out in the paper today."

The police officer shrugged as he looked at Jonah. "Sounds like he doesn't know."

"It does sound that way," Jonah conceded. "However, he has assured us that he can use his above average investigative skills to uncover who did."

"Well, that is a relief." Pearson turned his attention to Madeline. "I don't believe I have seen you here in Galveston before. Are you just visiting?"

"I am here with my employer on assignment," she told him.

Townsend's eyes widened. "There are others from the *Picayune* staff here in Galveston? How was I not made aware of this?"

Madeline shook her head. "No, this has nothing to do with my job at the *Picayune*. My employer is a widow lady," she said. "I am recording her memories for her."

"Anything interesting?" Townsend said as he leaned toward her.

"Mr. Townsend," she said in that I-cannot-believe-you-said-that voice that Jonah knew too well, "everything I record for my employer is private information. I'm sure you understand."

"Sure, of course," he said. "Forget I asked. Unless you change your mind, that is." Townsend laughed at his own joke, but no one else joined him.

Jonah stood, and Officer Pearson joined him. "I think we're done here."

"So soon?" Townsend said. "I had some questions of my own. Remember, I did promise to find out who is behind the article and digging."

Jonah frowned. "If you're as good as you say you are, you will bring me a name soon."

Townsend said his goodbyes and walked away. "Pearson," Jonah said. "Would you mind seeing he gets at least to the end of the street? I don't want him coming back here without an invitation."

"Sure will." He tipped his cap to Madeline and then shook Jonah's hand. A moment later, he was gone.

"So," Madeline said once they were alone. "What do you think about all that?"

He thought Townsend had something to hide. What that something was, Jonah had not yet determined.

"I am still deciding," he said. "What about you?"

"Yes, I am as well." She rose. "I should go. Madame is going to wonder why I have been gone so long."

Madeline took a few steps toward the edge of the property before Jonah caught up to her and offered her his arm. "Considering what happened in Indianola, I plan to see you safely back to Mrs. Smith's home."

She looked as if she might be about to protest, and then she nodded slowly. "Yes, all right. I don't suppose that's a bad idea, although no one in Galveston has fired a shot at me yet."

They walked in silence for a few minutes, and then Jonah decided to voice the question that had been on his mind since he saw Madeline coming out of the newspaper offices with Townsend. "Why did you go see that reporter, Madeline?"

Madeline did not miss a step even though her attention jerked in Jonah's direction. "I saw the same headline you did," she said.

"And you thought you'd finally get your information about the Lafitte treasure?"

❤

Of course that is why she sought out Walter Townsend, but Madeline would never admit anything of the sort to Jonah. She understood his need to protect his family from strangers who might seek to profit, but she also had an investigation to conduct.

"Madeline?"

"No," she admitted. "He claims to know nothing about it. You arrived before I could decide whether he was telling the truth."

They paused to allow a cart laden with hay to pass by, and then Jonah led her across the street. She matched his pace as she tugged at the ribbons on her hat to keep the wind from blowing it away.

"We had the same inclination in going to speak to Townsend." Madeline looked over and offered him a smile. "I just got to him before you did."

"Yes, I suppose you did," he said. "So what did he say before I arrived?"

"He said hello. He tried to be charming by inviting me to join him on some investigation he was headed to, and then he left his office and assumed I was following."

"Which you were."

"Only because there was no reason to stay behind in the building." Madeline stopped short and turned to face him. "Just accuse me of whatever you think I did so I can defend myself properly."

He looked away then returned his attention to Madeline. "Look, I'm sorry. For you this is an investigation, but for me this is personal." Jonah paused. "But that does not excuse bad behavior."

"No," she said as she watched him appear to struggle with what he was about to say. "It does not. But I understand."

And she did.

"Thank you." He took her elbow and urged her to continue their walk toward Madame's home. "I am just trying to fit these pieces together, and so far I'm not making much progress. I have decided you didn't dig those holes."

"Well that's nice," she said as she shook her head. "Dare I ask why?"

"Like Townsend said, if you had, you'd have covered up the evidence.

But more than that, if you had, I think you would have somehow convinced me to help you dig."

Madeline smiled at the reminder of a certain investigation she'd carried out back when she and Jonah were still a couple. Her informant sent a map along with the assurance that the evidence she needed to prove the suspect's guilt would be left on the property.

She had brought Jonah along on the pretense of not wishing to go alone and then surprised him upon arrival with the fact that the evidence they needed had been buried in the suspect's yard.

"Ah, the Valmont story," she said as she nudged his arm with her elbow. "I won a prize for that investigation."

"And I got a sore back and a job offer as a day laborer."

She joined him in laughing and then allowed the conversation to fall into companionable silence. By the time they turned onto Broadway Avenue, Madeline's thoughts had turned to a question in dire need of asking.

"Jonah, I have been wondering about something," Madeline finally said. "I have not seen all the documents you have, but I did look through the registry in Indianola and I listened to you talk to the sheriff and the other men. In all of this, have you formed an opinion as to whether Mrs. Smith's granddaughter is out there to be found or not?"

"I hope she is," he said as he held the gate open for Madeline then closed it after they both stepped inside the property. "That old lady sure wants her to be. As to whether I have found any concrete facts that point to finding her? Not yet, but I am going to keep trying until I do or until she finally tells me to stop."

"Us," Madeline corrected. "We're a team now, according to Madame."

"That was a surprise," he said.

"I agree." Madeline stalled to look up into the Pinkerton's eyes. "Jonah, I wish things were different between us."

He looked away and then returned his focus to her. He said nothing.

She sighed. "And that is my fault. I know I keep saying this, but I am sorry."

To her surprise, Jonah chuckled. "I keep saying it too."

"Aren't we a pair?" she said. "Some team we are."

Jonah's smile was slow to appear. "We used to make a great team, Madeline."

"We did," she said as she reached over to touch his sleeve. "Do you think we can again?"

He seemed to consider the question and then finally he nodded. "I do."

"Me too," she said, "but only if we start over. Completely, I mean. With neither of us having to continually apologize or try to get over the stupid things we did in the past. Can we do that?"

Jonah placed his hand on top of hers. Unlike that simple touch beneath the stars aboard the *Haven*, this time he looked into her eyes. "Hello, Madeline."

"Hello, Jonah," she said as she felt herself giving in to the pull of those eyes, of that smile. "It is very nice to meet you."

The front door opened, and Gretchen stepped outside, jerking Madeline from her thoughts. "Monsieur Cahill, Madame asked that you pay her a visit in the parlor as soon as possible. I was about to have the stable boy deliver the message, but here you are." She looked down her nose at Madeline. "You are to attend to Madame as well. Immediately."

Madeline pressed past the maid and walked down the hall to the parlor with Jonah behind her. At the door, she knocked.

"Oh do come in," Madame said. "I have the best news and. . .oh. . . Detective Cahill is with you. Excellent. Sit. Both of you."

Madame indicated the small settee nearest her, and Madeline complied. Rather than join her on the cramped furniture, Jonah walked around her to sit in the window seat.

"Detective Cahill, this will likely not take you by surprise, but I have only just learned this morning that our president will be visiting in a few days."

"Yes, ma'am," Jonah said. "I did know that."

"Did you also know that I have secured an invitation to the ball that the Browns are throwing in his honor on the 25th?"

"That's wonderful," Madeline said. "I will be happy to help you prepare for the ball. It will do you good to get out and enjoy yourself."

"Oh no, child," she said with a smile. "I am not going. You and Detective Cahill are."

"Why?" they said together.

Madame chuckled. "Oh listen to you. You even sound like a team." She sobered. "You are going because the people you need to meet will all be there. Imagine a gathering where Sealeys, Moodys, and all of Galveston society will be there. All the two of you have to do is watch, listen, and if possible ask a few questions. More important is to make a good impression. Mingle. Get invited to more gatherings so you can travel in that social circle. If you do that, I have a feeling you will find my girl."

She reached over to ring the bell, and Gretchen tumbled into the room. Of course once again she had been listening in the hallway, so her distance to travel was extremely short.

"Help me to my room, dear," she told Gretchen. "I am ready for my nap. And have Cook bring out tea and cookies for our guest."

Gretchen glared at Madeline over her shoulder and then disappeared out into the hall with Madame.

"I don't think your maid likes you," Jonah said with a lift of his brows.

"That is an understatement." Madeline rose and moved toward the door.

"Where are you going?"

She glanced back at him over her shoulder. "Unless you wish to stay for tea and cookies, I need to put a stop to the refreshments before Cook goes to the trouble of preparing them."

"I suppose that's fair," he said. "I've got some work to do anyway."

"Wait just a minute, Detective Cahill," she said. "Would this be work that you should be sharing with your partner?"

Jonah grinned as he pressed past her, but he said nothing. "Jonah," she called, following him out onto the porch. "You better not be working on this case without me, do you hear me?"

"Loud and clear," he said as the gate slammed behind him. "But that doesn't mean I am listening."

"You wait right there," she called. "I am coming with you."

Jonah turned around to come back to the gate but remained out on the sidewalk. "Do you understand what Mrs. Smith just required of you?"

She shook her head. "To go to a ball and talk to people?"

"For a reporter you sure do miss the obvious, Madeline." He glanced over at the Browns' home and then back at Madeline. "Our boss has insisted you and I pretend to actually like one another. In public."

"Well," she said with a laugh, "I like you. Sort of."

"And I like you. Sort of." He shook his head. "But we are going to have to do better than that if we want to play a convincing couple."

She gave him a mock-serious look. "I do see the dilemma."

"We've both got investigative experience," he said. "What do you suggest?"

"Well, now, I think you will have to decide what role you're playing and then present yourself as that."

"So since Mrs. Smith wants us to go to this fancy party as a couple, I need to act like I am crazy about you?"

Madeline could only laugh as Jonah made a silly face. "Yes, exactly. But I think that's the wrong kind of crazy. You should act like you are in love with me, Jonah. Pretend."

His expression slipped for a split second, and then he glanced down Broadway Avenue before looking back at her. Jonah motioned her over to the fence just as a well-appointed carriage rolled to the curb across the street.

"Remember," he said as he leaned close to whisper in her ear, "we love each other."

His hand wrapped around the back of her neck as his lips found hers. Just as they had done so many times. Despite herself, Madeline leaned in to the kiss and allowed herself to pretend too.

And then, just like that, Jonah stepped back, leaving her to hold tight to the fence to keep her knees from buckling. He turned before she could speak, a good thing considering she likely could have said nothing that made sense.

"Oh, hello, Mrs. Brown," he said to the elegant woman stepping out of her carriage across the street. "Beautiful weather we are having, isn't it? Looks like it agrees with your roses."

"Jonah Cahill, is that you?"

He grinned. "It is, and this is Miss Latour, my very dear friend."

"So I see," she said with what appeared to be amusement. "I take it the two of you will be attending my ball. We have quite the important guest, and I wouldn't want you to miss it."

"We will be there, ma'am," he said as he casually slipped his arm around Madeline, who was grateful for the assistance in remaining upright.

When Mrs. Brown had disappeared inside her home, Jonah took a step back from the gate, his expression completely changed. "Well, Madeline, that should do it."

Somehow she managed a nod. And a good excuse to hurry back inside before she asked him to repeat that performance for the milkman who was passing by.

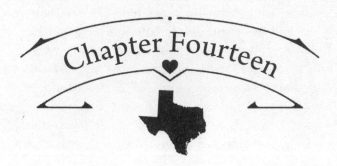

Chapter Fourteen

On the evening of the ball, Madeline watched the preparations from her third-floor window most of the day. The lovely dress Madame had delivered for her now hung on the peg, and her dancing shoes waited on the floor beside it.

The gown was an evening dress of blue silk made in the princess shape with a low corsage and short sleeves. The skirt was trimmed with four knife pleats, and the drapery atop it was white satin de Lyon that had been made to fall in a very long train in the back.

Madeline had indeed felt like a princess each time the seamstress arrived for a fitting. Just looking at it now made her smile.

Gretchen had been called in to tie up her corset and arrange Madeline's hair into something worthy of a formal occasion. The maid now stood behind her at the mirror, comb poised and her usual surly look in place while Madeline struggled to take a deep breath.

"You know what?" Madeline said as she reached to take the comb from Gretchen's hand. "I think I can manage this myself."

"Like you managed getting off that ledge," she said.

"I could have gotten off that ledge just fine if you hadn't closed the window." She watched Gretchen's expression closely. "Or rather if you hadn't locked it."

"I do as I am told," the maid said as she snatched the comb back. "And tonight I am told by Madame to do something to make your hair acceptable for the party."

"Acceptable. Well, as long as you have high standards," Madeline said sarcastically as she turned around to endure a full hour of torture. Finally the pain ceased and Gretchen offered her the mirror.

"It is now acceptable."

Madeline gasped. Her hair had been arranged in chatelaine braids fastened by a large bouquet of roses, presumably from Madame's collection downstairs.

Much as it pained her—literally—Madeline had to admit that Gretchen did have considerable hairdressing skills. "Where did you learn this?" she asked when the ordeal was over.

"I was taught," she said simply.

"Taught?"

"Yes," she snapped. "Someone teaches a skill and you learn it. It's a simple thing, no?"

"No, I mean yes, I suppose."

Gretchen looked away. "No. And we are done here. If you need help getting into that dress, you ring for the scullery maid, understand?"

"Gretchen," she said as the maid stepped out into the hall. "I am sorry for whoever hurt you."

The maid looked as if she wanted to say something. Instead, she slammed the door, her footsteps echoing in the corridor outside.

Madeline stared at the closed door. What in the world had possessed her to say that? The words had come out, unbidden and certainly unexpected.

Madeline walked over to where the rest of her ensemble had been laid out. Due to the cut of the neckline and the jewelry Madame had chosen for her, the necklace she had worn since the last time she saw her papa would have to come off for the evening.

Lifting the chain over her head to place it on the table beside the mirror, she keenly felt its absence as she heard Papa's words of warning. *"Keep this close to you and never take it off, do you understand?"*

Surely he wouldn't mind if she left the bauble for a few hours while she was only across the street. What could possibly happen in such a short time?

Madeline managed to dress without calling for help, but she thought she might have to ring for someone when the sapphire necklace Madame insisted she wear refused to latch. Finally she managed the feat.

Gathering up her gloves and the beaded reticule Madame had also procured for the evening, Madeline slipped her feet into her evening shoes.

Now what? She couldn't sit for fear of wrinkling the fabric and crushing the roses and greenery attached to her gown, so she went to the window with the idea of looking up at the stars. Instead, she spied Jonah arriving at the gate.

At least she thought it was Jonah, though she had never seen him look so handsome.

When he looked up in her direction, Madeline stepped back from the window. It wouldn't do at all to be caught peeking at him before he came inside.

She closed her curtains and moved toward the door. "We are employees of Madame Smith on assignment to discover clues as to what happened to her granddaughter."

Madeline sighed. All of that was indeed true, but wearing this dress knowing she would be going to that party with that man did feel very much like a social occasion.

Worse, it felt like the old days when they were happy together. She managed a smile. "I miss those days," Madeline whispered, "though I wish I didn't."

"Your escort is here," Gretchen said as she threw the door open without bothering to knock.

"He is not my escort," she said but without much enthusiasm.

One hand on the doorknob, she looked back at the necklace on the table and let out a long breath. Hurrying over to scoop it up, she dropped the chain and key into her reticule and closed the door behind her to move toward the stairs.

Jonah's voice carried up the three levels of the staircase to reach her as she made her way down. Madame's laughter joined his as they shared some amusement.

Instead of thinking about how handsome the Pinkerton detective had looked in the moonlight, she decided to go over the facts of the case as she knew them. The two of them were, by Madame's instruction, part of a team looking to infiltrate Galveston society and find a missing woman.

Taken as a whole, there was very little for a newspaper reporter to build a story on. Madame had been apologetic when Madeline pressed for details, claiming they had been lost in time or were merely memories of letters long gone to the ruin of hurricanes or floods.

Oh, but the story of Lafitte and his treasure, now that one had much more substance. Evidence existed that the pirate Lafitte had left substantial coin and other items of great value in places where he planned to return and retrieve them.

But had he? There was the conundrum. To prove he had, one would have to prove he survived beyond those years when documented sightings of the pirate existed. For unless he had survived, the treasure still lay in wait for his return and retrieval.

But if he did survive, if he managed to live beyond the years in Cuba and his subsequent documented scuffles with the navies of multiple countries, then anything was possible.

In fact, it was entirely possible that a man such as Lafitte who was well schooled in subterfuge did exactly that. And what if he took his ill-gotten gains and retired to live in comfort? Madeline touched the sapphires at her neck. What if he finally decided enough was enough?

Enough coin.

Enough baubles.

Enough fighting and endlessly looking behind him to worry who might be coming after him next. What would a man like that do?

Madeline paused on the second-floor landing, her hand gripping the rail as she followed the trail of reason rather than think of the fate that awaited her downstairs. A man like that just might settle down, find a good woman, and perhaps even begin again to raise a family.

Of course age was a factor, as Lafitte would have been well into his fortieth year when he disappeared from history. But a man of forty or even fifty might still find a bride willing to settle down to a quiet life of children and then, eventually, grandchildren.

Or, more specifically, a granddaughter born in 1855.

Madame's laughter once again resonated from the foyer below. It would take a special woman to love a man with such a past. But the story, more of a theory she'd researched for many years, was certainly one that could have happened.

It was the story that led her to Madame. Now Madeline would see if the facts led her there too.

Madeline took a deep breath and straightened her spine. The corset impeded her breathing but not by as much as it might have if Gretchen had her way.

By the time she reached the turn in the staircase that brought her in view of the first-floor landing and the foyer beyond, Madeline thought she had it clear in her mind that this was merely a business event. Just two people working on a shared investigation.

A project.

Anything but a social occasion.

Yes, he had kissed her, but that was only in the line of duty. And she hadn't enjoyed it.

Much.

Then she spied Jonah speaking with Madame, and her best efforts evaporated. His back was to her, allowing Madeline to study the Pinkerton detective at her leisure.

Her escort for the evening was wearing a black dress coat and trousers. His hair had been tamed, possibly even barbered, and the everpresent gun he carried at his waist had disappeared. A pair of fashionable gentleman's shoes had replaced his usual boots, making the transformation from detective to dandy complete.

The man looked, in a word, breathtaking.

But this was not personal.

Madeline squared her shoulders and continued down the stairs. The Pinkerton detective turned her direction. His eyes swept the length of her in a rakish glance, and then he smiled.

"Hello, Madeline."

"Detective," she said, as much to remind herself as to remind him that they were attending this ball for purposes of work and not pleasure.

"You look lovely," Madame told her as she pressed something into her hand. She looked down to see an exquisite jeweled notebook with a pencil attached. "Should you need to make a note of any discoveries this evening."

"Yes, of course," she said as she tucked the notebook into her bag and looked past Madame to find Jonah studying her.

❤

Jonah had heard the word *breathtaking* used in regard to beautiful women before. But not until he saw Madeline Latour walking down Mrs. Smith's staircase had he experienced this feeling for himself.

Gone was the irritatingly nosy reporter with her incessant comments and refusal to cooperate with good sense, and in her place was a stunning woman who looked as if she came out of a storybook.

The woman he once thought he would spend his life with.

The woman he wanted to kiss again.

Mrs. Smith led her over to him because he hadn't had the good sense or presence of mind to do anything except stand there gaping like a fool. She put Madeline's hand in his and said something about them leaving.

Jonah heard hardly any of it.

"Something wrong, Jonah?" Madeline said.

"No," he managed. "Nothing's wrong."

The reporter gave him a look that told him she thought he'd lost his mind. If he could have managed to speak with any good sense, he could have told her she was right. He had.

Somehow he managed to get out the door and all the way to the front gate without any major mishaps. Then he realized his fumbling fingers could not open the gate.

"Oh for goodness' sake." Madeline reached over his arm to easily accomplish the task.

Instead of walking through the now-open gate, Jonah pulled it shut once more and turned to face Madeline. "Okay, something is wrong."

"What?" She lifted her hand to touch her hair. "Has Gretchen put something awful up there? Did she weave poison ivy in with the roses? I wouldn't be surprised. I have no idea why that woman dislikes me so much, but she certainly—"

Jonah pressed his finger to her lips, temporarily ceasing the barrage of words. "None of that," he said. "But there is a problem."

Overhead the stars sparkled as only they could in this part of Texas. Just behind them the noise of carriages approaching and leaving, of couples arriving, mingled with the chorus of musical instruments each time the front door to Ashton Villa opened.

But here on this side of the fence, with the uncomfortable fancy shoes his sister insisted on him wearing pinching his feet, he needed to get one thing straight with Madeline Latour.

"You were not supposed to look so beautiful."

"Thank you?" she said as she shook her head.

"Don't thank me. This is a real predicament."

The moonlight painted her features in silver as she shook her head. "Stop teasing me, Jonah. I know this isn't what I normally wear, but you don't have to be cruel."

"I assure you I am not being cruel." He looked up into the night sky again and then back down at her. "We are going over there as guests of the Browns, but you and I both know we are investigators looking for clues to find that woman. To that end, we should be inconspicuous."

"Well, of course," she said.

"Darlin', in that dress the last thing you could possibly be is inconspicuous."

Chapter Fifteen

Madeline crossed Broadway Avenue on Jonah's arm. She slid him a sideways glance but found his attention focused straight ahead.

Giving way to a carriage filled with well-dressed men and women, Jonah led her around to the sidewalk in front of the magnificent home known as Ashton Villa. Though she had seen this home nearly every day since she arrived in Galveston, tonight was the first time she had really looked at the magnificent structure.

Standing every bit as tall as Madame's rented home, the Browns' mansion had been lit with a multitude of lamps and lanterns for the occasion. The home was a three-story brick structure made in the Italianate manner with black frilled iron railings on the front balcony and porch below.

Madame had told her that President Lincoln's notice of emancipation for the slaves had been read by General Granger of the Union army on that very balcony some fifteen years ago. Tonight the balcony had been festooned with more lanterns and now played host to a pair of gentlemen who were likely also in the employ of either law enforcement or the former president himself.

Jonah tipped his hat to the men on the balcony and got a greeting in return. "Remember our purpose tonight, Madeline," he told her.

"I will try not to detract from it," she said with a jab of sarcasm.

"See that you don't." His tone did not betray whether he was serious or merely continuing the joke. After all, they did have an agreement that required them to pretend a relationship that had once been real.

Jonah stepped forward, and Madeline took the opportunity to look around.

As she approached the house on Jonah's arm, several men came up to stop them. She recognized one immediately. "Hello, Detective Donovan," she said. "Are you assigned to President Grant?"

"I am assigned to his safety," he said. "I assure you there will be nothing to worry about as long as the Pinkerton Agency is in charge."

Jonah shook his head. "You might also want to credit the Galveston police and a few other government agencies, Donovan. Don't try to make her think you're doing all of this alone. Miss Latour is far too smart to believe you."

He grinned and dipped his head. "Detective Cahill is, as always, correct."

Madeline smiled, but something in the detective's tone troubled her. "Is he a friend of yours?" she asked when they'd moved past him toward the door.

"Of sorts," Jonah said. "We joined the agency within a few years of one another and have worked on several cases together." He glanced over at her as he stepped onto the porch. "Why?"

She shook her head. "No reason."

The door to Ashton Villa swung open, and Jonah ushered her inside. To Madeline's right, a magnificent staircase rose beneath a crystal chandelier aglow with what seemed to be thousands of lights. Up ahead she could see a crowd had gathered in a room adorned with floor-to-ceiling windows that were topped with cornices of what must be pure gold.

From each cornice, curtains of filmy gold fell and puddled on the polished wood floors. The walls had been papered in a similar shade of gold, making the room feel both opulent and cozy.

A frenzy of conversation died down just as Jonah and Madeline stepped into the room. "My friends and neighbors," a man who must be their host called. "Rebecca and I are most honored to welcome you into our home. But even more so are we honored to have in our midst not only a hero but also a man of great learning and expertise."

At the word *hero*, an older fellow next to Madeline groaned. "Not all of us have forgotten the war years," he commented to her. "Though he did turn out to be a decent president, I will say."

"So with no further ado," Mr. Brown continued, "I present the eighteenth president of the United States of America."

As President Grant rose to begin speaking, Madeline glanced around the room. Most of the guests were dressed in the same evening garb she and Jonah had chosen. A few of the men, however, wore military uniforms with buttons and sashes that indicated their rank and importance.

One of them, a gentleman easily as old as the former president, caught her looking and smiled.

"Flirting already?" Jonah whispered.

"I am doing my job. Who is that man over there by the staircase?"

Jonah glanced past her then returned his attention to Madeline. "That would be Commander Horace Montlake, former aide to Rear Admiral Rogers during his voyage to Korea back in '71. Small amphibious assault on the forts protecting Seoul for the purpose of getting an apology for murders of Americans."

"Oh my. I don't know anything about that," she said.

"I would say you should ask him, but likely he'll offer the information. Likely also he'll introduce himself exactly as I said. He always does."

"So you know him?"

"Madeline, everyone in Galveston knows the commander."

She caught a movement out of the corner of her eye. "He's coming this way."

Jonah grinned. "Then I suppose you've just hit on the topic of conversation. Now if you'll excuse me, I am going to go and do the job I was hired to do. I see Mrs. William Ballenger, and I intend to ask her if she has any recollections that might be helpful."

Madeline nodded and then watched as Jonah walked over to an elegant older lady and began speaking with her. Commander Montlake pressed past several guests to stand beside Madeline as clapping sounded all around them indicating that President Grant had finished speaking.

"Not quite the orator of his predecessor but he'll do." The elderly sailor smiled down at her. "I don't believe we've met. I am Commander Horace Montlake, former aide to Rear Admiral Rogers during his voyage to Korea back in '71."

Madeline stifled a giggle and then offered him her most neutral expression. "Pleased to make your acquaintance, Commander. I am Madeline Latour."

"Well now, Miss Latour. It is certainly pleasing to see such a lovely young woman in our fair city. Are you newly arrived?"

"Of a sort," she said. "I understand you are a hero."

The commander's face flushed, and a broad smile rose. "I don't know about all that, but I did serve our country and still do, although back in '71. . ."

While Commander Montlake was waxing poetic on the strategy behind the campaign he apparently still remembered as if it happened yesterday, Madeline used his inattention to her to make note of the other guests in the room.

Seated on one of the settees that lined the room was the elderly Mr. Sealey. Beside him, his wife waited in attendance to him while expertly fending off the conversation attempts of several talkative matrons. Several others whose faces she recognized as being among Galveston's wealthy elite mingled around her.

Gradually, Madeline became aware that the commander had stopped talking. She turned to him with a smile. "It appears you've had quite a lot of experience in handling situations of importance," she said, and he beamed. "I wonder if I might trouble you to get some advice."

"Certainly," he said as he inclined his ear. "What is it exactly that you need advice in regard to?"

"It is like this," she told him. "A dear friend of mine is looking to locate someone who she believes is living in Galveston but has little information. I wonder what sort of advice you might have for her."

"This someone, might this be a man or a woman?"

"A woman," she said. "Trésor Smith is her name, but I don't know what she looks like. And it is possible she doesn't know who she is."

He smiled. "Look around you, then. Anyone in Galveston of any importance is here. I would tell your friend that if she is not here, she should be. Your friend is Madame Smith, yes?"

"How did you know?" she asked.

"My dear, I have known Madame Smith for quite some time. I paid her a visit just a few days ago and she told me she had hired you and that Pinkerton man over there to investigate on her behalf."

"I see." She paused to consider her next question. "And what else did she tell you?"

"That she had the greatest confidence that you would find the child she has lost." He looked away to greet another guest and then returned his attention to Madeline. "I believe the woman you seek is in this room."

"She is?" Madeline's heart jumped. "And how do you know this? Have you seen her?"

He smiled. "As a child, yes. She was most beautiful. I can tell you she had her grandmother's smile and her grandfather's eyes."

"So you knew Mr. Smith, then?"

"Quite well," he said with a grin. "Since I was a child, you might say."

"This is wonderful news." She pulled her notebook out of her bag. "Would you mind if I jot down some notes? If you please, I need a more detailed description. We have very few details about her."

"Miss Latour, I am afraid I have told you all I can."

She tried not to show her disappointment. "Yes, all right. How can I contact you?"

He offered her a formal bow. "I see Mrs. Moody needs saving from the Franklin sisters again, so I fear I must come to her assistance."

"But sir, finding her is of great importance. If you say you believe she is in this room. . ."

"I am an old man. Perhaps I am wrong," he said. "But when you ask about her, do not ask if someone knows this girl. You know your employer. This is her grandchild. Just look with your heart and you will find her."

"Look with my heart?" she asked as he walked away, obviously oblivious to her confusion.

"Any luck with the commander?" Jonah asked, whirling her around to face him.

"No, and yes," she said. "No, he didn't exactly point her out here in this crowd, but he did say he knew both Madame Smith and her husband and that he remembered the granddaughter as a child."

"So is she here?"

"He said he could not point her out but felt she must be here."

Jonah shook his head. "That makes no sense. How does he know she is here if he cannot point her out?"

"That's the strange part. He told me to look with my heart."

"And that means what?" Jonah asked.

"I have no idea," she responded as she allowed her gaze to travel around the room. "Oh, wait. What color eyes does Madame have?"

"I have no idea," he said.

"Oh, I remember. They are brown," Madeline recalled. "So now we just have to look for the woman with brown eyes. If she was born in 1855, we are looking for a woman who is twenty-five. If we also guess she has similar characteristics to Madame Smith, then I would guess she also has dark hair."

Jonah seemed to consider her statement. "I agree. Come with me." Jonah led her out of the parlor where the older folks were still congregating and into the ballroom where most of the younger guests had gone.

She glanced over her shoulder to see that the commander was still in conversation with Mrs. Moody. It appeared that he was doing most of the talking.

Madeline felt a tug on her arm. "Time to go to work," Jonah told her as he pulled her into the crowd of dancers. "Remember," he said against her ear, "we are in love."

"Love, right," Madeline echoed, and yet she had no trouble leaning in and allowing him to lead her across the dance floor like they were indeed a couple.

For a man who made his living as a Pinkerton detective, Jonah Cahill was quite a dancer. But she already knew that.

As he spun her around and moved between the couples with ease, Madeline forgot she was supposed to be looking for a brown-eyed woman. Forgot everything about this assignment except for the fact that she was dancing on the arm of the handsomest man in the room while wearing sapphires around her neck, roses in her hair, and a gown that had been made just for her.

And though her shoes had begun to pinch and her corset had been laced so tight she could barely breathe, Madeline felt like the belle of the ball. When the song ended and another began, they danced on.

Finally the music stopped, and Jonah leaned down. "Did you see any likely candidates?"

Oh. "Not yet," she said. "But if the commander believes she is here, I suppose we owe it to the investigation to keep dancing."

Chapter Sixteen

The music began again, and Jonah escorted Madeline back out on the dance floor. They danced and then they danced some more, but he knew good and well that woman wasn't looking for their suspect.

She wasn't even looking at all most of the time, not with her eyes closed and her head resting on his shoulder. Oh, but when she rested her head there and tucked her hand in his, Jonah felt like the luckiest man in the room.

He felt as though all the things that happened to tear them apart no longer mattered. It was a dangerous feeling, but Madeline had always been dangerous to his heart.

So he danced and danced until finally he couldn't dance anymore. "All right, Cinderella," he said to her as he led her off the dance floor. "Let's find some refreshments and a quiet place to compare notes on what we've discovered."

A few minutes later, they found a curtained alcove off the second floor opposite the balcony and crowded into the tiny space. Madeline sipped punch and sat quietly for a moment while Jonah watched her, their knees touching.

"You always did like wearing roses in your hair and being the belle of the ball, didn't you?"

She looked up sharply, as if he'd guessed her secret. His Pinkerton training told him Madeline would likely deflect the question with a question of her own.

"I do actually."

Of course his Pinkerton training was completely useless when it came to Madeline Latour. It always had been.

"Then drink up, Madeline. We have dancing yet to do."

"And an investigation to conduct," she reminded him with an expression that he figured she meant to look serious.

"Yes, that."

Madeline opened the silver bag she'd been wearing on her wrist and retrieved a notebook covered in sparkling gems along with a pencil. Before she tightened the strings, Jonah noticed that the necklace she always wore, the one with the key attached, was nestled in the bottom of the bag.

"Is there anything we can say we have learned from tonight so far, other than the information from the commander?"

"Yes," he said. "I have learned that next time I plan to dance this long, I will ignore my sister and wear my boots."

Madeline laughed and then began to write in her notebook. He watched her, allowing his gaze to settle on the curve of her neck, the way she pursed her lips as she appeared deep in thought, and the long lashes dusting her cheeks when she closed her eyes. If their shared past didn't prevent it, Jonah might have considered spending more time with her after this investigation ended.

That insight should have felt better than it did. Somehow getting rid of the woman as soon as possible was no longer a goal he wanted to pursue.

So maybe, just maybe, he would seek her out. Just to see how she fared. Nothing more. Nothing to do with the way those brown eyes melted him or how the feel of her on the dance floor made him forget everything but the two of them.

And the fact they had agreed that their past was just that—the past—and that they were starting all over. So maybe there was hope for them yet.

Who was he kidding? He couldn't imagine life without this woman, could he?

Jonah dismissed the crazy thoughts—along with the desire to kiss her—with a roll of his shoulders while Madeline, unaware, continued to write in her notebook. A young man and his lady friend strolled past, their laughter preceding them. When they were gone, Jonah rose and offered Madeline his hand to help her up. "What color were that woman's eyes?"

"The one who just walked past?" She shrugged. "I wasn't looking."

"Go find out, then." She appeared ready to protest. "Go on. I will save your seat here in the alcove."

Though she still looked as though she was formulating an argument against it, Madeline dropped her notebook and pencil into her bag and pressed past him, leaving the scent of roses in her wake.

Jonah settled back down on the opposite chair where he could watch as Madeline walked over to the pair and struck up a conversation. A moment later, she returned.

"Blue eyes, so not our suspect." She sat back down. "What was the point of that exercise?"

He feigned innocence. "I have no idea what you're talking about. We are here working on an investigation and it was your turn."

Her eyes pinned him to his chair. "To go look into someone's eyes?"

"Yes, actually."

She leaned back against the papered wall and grinned. "So this was a test?"

"No, it was your chance to actually do some investigative work."

"I have been."

"Have you?" He paused. "With your eyes closed and your head on my shoulder?"

Was that a blush that crossed her pretty cheeks? "I think we've been here long enough," she said though she made no move to leave.

"Probably." He smiled. "But I'm enjoying myself."

She nodded toward the hall beyond the curtains where a trio of gossiping women was comparing notes on the clothing choices of the females in the ballroom. "Go enjoy yourself by checking those three."

Jonah lifted a brow. "I am the Pinkerton detective in this investigation, Madeline, and you are the newspaper reporter. I give the orders."

"That may be," she countered, "but which of us do you think they would be more forthcoming in speaking with?"

He frowned. She was right.

"Go on. I will save your seat here in the alcove." She patted the place where he'd been sitting then offered a broad smile.

Jonah felt Madeline's eyes on him as he walked over to the ladies. "Excuse me," he said, and they all turned to look at him.

All three had dark hair and were approximately the correct age. He looked at their eyes. Blue. Green.

Jonah groaned when his attention reached the third one. She was wearing colored spectacles that made her eye color impossible to discern. Now he understood the women's discussion regarding the appearance of all the others on the dance floor. Their companion was blind.

"Sir?" Green Eyes said. "Is there something you needed?"

"There is, actually," he said. "Do you see that lady over there?" Jonah waved to Madeline, who gestured back reluctantly. "She and I were just talking about something rather interesting. You see, my companion believes there are more women here with blue eyes, and I say there are more whose eyes are green like yours."

Green Eyes smiled. "Well indeed there is one of each here."

Blue Eyes nodded.

Jonah pondered a way to ask politely about their friend but could think of nothing that might not sound impolite. Green Eyes must have sensed his discomfort.

"My friend's eyes are also green," she said, and the blind woman nodded.

"Thank you. I will tell my friend that I am in the lead," he said as he walked away.

"Sir," the blind woman called. "And your friend? What color eyes does she possess?"

He thought a minute. "I believe they are brown."

She laughed. "Well that does make things interesting, doesn't it?"

"It does," he said as he wandered back to take his seat in the alcove.

"Well?" Madeline asked.

Jonah studied her face and then shook his head. "None there. Two sets of green and a blue."

"So no brown eyes yet, then?"

"Only you, Madeline." He stared openly. "Wait just a minute." Jonah leaned closer until their noses almost touched.

"What are you doing?"

He sat back. "Just testing a theory."

"And what theory is that?"

"The theory that you are the Smith granddaughter."

Her eyes widened. "Me? What kind of idiocy is that? I have a father in New Orleans who is alive and well and will attest to the fact he is not the deceased Samuel Smith, and I also have a mother who delights in telling the story of how incorrigible I was as an infant. Now my brother, he would probably be delighted if we were not actually related, but that is another story altogether. Then there's the problem of me not yet having been born in 1855."

"Madeline, I am joking. Your birth records clearly rule you out. And yes, I checked," he said as he rose again and helped her to her feet. "Enough of this. Back to work."

Her laughter followed him past the three ladies and all the way to the stairs. However, when he turned to look over his shoulder, he found Madeline disappearing up the stairs in the opposite direction.

"Where are you going?" he asked as he fell into step beside her.

She grinned but said nothing until they reached the third-floor corridor. It was dark up here, the lights being reserved for the lower two floors, but Madeline appeared not to care.

Traversing the length of the hall with nothing but moonlight to guide her, Madeline reached the floor-to-ceiling window at the end of the corridor and lifted it. She turned around as if to beckon him and then giggled softly.

"What are you doing?" he demanded as she disappeared out the open window to what must be the roof of the balcony below.

"Come on," she whispered, "but be quiet about it."

Jonah followed her outside and then stalled. She was nowhere to be found.

"Over here," she whispered. "Around the corner."

Jonah looked over the edge to see that the grounds three stories below were filled with men milling around and guests arriving and departing. From the sounds of laughter, there were also guests on the balcony below.

The former president's private carriage remained in its place up front, so likely many of these men were in his protection service. Jonah groaned. The last thing he needed was to have some fellow with a gun and a badge find him skulking around so near to the roof.

He crawled around the corner to find Madeline sitting with her back against the redbrick wall. Being as careful as possible not to be seen, Jonah settled beside the infuriating reporter.

"This is madness."

"I know," Madeline whispered in that same dreamy tone she had used under the stars aboard the *Haven*. "Isn't it wonderful?"

❤

For a moment she did not think Jonah would answer. Then he turned to look at her. "I repeat, Madeline. This is madness."

"Oh come on, Jonah. Relax. We have plenty of time to circulate through the guests and look for the Smith woman. But how many opportunities will we have to sit out here under the stars on such a beautiful night?"

"With people on the porch below us and half the law enforcement in the city on the lawn?" He shook his head. "I do not know how you talk me into these things."

"These things?" She shook her head. "Maybe I am wrong, but it certainly looked like you got over here of your own free will. But maybe I just have that kind of power over you. If that's the case, then I wish you would let me know so I can better use it when I really need you to do something."

"Oh, you always did have power, all right," he grumbled as he adjusted his coat. "The power to drive me completely out of—"

"Hello," someone said from below them. "Is someone out there?"

"I'm with the Pinkerton. Everything is fine," Madeline called in her best imitation of a man's voice.

"All right, then," the man below responded.

Jonah leaned close until their shoulders were touching. "You are completely incorrigible."

"What?" Madeline turned to face him, and their noses almost touched. "I told the truth. I *am* up here with the Pinkerton, and everything is fine."

To avoid looking into those far-too-familiar eyes a moment longer, she turned her attention to the night sky. "See, look how beautiful it is up here."

From their vantage point, the rooftops of neighboring homes gave way to the waves of the Gulf of Mexico to the east and the sparkling waters of the bay to the west. The lights on the first and second floors of Madame's home had been doused, but there were still a few windows on the third floor that showed evidence of lamps that were lit.

One of those was her own room, visible now as she craned her neck to look around the palm tree at the corner of Madame's property. Funny, she didn't remember leaving her lamps burning.

She leaned over just a bit more to make sure she was looking at the correct window. Her hand slipped and so did she. Jonah's strong grip hauled her back against him.

"What in the world are you doing?"

"Just looking," she said as she adjusted her bag back up safely on her wrist.

Madeline gave the windows one more look and decided she must have left the gas lamp burning after all. Vowing to be more careful, Madeline leaned back against the brick wall, caring nothing for the fact that she might be crushing the roses in her hair.

There was too much beauty in the night skies above right now to worry about silly questions like whether a lamp was lit. Indeed, the moon was one day away from being at its fullest, so there were fewer stars to be seen. Still, she easily found the North Star, Orion, and the Big and Little Dippers.

She might have pointed them out to Jonah, but that would require her turning to look at him. And when she turned to look at him, he was close.

Too close.

And when Jonah was that close, all Madeline could think of was that kiss. Much as she felt she knew the answer, she still wondered if maybe

Jonah hadn't been pretending in front of Mrs. Brown.

"Something wrong?" he asked.

There was, but she would never admit it.

She felt strange inside. Soft and. . .something she couldn't define and didn't particularly like, considering the past history between them.

It had happened under the stars on the *Haven*, and it happened again just now. The past was crumbling, and a possibility of a future together beckoned. Or did it?

"Madeline, look," he said as he pointed to a spot in the eastern sky.

Following the direction he pointed, she saw a falling star streak across. "Oh," she said softly. "So beautiful."

"Yes," Jonah said as he gave her a sideways look. "You are."

Looking as if he was surprised at the words he spoke, Jonah returned his attention to the skies overhead. "We're due for a meteor shower soon," Jonah said. "I can't remember the name."

Madeline smiled and supplied the name as she dared a look in his direction. She quickly looked away again.

"Yes," he said softly. "That's the one. So you really are interested in astronomy, aren't you? Is this recent?"

"No," she said. "I suppose I just didn't think to mention it before, but I would give up being a reporter if I had any hope of becoming an astronomer. Which I don't, of course," she hurried to add.

Jonah chuckled. "Anything that would make you give up being a reporter is something you should consider," he said as he offered a grin. "Just let me know how I can help."

"Oh I'm sure you would like that. Then who would irritate you?"

"My point exactly," he said as he motioned in the direction of the window where they'd climbed through. "Inside with you, Madeline. The stargazing is over for this evening."

"No, not yet," she said as she suppressed a shiver.

"You're cold," he said as he wrapped his arm around her. "Let's go. It's much warmer inside."

Her chill instantly banished, Madeline looked up at Jonah. "I'm fine now. Really. Let's just keep looking at the stars a little longer, shall we?"

"Oh," he said as he pressed an errant curl back into place behind her ear, "looking at the stars is dangerous for us, Madeline."

"How so?" she asked with the beginnings of a smile. "It seems fairly safe to me."

"Nothing about you is safe," he whispered as he moved closer.

"Are you going to kiss me?" she whispered.

"Do you want me to?"

"You there! No one is supposed to be up there," a familiar voice called from the porch below. "Whose voices am I hearing?"

Jonah leaned back against the wall and gave her an I-told-you-so look. "I am Detective Cahill of the Pinkerton Agency. Who are you?"

"Jonah? It's Donovan. What are you doing on the roof?"

"Surveillance," he said and then winked at Madeline.

"Alone?" he asked.

Jonah looked at Madeline and then up at the skies as if searching for an answer. Or perhaps his sanity. "No, Donovan," he said. "I am not alone."

"So you've brought backup, then. Good man. Carry on, then," Detective Donovan said.

Madeline giggled, but Jonah was not amused. The chance to share a kiss under the stars had obviously passed. She sighed. "So it's back to dancing, then?"

"I'm afraid so," he said as he moved toward the corner of the house.

Madeline shifted positions and felt her dress tug. She tried again. Something was wrong.

"Jonah," she whispered, but he had already disappeared around the corner. She tried moving again with the same result. "Jonah," she repeated, this time a little louder.

Finally his face peered back around the corner. "What?"

She reached around to try and free her skirt from whatever held it. "I am stuck."

Jonah's face reflected exactly how Madeline felt about the matter. "How is that even possible, Madeline?"

"It is possible," she said as she continued to try and free herself, "because it has happened. Beyond that I really cannot. . .oh!"

The dress gave way, and she tumbled forward. Once again, Jonah caught her before she landed two floors below on the lawn among the lawmen. She barely snagged the strings of her bag before it went tumbling as well.

From the sudden cool breeze in the vicinity of her backside, she knew exactly why she was free. A glance behind her revealed that the nail that had caught her dress now had a substantial fragment of her dress attached to it.

Madeline scrambled away from the Pinkerton detective, thankful for the shadows in this part of the roof for preserving her modesty. This was awful. Just awful.

Her breath caught, and not just because the stays from her corset had dug so deep she could barely move. She fought back tears.

"I am beginning to see how you ended up in that palm tree," he said. "I just wonder how you've managed to stay alive this long. Something else I never knew when we were together, Madeline: Do you enjoy sliding off roofs, or do you prefer to jump?"

"It's not funny, Jonah," she said as she scrambled to think of a remedy for the situation.

Her dress was torn, and from the feel of it there was no way to hide the damage. Though Madame's house and the third-floor room where Madeline would love to be right now were just across the street, there was no easy way to get there.

Either she must find a way to climb down from out here—and without palm trees or a ladder nearby, it was likely impossible—or she must figure out a way to walk down the stairs and out the front door without any of the guests noticing her predicament.

Madeline sighed and leaned her head back against the brick, absolutely certain that the situation could not get worse.

"Miss Latour, is that you?"

She opened her eyes again and followed the sound of the voice to a third-floor window just beyond the porch. Even in the dim light, there was no mistaking the face that smiled back at her.

"Mr. Townsend."

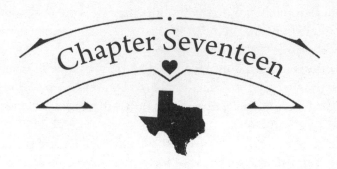

Chapter Seventeen

Jonah suppressed a groan. "Townsend, what are you doing here?"

"Just doing my job," he said as he lifted the window sash a little more to stick his head out. "Same as you."

"I am an invited guest," Jonah said, his jaw clenched. "I doubt you are."

When Townsend didn't respond, Jonah had his answer. "Donovan," he called. "You still down there?"

"I am," came the familiar voice from the porch below.

"We've got an uninvited guest up here. A reporter. Light hair, slender build, carrying a notebook. Northeast corner room on the third floor. I have a visual right now and would handle him myself but I am currently working on another problem."

"That's not funny," the reporter said. "Look, I am just trying to see what kinds of articles I can write, but hey, I am still researching the source of that article you asked me about. This morning, though, I had thought to get an interview with the former president, but apparently the fact I voted for him was not enough to get on his schedule yesterday. This seemed like the best way to see him."

Jonah heard a ruckus down on the lawn and leaned over to see the cause. When he spied the guest of honor and his security detail walking toward the street, he laughed as he turned back to the reporter.

"Well, Townsend, it looks like you've missed your chance. They're escorting President Grant to his carriage right now."

Disappointment showed on the man's face. Then he smiled. "Oh well, I suppose I will just have to find another story to write." He paused to leer at Madeline. "What exactly are you and the detective doing up here, Miss Latour? Has there been a break in the investigation, or were the two of you investigating something else? Like each other."

Before Madeline could respond, Jonah cut in. "She has nothing to say to you, Townsend."

"I'm afraid he's correct," Madeline said, although much more politely than Jonah had responded. "I would be very grateful if you would leave."

"Oh." A smile dawned on Townsend's face. "Oh," he repeated. "I see. You two are. . .that is, you're out here for. . ." His grin interrupted his words. "So what we have here," he continued, "is a man employed by the Pinkerton Agency and a reporter from the *New Orleans Picayune* conducting a covert liaison right here under the noses of half the city of Galveston and one former United States president."

"Of all the nerve," Madeline said as she wriggled closer to the wall. "You are wrong."

"Am I? You two were engaged to be married a year ago and then that engagement was ended. I'm still working the sources I have to find out why, but I will, don't you worry. So, see, I do my research."

"Commendable," Madeline said. "But again, you have it all wrong."

Townsend smacked himself on the head with his palm. "Of course. Why didn't I see it? Sure I do, honey."

Anger rose as Jonah's fists clenched. "If the word *honey* ever crosses your sorry lips in reference to Miss Latour again, I will make sure it is your last."

Though the reporter's expression showed fear, he soon realized there was a gap of space between the porch roof where Jonah was seated and the third-floor window across the way. In order for Jonah to reach him, he'd have to crawl around to the front of the home, climb back in the window, and then follow the corridor around the corner to the room where the reporter was hiding.

As mad as he was, Jonah was willing to do that. But he was not willing to leave Madeline up here alone.

"Ignore him, Madeline," he told her when she looked his direction.

She nodded but continued to stare. "He's going to put this in the paper," she finally said.

"I just might." He looked down toward the front lawn and then back up at them. "And I have plenty of eyewitnesses to corroborate my story."

Jonah looked past her to fix his eyes on the man from the *Daily News*. "If you do, you will have me to answer to, Townsend. And trust me, I won't play nice this time. You will wish you never heard of either of us."

Before the reporter could respond, he was snatched back from the window. Detective Donovan's smiling face replaced the reporter's.

"Thanks for the tip, Cahill," he said. "This guy's been pestering the men downstairs all day trying to get in. Don't know how he got past them, but he won't bother you anymore."

"Thank you," Jonah said.

Donovan remained in the window. "So, um, what exactly were you doing up here? I mean, I can see you two were investigating something. I just can't tell exactly what."

"I'm surprised you can't, Mr. Donovan," Madeline said. "Do you see that house across the street? The white one with the palms on either side?"

"I do."

"The woman we are both employed by has rented that home. From our vantage point here, we are not only providing safety to an old woman left alone with only her staff to protect her, but we are also watching to see that no one goes in or out who might intend her harm."

Jonah looked past his companion and offered a smile. "Yep," he managed without laughing. "All of that and helping you catch a trespasser."

Donovan looked like he swallowed a fly. "Well, all right, then. Carry on."

When the detective had disappeared from the window, Jonah looked back over at Madeline. "Providing safety to an old woman left alone? Where did that come from?"

She smiled sweetly. "Actually, before I became stuck to the roof, I was looking over at Madame's home and wondering whether a light that is on should be. So, I did not tell a lie. If someone had gone in or out of there since we have been up here, we would have seen the person."

He looked over and saw several lamps lit in windows on the third floor. Other than that, the building was completely dark. "Unless the person decided to go out the back door and down the alley."

"Yes, well," she said as she frowned. "I guess there's that."

Jonah shrugged. "If you think there's a light on that shouldn't be, then it is my duty as an employee of Mrs. Smith to go and check on it. I believe we can skip the dancing. I know my feet would appreciate it."

She nodded. "I suppose, given the fact that my dress is no longer intact."

His eyes narrowed. "What exactly does that mean, Madeline?"

"It means," she said slowly, "that certain portions of this roof are very cold."

He thought a minute and then shook his head. "So when you were stuck?"

"Yes. I became unstuck, but a certain part of the back of my dress remained behind." She nodded to a nail on the roof that had a patch of cloth the same color as her dress wound around it. "And that is the situation."

He leaned over to snatch the fabric from the nail. "I don't guess you can just put it back."

"Hardly. Even if I had needle and thread, which I do not, the location of the. . .the situation is quite impossible for me to reach, and I assure you I will not allow you to help."

"Oh," he managed as he tried not to laugh.

"You are not helping," she snapped. "Somehow I need to get from where I am here to where that light is on over at Madame's home without revealing my, well, situation. Since you are a highly trained Pinkerton agent, do you have any suggestions?"

He thought a minute. "I do. Scoot over here closer," he said as he tucked the fabric square into his pocket. "We're going back downstairs the same way we came in."

"Jonah, that's not possible considering the damage I've done to this dress."

"Leave it to me." He nodded toward the corner of the porch roof.

"I'm going back inside. You follow me. I promise if I see anyone in those windows, I will warn you."

She looked skeptical but, to Jonah's surprise, did not argue. He made his way to the window and then climbed inside to wait for Madeline to appear.

❤

Madeline edged her way around the building, acutely aware that her ruined dress was in plain sight of anyone else who might be hiding in the third-floor rooms behind her. How in the world did she keep getting into such messes?

She turned the corner and found Jonah waiting for her inside. If her corset had allowed, she might have taken in a deep breath of relief. As it was, she merely made the attempt.

"Come on inside, the coast is clear," he said as he extended his arms to her, "but be sure and keep your, um, situation out of sight as you do."

"Very funny." She climbed in, being careful to show only the front side of her dress to him as her feet landed on the carpet.

Jonah handed her his coat. "Put this on. You said you were cold, so that's what we will tell anyone who dares to ask."

She threaded the bag off her arm and handed it to him then shrugged into the coat. Instantly the feeling of warmth and the scent of fresh soap and something woodsy enveloped her. Even better, the length of the coat reached all the way to the back of her knees, providing ample coverage for the missing fabric of her dress.

Handing her the bag, Jonah gave her an appraising look. "Ready?"

Madeline tucked her bag into the jacket's interior pocket and nodded. "Ready."

Jonah offered his arm and ushered her toward the staircase. "I know from experience you're generally hopeless at following directions," he said then grinned when she made a face. "But I want you to walk down those stairs like you own the place. Do you understand?"

She shook her head. "No."

"I want you to have your head held high and not give a care for what anyone thinks of you. Just walk. I promise that'll settle most of the tongues that want to wag. If you act weak, they're going to pounce."

"So just like I own the place," she repeated. "Got it."

Squaring her shoulders, Madeline called on every ounce of ability she learned in the one theater class Papa allowed her to take at the convent. While her expertise was limited to acting as one of the women at the tomb of Jesus on resurrection day, she thought she just might be able to manage this I-own-the-place performance.

Giving Jonah a nod and a quick smile, she allowed him to escort her down to the second-floor landing. From where they stood, Madeline could see the guests still milling about below. A pair of young ladies came hurrying up the stairs to press past them, neither bothering to pay any attention.

Madeline made a quick check of their hair and eye color. One blond, one brunette. Both had blue eyes.

"See," Jonah said. "I told you so."

"And none were our suspect," she added.

"Exactly," was his quick response.

With a nod, they were off again. Each step brought the noise of the crowd louder until they reached the first-floor landing. Madeline let out the breath she didn't realize she was holding and then stepped down into the throng of guests.

Owing to the size of the home, the door was quite a distance from where she stood. Still, they had arrived undetected on the same floor as the exit, and that was something to be celebrated.

Linking arms with her, Jonah nodded toward the door. They made it halfway across the room without drawing attention. Then someone called Jonah's name.

He paused to turn around to speak to their host. "And who is this lovely lady?" Mr. Brown asked, turning his attention to Madeline.

"Madeline Latour," she said as she managed a smile worthy of their host. "I am very pleased to make your acquaintance."

Mr. Brown clasped his hand on Jonah's shoulder. "Come join us," he said. "I've been listening to Judge Harvey advocate his plan for deepening the harbor at Sabine Pass for the last thirty minutes. Surely you've got a more amusing tale to tell than that." His gaze swept the length of

Jonah and then did the same to Madeline. "In fact, I'm certain of it."

"As much as I would enjoy that, sir, I am afraid I am going to have to decline. My friend here, Miss Latour, has caught a chill and I need to get her home."

"Oh no," he said. "Such a pity. I had hoped to speak to both of you regarding an investigation I have learned that you are conducting right here in my home."

"Investigation?"

He chuckled. "Yes, well I don't suppose you would realize I knew, but I have heard of the thing you are investigating for my esteemed neighbor, and I do think perhaps I might have some information to offer."

"What sort of information?" Madeline said, no longer caring if she drew stares as she fumbled for the notebook in her bag.

"Well now," he said. "It all goes back to the rose garden my wife does love so much." He leaned closer. "The gardeners have found interesting things there."

"Treasure?"

Mr. Brown chuckled. "Perhaps the occasional coin. But the most interesting is the man we found hiding out there when our security fellow did his check in the middle of the night a few days ago. He would not give his name and said he was supposed to be watching the Smith home, but he gave no details as to who was paying him."

Jonah frowned. "And this was a few days ago?"

"Oh yes," he said.

"What did you do with him?"

"Why, I suppose our security fellow turned him over to the authorities." Mr. Brown paused to look beyond Jonah. "There he is. You can ask him yourself."

"Donovan?" Jonah asked him.

"Yes, that's him."

"Thank you, sir," Jonah said, shaking his hand. Madeline echoed his thanks and then followed Jonah toward the center of the room where Detective Donovan had been captured by a young lady insistent on challenging him to dance with her.

"Oh, look, there's my fellow Pinkerton agent," he said to her as he made good on his escape. "Thank you," he added when they had reached the door. "Why are you dressed like that?" he said to Madeline.

"Never mind," Jonah told him. "I want to talk to you, and we need a place where you won't be embarrassed if I punch you."

"Hey now," he said, although he allowed Jonah to lead him out onto the lawn without a fight. "I wonder what's going on here, Miss Latour. Can you enlighten me?"

Madeline kept the coat gathered close and ignored the ginger-haired Pinkerton agent. The last thing she intended to do was get in the middle of whatever was about to happen.

Jonah opened the gate to the rose garden and led Donovan inside. When the gate closed behind them, Madeline went to settle onto a bench to watch and stay out of the way.

"I hope you've got a good reason for this, Cahill," the detective snapped. "I may not have wanted to dance with that woman, but I certainly didn't want to be taken off duty to argue with you over something either. So what is it?"

"The rose garden," he said evenly. "I wonder if you might remember something that happened here a few nights ago."

Donovan's eyes narrowed. "Be specific. It's been a busy week."

"How about a man who wouldn't give his name but said he'd been paid to hide here and watch the Smith house? Does that sound familiar?"

Even in the moonlight, the flush on the man's cheeks was evident. "Now that you mention it, I do remember that. What about it?"

"Don't play dumb, Donovan. You don't fool me." He leaned forward. "You withheld information pertinent to a case you knew I was actively working. Why?"

"I didn't withhold anything, Cahill. With all the work I've been doing getting ready for Grant's visit, I just plain forgot."

Jonah shook his head. "Then you're either lying or a lousy Pinkerton agent."

Chapter Eighteen

"I am neither of those." Detective Donovan's fists rose. "If you want to fight about this, go ahead. I'm ready. But that man we found here in the rose garden could have been any sort of lunatic. I didn't believe him when he said what he was doing because he wouldn't tell us his name or who he worked for."

"Go on," Jonah said, his tone low and menacing.

"I did have one of the staff here stop by the next day and leave a note with the maid letting the lady of the house know the fellow had made those claims. Never heard anything back from her so, like I said, I forgot about it."

"Did you follow up with the messenger to see if the note was delivered?"

Donovan shook his head. "As I said, I got busy and forgot about it, so no."

"Where is the suspect now?"

"Galveston jail, I guess. Unless he got let out. I didn't follow up because it had nothing to do with what I was working on." He shook his head and lowered his fists. "I realize now I ought to have told you about it, but it just didn't seem like it mattered."

"Everything matters when you're working an investigation," he said. "You know that."

"I do, and like I said, I'm sorry. Do you want me to go see what happened to him? Can't be until tomorrow because I've got loose ends to take care of here once the party ends."

"No," Jonah said. "I will handle this from here. You just let me know if you get anybody else hiding in the rose garden and claiming to be watching the house, you hear?" At Donovan's nod, he continued. "For that matter, you let me know if you hear anything from anybody regarding this case I'm working. If you don't, then I might have to decide you're on the wrong side of the matter. Got it?"

"Yeah, I got it." Donovan's nervous laughter echoed through the rose garden.

Jonah nodded to Madeline. "Let's go."

She rose to stand beside him and then allowed him to lead her toward the gate. Madeline cast one last glance up at the stars, inhaling the rose garden's sweet scent of roses and salt air.

"Hey, Cahill," Donovan called. "Now I'm the one who ought to be calling you out, Cahill. Don't you ever accuse me of being on the wrong side of a case."

Jonah escorted her through the gate and then let it slam before turning around to face the Pinkerton agent. "Then don't get on the wrong side and we won't have a problem."

He stood with his hand on the gate latch looking as if he might go back inside. When Detective Donovan shook his head and said nothing further, Jonah turned away.

Jonah guided her to a side exit, avoiding the guests and lawmen still gathered on the lawn. When they reached the street, he paused.

"He's lying," Jonah said.

"Why do you think so?"

Jonah glanced down at her. "I don't know, but he is."

"All right." Madeline allowed Jonah to guide her across the street as she looked up at the house. The light in her room was off.

"Jonah," she said. "You do remember me saying the light was on in my room. That would be the first window on the left on the third floor."

He followed her gaze. "It is off now." Picking up his pace, Jonah led her to the front door with his gun drawn.

"Is that really necessary?" she said. "It's possible Gretchen saw the light on and turned it off because she knew I was at the party."

"I suppose," he said. "But since I am in Mrs. Smith's employ, I intend to make sure that's what happened." He opened the gate and let her inside and then looked up at the window once more. "Wait for me on the porch, but don't stand in front of the door or that window. Got it?"

Madeline nodded and hurried up to the porch. A moment later, Jonah joined her and opened the door. "Stay behind me," he said as they went inside.

The house was dark, but moonlight streamed through the windows, offering enough light to lead them to the staircase. Madeline looked around as she walked behind Jonah. Nothing appeared to be amiss.

"I truly think this is not necessary," she said.

Jonah turned around. "Humor me."

"All right." She followed him up to the second-floor landing where they paused.

"Do you see anything out of place?" When she shook her head, he continued. "And those rooms, are the doors always shut?"

"Yes," she said softly. "No one sleeps on this floor. Madame's chamber is downstairs, and the staff has the third floor."

He stood there a moment longer, his gaze scanning the corridor. Then he turned and nodded toward the staircase.

Madeline stayed behind him until they arrived on the third floor. As with the ground floor, the large windows on either end of the corridor let in plenty of light to allow them to see quite well.

Jonah turned to look down at her. She shrugged.

"Yours is the door at the end?" he asked.

She nodded, and they set off, Jonah in the lead and Madeline a step behind. When they reached the door, Jonah motioned for her to stand out of the way. Gun drawn, he opened the door slowly.

A moment later, he nodded for her to join him. Madeline fumbled for the lamp and lit it. Temporarily blinded, she waited until her eyes adjusted.

"Well?" he said. "Is everything the way you left it?"

She looked around. "I think so."

"All right, then. I have no explanation other than maybe the maid did find the light on and turn it off." He paused. "But I will be happier once I hear that from her."

"You want me to wake Gretchen? I don't think that's a very good idea."

"Then tell me which room is hers and I will ask her myself."

"No," Madeline said. "It is late. Don't you think this can wait until morning?"

"No, I don't, but I can see that you do." He paused to step out into the hallway and look both directions. "I'm going to check the doors before I leave. If you notice anything out of the ordinary, you send someone to get me or find a policeman."

"I promise. Now let me walk you down."

She trailed behind him all the way to the first floor then waited while he checked the halls and kitchen. Satisfied all was well, he returned to stand beside her.

"Look," he told her. "I can stay here tonight if there's any thought of a problem."

"I told you there wasn't," she said. "I'm sure Gretchen will give us the answer as to why the light was on and then off, but in the meantime I plan to get some sleep, and I suggest you do the same."

Jonah looked doubtful but nodded all the same. "I will follow up with the Galveston police in the morning and see what I can find out about the man in Mrs. Brown's rose garden."

"All right," she said. "And I will speak to Gretchen first thing. Should we meet to discuss our findings sometime tomorrow?"

"Yes, that's a good idea." He smiled. "Unless you've got other plans, I can come here after I leave the police station."

"No, that's fine. Oh," Madeline said. "Your jacket."

Madeline shrugged out of the coat and instantly felt the chill even though the air was not that cold. She watched him fold the jacket over his shoulder, her fingers gripping the door frame.

He caught her studying him and smiled. Then his expression sobered. "About that kiss," he said softly.

"There was no kiss," she reminded him.

Jonah gave her a curt nod. "Right. There wasn't."

They said their goodbyes, and Madeline hurried back upstairs, rethinking her comment about the kiss with each step. After slipping out of the ruined dress and awful corset, she donned her nightgown and then went to the table to remove the necklace she'd worn.

As she placed the sapphires on the table beside the brush, Madeline realized the necklace her father gave her was still in Jonah's pocket inside her bag. After a moment of panic, she shook her head. What safer place for that key to be than in the hands, or rather pocket, of a Pinkerton agent?

Madeline unwound the roses from her hair and placed them on the table beside the sapphires then combed out her braid. She reached for the mirror and then spied it on the floor beside the table.

Odd. She specifically remembered putting the mirror on the table before she left. And if it had broken when she returned, she would have heard it.

Maybe she was remembering wrong. That was always possible.

Just as she was about to turn out the light and climb into bed, she heard something hit the window. Then it happened again.

She turned off the light and then crept to the window just as she heard the sound again. Someone was throwing pebbles.

Daring a look, she spied Jonah and opened the window. "What are you doing?" she said as softly as she could.

He held up her bag. She pointed to the back door, and he nodded and disappeared off in that direction. Madeline threw a blanket over her nightgown. Hurrying down to the kitchen, she opened the door and leaned out to take the bag.

"Thank you." He was just turning to go when Madeline remembered the mirror. "Oh, Jonah, it's probably nothing, but I noticed something in my room. Do you remember if you might have knocked my mirror off the table?"

"No," he said slowly.

"It's fine. I probably did it."

Jonah shook his head. "I don't like the sound of this. Where was it?"

She shrugged as she tugged the blanket tighter around her. "I'm fine, Jonah. Really. It was on my dressing table. I found it on the floor beside the table."

Jonah stepped inside without being invited. She was about to protest when he closed the door and turned the lock. "Are the doors and windows locked on the first floor?"

"No," she said. "We never lock them. Why?"

"Because until I get an answer from the police and you get an answer from the maid, we don't know what we're dealing with. I can't think of a good reason for anyone to be in your room while you're away, can you?"

She huddled inside the blanket, acutely aware that Jonah seeing her like this was highly improper. "Truly, Jonah. You're worrying for nothing."

"I might agree if you hadn't been shot at less than a week ago." He peered out the kitchen window and then turned back around to face Madeline. "Twice," he added.

He stalked down the hall, and she followed him. "We don't know if that was intended for me or just an accident."

Jonah had reached the front door and bolted it. "Until we're certain, I cannot let you ladies stay here alone."

"And you cannot stay here, Jonah. It would be—"

"It would be a favor to me," Madame said from behind them.

Madeline turned around to find her employer wrapped in a bathrobe and standing in the hallway. "Detective Cahill, in your capacity as a detective hired by me, I find nothing improper about you taking a room on the second floor for tonight."

"Thank you, Mrs. Smith," he said, "but if it's all the same to you, I am going to stay down here and guard the doors. Last thing I want is for someone to come in here uninvited."

Her brows rose. "Do you have reason to suspect this might happen?"

"I discovered new evidence that this house might be under surveillance. Tomorrow I'll speak to Officer Pearson and see what he's learned about this." He slid Madeline a look. "There's also a question as to whether Madeline left her light on in her room when she left for the ball."

Madame turned toward her. "What kind of question?"

She fumbled with her blanket before looking up at Madame. "I was certain the light was off, and then I spied my window from the

Browns' home and it was on. The detective and I both saw it. Then when I returned it was off again."

"Tell her about the mirror."

"It was on the floor broken when I returned. We used it when Gretchen dressed my hair, and I have no recollection of it breaking in my presence."

"I see," Madame said slowly. "Well, tomorrow we shall speak to Gretchen to see if she heard anyone or heard glass breaking. In the meantime, please see that Detective Cahill has a blanket and pillow, preferably not the blanket you are wearing."

She felt her cheeks flush. "Yes, Madame. And as to the blanket I am wearing, you see, I was preparing for bed when—"

"There is no need to explain. I trust you both implicitly until such time I have reason not to." Madame shifted her attention to Jonah. "And I will once again thank you for your attention to our security needs here, Detective. If this proves to be an ongoing issue, I would very much like your recommendation on the hiring of a night guard so that you do not have to do this every night."

"Yes, ma'am," he said.

"All right, then," Madame said. "I will bid you both good night."

Madeline echoed her sentiment, as did Jonah. "I'll just get a pillow and blanket for you," she said as the door closed to Madame's rooms.

She returned with the promised items and found Jonah had moved a chair from the parlor and positioned it in front of the door. "Are you sure you won't consider taking a bed like Madame offered?"

He looked affronted. "Thank you, but no."

"All right, then," she said as she backtracked to the kitchen to retrieve her bag and then hurried up the stairs. At the second-floor landing, she stopped to look down at Jonah, who had already folded his oversized frame onto the chair.

"You look uncomfortable," she told him.

"Madeline, I have been uncomfortable ever since the minute I laid eyes on you," he said in that Texas drawl of his, "so go to bed and leave me to what I do best."

"Grumbling?" she quipped.

"Taking care of you." He paused. "When you let me, that is."

The truth of that statement made her smile. "Good night, Jonah," she said. "And thank you."

"Good night, Madeline."

When she reached her room, Madeline closed the door and dropped the blanket on her bed then set her bag on the table. Retrieving her necklace, she slipped the chain over her head and tucked the key into the bodice of her gown.

She slept well that night despite the brightness of the moon streaming through her windows and the fact that Jonah Cahill remained two floors below. Or perhaps Jonah's presence was why she slept.

Whatever the reason, by the time she drifted downstairs for breakfast, Jonah was long gone. Gretchen set a plate of cold eggs and sausages in front of her with her usual ill humor.

"Madame asked me about the light and the mirror."

"And?" she said as she picked up her fork to stab at the eggs.

"I know nothing of the mirror, but I will confess to lighting the lamp in your room and then returning to extinguish it."

"Why would you do that?"

She paused as if considering her answer. "Despite all the empty rooms on the second floor, I share my room with the scullery maid. Did you know that?"

Madeline indicated that she did not.

"I thought not." She paused. "I wished to read, and she complains if there is a lamp on in the room. Most nights I ignore her, but last night she claimed she felt ill, so I used your room and your lamp because I knew you were away for the evening."

"I see."

Gretchen gave her a fierce look. "But the mirror, no, I did not do that. Why would I? It was my mother's."

"Your mother's? Oh no. I am so sorry."

"Why would you be? You did not do it."

"No," she said. "I didn't, but I will find out who did. Are you sure the scullery maid didn't sneak in there for some reason? Nothing was taken, so I am not making accusations, but perhaps she also wanted privacy?"

"That little mouse? No. She wouldn't."

The vehemence with which Gretchen answered the question gave Madeline the assurance that the maid was telling the truth. "All right. Thank you for letting me know."

"So your Pinkerton man, what is the relationship with you and him?"

"We are working together on an investigation for Madame," she said.

"I see." Gretchen walked back to the cupboard. "And that is why he comes throwing pebbles at your window past midnight and takes you up to your room in your nightclothes? Interesting assignment that requires all of that, yes?"

"What are you implying?" she said as her temper rose.

"I am implying nothing. I am saying that if you do not watch yourself with that man, you will fall in love with him." Gretchen paused and looked as if she might be assessing her. "Perhaps you already have."

Madeline laughed at the thought. "I am not going to dignify that with an answer. Jonah Cahill barely tolerates me, and the feeling is mutual."

Gretchen's smile was all the response she would offer.

"No, really, there is nothing between us, Gretchen."

The maid shook her head and walked out of the kitchen, leaving Madeline to her breakfast and the morning edition of the *Galveston Daily News*. There on the second page beneath a story chronicling the benefits of Dr. C. McLane's Liver Pills and beside an advertisement for the Hazard Powder Company Blasting and Mining Powder was a headline that read, Miscellaneous Notes from the Event of the Arrival of the Former President of the United States at the Home of the Illustrious Browns.

Intrigued, Madeline folded the page and began to read. A moment later, she stalled on this sentence: *Of particular interest to this reporter, and later to the guests assembled three floors below, was the conduct of a certain employee of the Pinkerton Agency and a certain resident of New Orleans lately employed both by the grand and highly respected* Picayune *newspaper and a widow of high regard who has taken temporary but quite fine lodgings in this fair city.*

There was no byline anywhere, but the author was obviously Walter

Townsend. She slammed the paper down on the table. "Of all the nerve."

Though she did not want to read any more of Mr. Townsend's tirade, she had to see what other rubbish the readers of the paper would have read about her and Jonah. By the time Madeline had read two more paragraphs—the contents of which included a commentary on the question of whether a Pinkerton agent ought to be courting while on duty and a rumination as to how the lady reporter's dress had become torn after an assignation with the Pinkerton on the roof of the second-floor porch while the former president was being feted on the ground floor—she was furious. Stating in print that she and Jonah had a former romance that was being rekindled with a kiss under the stars was the absolute last straw.

"We did not kiss," she said to the paper in her hand.

Tucking the newspaper under her arm, Madeline pressed past Gretchen. "Has Madame awakened from her nap?"

"She has not," Gretchen told her. "What's got you all riled up? And who did you not kiss? Is it that Pinkerton man?"

"Please let Madame know I am going out," she said, ignoring the maid's question. "Depending on how long it takes me to find that weasel, I may be gone a while."

"There are no weasels in Galveston," Gretchen protested. "Rats and mice, yes, but no weasels."

Madeline snatched up her hat and then turned to look over her shoulder at the maid. "That isn't true. I know for certain there is at least one at the *Galveston Daily News* offices."

She stormed to the front door and opened it only to find a young woman in a yellow frock and matching hat about to knock. Madeline stopped short and collected herself and then offered a polite smile.

"Is this the Smith residence?"

"It is, but I am terribly sorry," she said. "Madame is indisposed, but I can leave her your calling card."

She smiled. "Oh no, that will not be necessary. It is not Mrs. Smith I am here to see. Might you be Madeline Latour?"

"I am." She took note of the stranger's honey-colored hair and dark blue eyes. Something about her was familiar, but Madeline couldn't quite figure what that was or why she might think so. "I'm sorry. Do I know you?"

"You do not, but I feel as though I already know you."

Her voice was gently bred, her accent definitely local. Still Madeline could not place her. "Well now," Madeline managed. "You do have me at a disadvantage."

"Hello, Miss Latour. My name is Susanna Cahill, and my brother is hopelessly in love with you." She paused. "Again."

Chapter Nineteen

Madeline shook her head and suppressed a groan. Of course. Though she had not met Jonah's family when they were engaged, plans had been in the works when the engagement ended.

"Please do not believe what the newspaper says. I was just on my way to the *Daily News* office to lodge a strong protest."

"What does a newspaper have to do with anything?" she said.

She gave the woman a sideways look. "You didn't see anything about your brother and me in today's *Daily News*?"

"No," she said slowly. "Why?"

"No reason," Madeline hurried to say as she reached behind her to place the folded newspaper on the breakfront nearest the door. "But if that is not the basis of your opinion of your brother's romantic life, then I think you must have me confused with someone else."

"I assure you I do not." Her smile was broad, her tone curious. "Although if I know my brother, and I assure you I do, you are likely confused."

"I am, actually. Oh, forgive my manners." Madeline stepped back into the corridor. "Won't you come in?"

Miss Cahill nodded toward the sidewalk and the street beyond where a buggy awaited. "I much prefer to take a ride if you're up for it." She returned her attention to Madeline. "I am harmless, I assure you. If that's why you're reluctant."

"I'm not reluctant," she said as she adjusted her hat and stepped out onto the porch. "However, I am still absolutely certain that you are mistaken about your brother's feelings toward me. I assure you we are just two people working on the same investigation."

Her smile sufficed for an answer as she nodded toward the buggy. "Shall we go?"

Madeline climbed in beside Miss Cahill. Glancing back at the house, she spied Gretchen watching openly from one of the front windows. As the buggy pulled away, Madeline thought she saw a curtain move in Madame's room. Was she watching too?

She sat back against the seat and focused on the road ahead. The traffic on Broadway Avenue was light this time of the morning although the sidewalks were heavily populated with pedestrians.

At Twenty-Third Street, Susanna made a right turn and headed into the wind down the road that led to the Gulf of Mexico. She drove very much like Jonah, throwing caution to the wind to fly past all the other vehicles on the road and yet being careful at the same time. It was an odd combination of driving skills that until now Madeline had believed belonged to Jonah alone.

She slid a sideways glance at Susanna and noted that the young woman also had Jonah's profile. That stubborn set to his chin that Jonah had perfected looked softer and quite lovely on his younger sister.

As they drove past the Ursuline Academy, she offered Madeline a quick glance. "I do appreciate your time this morning," she said. "And since I believe we will be seeing much more of each other once my brother finally comes to his senses, I would like it very much if you would call me Susanna."

"All right, Susanna," she said. "Then I am Madeline."

Silence fell between them until the road gave way to the beach. Ahead blue skies touched the water, which changed to a shade of darker greenish blue that deepened to muddy brown near the shore. A few wispy clouds floated by as if chased by the breeze.

Susanna brought the carriage to a stop at the edge of the sand. She swiveled in the seat and regarded Madeline with a smile. Though carriages and wagons traveled the road behind, the screech of gulls and waterbirds drowned out the *clip-clop* of the horses.

"My brother says I am too quick to speak my mind." She shrugged. "I do not disagree with him." She smiled. "However, I do not plan to mend my ways, so perhaps I should apologize now for being so blunt."

"I much prefer complete honesty, and to be perfectly blunt, I wish I had met you when Jonah and I were engaged to be married. But that was ages ago," she said.

"One year," Susanna corrected.

"But I do think you're mistaken about Jonah. He and I have been at odds since he broke the engagement. I don't suppose he told you I almost caused him to be arrested last year, so I cannot fault him with deciding not to go through with the marriage."

"The McRee case," she said as she pushed a strand of hair away from her face. "Yes, he did mention it. Several times, actually."

"Then you can see that he and I barely tolerate each other."

Even as she said the words, she thought of Jonah spending last night in a chair to keep the household safe. Of him putting his life on the line to get her out of danger in Indianola. And of him coming to her rescue at the Brown party when she might have been horribly embarrassed.

"Oh, I'm sure that's what my brother wants you to think." She looked up as a pair of seagulls flew past. "He calls me stubborn, but truly he's just as obstinate." Susanna returned her attention to Madeline. "It's not what he says about you but rather how much he talks about you."

Madeline shook her head. "I don't follow."

"Jonah is a private man. I would like to blame the Pinkerton Agency for that, but he was that way well before he joined. He always attracted the ladies, even when he was younger, but I can count on one hand the number of them he actually spoke about."

"Well," Madeline said slowly, "while I understand what you're saying, is it possible that he happens to be talking about me because we are working on an investigation together?"

"Oh yes, the investigation. Do you know he's said absolutely nothing to me about what you're investigating?"

"I would assume that is because it is confidential."

"Oh, I don't expect him to share details. That's not what I mean. He hasn't said what you're investigating, but he has said a lot about things that have happened during the investigation. For example, he talks about how brave you were when you were being shot at, how relentless you are when you are looking for answers, and how you and he share the same love of astronomy. Don't you think that is a lot to say about one person when you cannot say anything about the investigation?"

Interesting. Still. . .

"He can't," Madeline protested. "Nor can I. Being unable to discuss an investigation is not unusual."

"I am willing to agree to disagree," she said. "In fact, I bet he is frantically searching for you right now."

"Why?"

Susanna giggled. "Because I may have left him a message that I was taking the buggy to come meet you." She paused. "But I'm really not here to convince you. I just wanted to meet you."

"And now you have, Susanna." Jonah stepped around the buggy to stand beside Susanna. "Hello, Madeline. What has my sister done this time?"

"Well look who is here," Susanna said as she gave Madeline an I-told-you-so look. "You're right. I like her very much. She suits you perfectly, and I am wishing right now that you weren't too stubborn to admit this."

For the first time since Madeline met Jonah Cahill, he looked like he had no idea what to say. Finally he turned his attention to her. "I apologize for whatever my sister has done."

"Even the part where she told me how popular you've always been with the ladies?" Madeline teased.

"Especially that," he said with the beginnings of a grin. "Although you can believe it if you want to."

"See," Susanna said. "He even makes jokes around you. Jonah Cahill never makes jokes."

❤

Jonah stood his ground despite the fact that both his sister and his partner in the Smith investigation were grinning like fools. "All right, Susanna. That is enough."

Susanna put her hands on her hips, a sure sign she wasn't giving in so easily. "I see you got my message."

"Get out of the buggy," he said through clenched jaw.

As his sister climbed to her feet, Jonah looked over at Madeline. "Excuse us just a minute."

"What are you doing?" he demanded when he got Susanna far enough from the buggy to be sure Madeline couldn't hear them.

"Trying to get your attention," she snapped.

"Okay, it worked. Now what?"

"Now you can face the fact that you are crazy about that woman over there and maybe see you have too much still between you to ignore it."

Crazy about Madeline Latour? Where did this woman get her ideas? He looked down at his younger sister, temporarily speechless.

"We have a broken engagement between us, Susanna," he protested, trying not to think of that one kiss he just missed with Madeline. "I am not ignoring that."

"Maybe you should," she snapped. "Forget what broke you up and concentrate on what you have now." She paused. "I just want you to be happy, and I think you're not going to be happy if you miss this second chance, Jonah."

"I know you do," he said. "I'm just not convinced you're right about this."

"Yes you are," she said as she watched him closely in that way his sister had. "You are absolutely certain and absolutely terrified all at the same time."

He opened his mouth to protest and found he couldn't. Unfortunately, Susanna was right.

"Get in the buggy," he finally told her for lack of a better response before stalking over to the buggy.

When she so quickly complied, he realized why. Though he stood back to put her in the middle between him and Madeline, the infuriating woman got in on the other side. To accommodate the woman who was taking up far more room than her tiny body required, Madeline had to scoot so close to him that her side was wedged against him.

He looked beyond Madeline to catch Susanna staring in his direction.

"Ready when you are," she said as she squeezed her elbows out, causing Madeline to move even closer—if that were possible.

Later he would have a serious conversation with his little sister about the consequences of meddling in his life. Right now, however, he found conversation—and concentration—difficult.

Jonah turned the buggy toward home, his horse firmly tied to the back. They rode in silence until he pulled to a stop in front of the Cahill home.

"Give me a minute," Jonah said to Madeline as he jumped out and untied the horse then handed Susanna the reins.

Stowaway, the orange cat that had declared all of Cahill property its kingdom, hurried to thread itself around Jonah's legs. After bending to scratch the persistent beast under its chin, he rose to look down at Susanna.

"See to the horse. I'm taking Madeline home."

Susanna gave him her brightest smile. "Take your time, Jonah. Officer Pearson is coming for dinner on Friday. You and Madeline are welcome, of course."

She raised her voice when she delivered the dinner invitation. Of course that was his sister's way of making sure Madeline could hear.

"Thank you," Madeline said. "I think that sounds like a good time to find out what Officer Pearson knows, don't you, Jonah?"

His sister was already giggling by the time Madeline finished speaking. "Stop it," he told her.

"Do you really think I will?" Susanna said.

Several responses occurred to him, but he chose not to speak at all. Rather, he turned his back on the meddling female and stalked toward the buggy.

"I apologize for my sister," he said evenly as he climbed up onto the seat. "She loves me but doesn't use good sense when she speaks. That is sometimes a dangerous combination."

"Does that mean I am not invited for dinner on Friday?"

"What? No, I mean yes. Sure, you're invited for dinner." He looked past her to where Susanna was silently laughing as she held tight to the horse's reins. "Like you said, it will be a good time to see what Officer

Pearson knows. He wasn't at the station this morning when I stopped by."

"Oh, yes. I forgot you were going to see about the man in the rose garden."

"I found out plenty, but let me get somewhere a little less noisy then I will tell you what I discovered."

While he maneuvered the buggy around people and various types of wagons and carts, Jonah gripped the reins and wondered just how dangerous Susanna's words had been. True, he had spoken of Madeline to Susanna, but surely he'd said nothing that would prove embarrassing.

He squared his shoulders and ignored the worrying thought that Susanna had likely found a way to embarrass him anyway. Crazy about Madeline Latour indeed.

Preposterous idea.

Madeline slid him a sideways look. When she grinned, his heart flip-flopped worse than the time he got thrown from his horse when he was twelve.

Jonah guided the buggy down the avenue that ran alongside the bay and then turned onto a small road nearly hidden by tall sea grass and cattails. The sounds of carriages and horse carts faded as the shrill call of terns and egrets beckoned.

He'd spent many happy hours fishing at the end of this road, truly more of a nearly hidden horse path. He swiveled to face Madeline, took a deep breath, and let it out slowly. "Whatever my sister said, ignore at least half of it. Or more."

"We're in the middle of an investigation, Jonah," she said sweetly as she peered up at him from beneath the brim of her hat. "Shouldn't we just talk about that?"

Relief flooded him as he answered with a nod. So she was smart enough to see his sister's foolish attempt at matchmaking as just that—foolish.

"All right, Donovan may have handed the trespasser over to a police officer," he told her, "but there is no report of the arrest."

An egret rose from the bay to soar overhead, and the horse nickered. "How is that possible?"

"It isn't." He shifted positions and let the reins drop over his leg.

"Either the trespasser never went to the station or Donovan handed him over to someone who wasn't a police officer."

"Or Donovan lied." She shook her head. "I'm sorry, Jonah. I know he's a fellow Pinkerton detective, but we have to look at all the possibilities."

Much as he didn't like to agree, it was a logical assumption. "What did you find out from the maid?"

"Gretchen admitted to using my room to read while her roommate was sleeping, but she had no idea what happened to the mirror. I believe her."

Jonah shifted positions. "So the light is explained but the mirror is not."

"Yes. Especially given the fact it was hers and had sentimental value," Madeline said.

"I'm hoping Pearson can shed some light on this. Are you sure you want to come to dinner on Friday?" He thought of what his sister must have said to her and tried not to cringe. "I warn you, my sister will continue to persist in her matchmaking."

"I fully expect it," she said. "And I may know why, although she claims she did not see it."

"It being what?" he said.

"It being an article in the *Daily News* about the party at Ashton Villa."

"Go on," he said warily.

She shrugged. "I can't quote the author without reading the article, but let's just say he wondered whether a Pinkerton agent ought to be courting while on duty."

Jonah's temper spiked. "Of all the—"

"Just wait," she said. "There's more. He also wondered how 'the lady reporter's dress had become torn after an assignation with the Pinkerton while the esteemed general and former president was being feted on the ground floor.' That much I can quote from the story, although I am paraphrasing." She paused. "Then there was the allegation of the kiss between us."

"Townsend," he snapped as he tightened his grip on the reins. "I will see he never writes for another newspaper."

"Now Jonah," she said as she reached over to place her hand over his.

"Let's think about this for a minute. First, we don't know for certain it was Mr. Townsend. There was no byline on the story."

"Of course there wasn't. The man's a coward. He wouldn't put his name on it." Jonah slammed his fist down as he fought to tame his temper. "He saw us and threatened to write the thing. If he didn't, then who did?"

She studied him a moment. "Yes, you're right. I was on my way out the door to go down to the newspaper and demand a retraction when your sister arrived. I'm still very tempted to do that."

"The paper owes us a retraction." He leaned back against the seat. "I'm not worried what it said about me, but I don't want you embarrassed."

"Why would I be embarrassed? I have been linked with 'the most handsome Pinkerton detective currently employed by the force.'" She giggled. "Also a direct quote."

"Stop making that up," he told her.

"You don't believe me?" She nodded toward the road behind them. "Let's go. I have a copy at home that you're welcome to read for yourself."

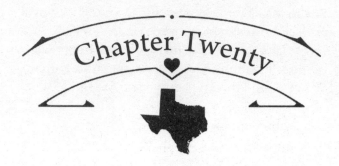

Chapter Twenty

Jonah gave Madeline a sideways look. Even riled up as she was now, Madeline Latour was beautiful.

But her beauty wasn't what had attracted Jonah to her back then, and it wasn't what he liked most about her now. Madeline's intelligence, her wit and curiosity, those were the reasons he had fallen head over boots for the lady reporter.

"So you've decided not to hunt down the reporter and force a retraction out of him?"

She looked over and caught him watching her. "I have decided to hear what Officer Pearson says first. Something tells me Townsend might know more about our trespasser in the garden than anyone else."

"Why him?" Jonah asked as he turned the buggy around.

"Call it a hunch, but do you remember when Townsend said he had eyewitnesses to corroborate the story of us courting on the roof?"

"Vaguely," he said. "I was so mad, I only remember threatening his life after he called you honey."

"I think you only threatened his career, but I could be wrong." She paused. "Anyway, before he made his threat about the eyewitness, he looked down at the rose garden. I wonder if that was some sort of clue that he had a man down there."

"I don't know," he said as he turned the buggy toward Twenty-Fifth Street. "The time line doesn't add up. Donovan says he turned the man over to the police a few days ago. Would someone risk another arrest by going back to the rose garden again? It makes no sense. If anything, I think he was referring to all the people standing on the lawn downstairs."

"I need to see the facts written down," she said. "I plan to spend the afternoon outlining everything that has happened in the past twenty-four hours."

"Please leave off the part where my sister made a fool of herself—and me."

Madeline smiled. "I assure you she did not make a fool of you. She actually said some rather nice things about you."

"Did she now?" He glanced at her briefly before making the turn onto Broadway Avenue.

"She did." Madeline paused. "I'm almost home, so I want to ask you about something I keep forgetting to ask. Have there been any more holes dug in your property?"

"No. Not since I returned to Galveston. Either the perpetrator is aware I am here and looking for him or the two events were isolated incidents and whoever did it decided to give up."

"It could be either," she said. "And if it makes any difference, I haven't come across any credible evidence other than hearsay that puts any of Lafitte's treasure on Cahill property. Most say Three Trees is a likely place, but too many have looked there and not found it."

Jonah nodded. "Or if they have and it is gone, no one has admitted to finding it."

"Nor would they, for obvious reasons." She paused. "If I can change the subject slightly, remember the commander thought Mrs. Smith's granddaughter was at the Browns' party but offered no facts to support that statement. What do you think of that?"

"Anything is possible, especially regarding a man of the commander's age."

"So you think he fabricated the story?"

"I think he believes what he told you," he said.

"Mrs. Smith swears she's in Galveston, so it wouldn't be out of the realm of possibility that she might have been invited and attended. And we didn't exactly look at every woman's eyes to check their eye color."

"Not that we can be certain they would be brown. That's merely a guess that we hope is correct."

"Exactly." She sighed. "We know very little, don't we?"

"We know more than when we began, but there is much more to learn." He paused. "So to answer your question, I think the commander is a nice man and that he may have information we need to follow up on. But I am not ready to say he was correct in his statement that she attended the Browns' party."

"I agree. One more thing. The investigation into my family still concerns me."

Jonah pulled the buggy to a stop in front of the Smith home. "I know it does, and I don't blame you. But I don't know anything about it."

"I believe you. The last letter I got from my parents indicated there had been nothing on that subject. Still, I just can't get it out of my mind."

"That's because you're a reporter. You won't rest until you've chased down all the leads."

She smiled. "True. And speaking of reporters, let's go get that paper so you can enjoy the article as much as I did. Then we can talk about whether to force that retraction out of my colleague from the *Daily News*."

Jonah laughed and hurried over to help her down from the buggy. He followed her down the walkway until she stopped short. "Jonah, I never thought I would say this, but I'm glad we're working together on this investigation."

"So am I," he said and meant it as he took one last look around the perimeter and then followed her inside.

"Second page under the advertisement for Dr. C. McLane's Liver Pills," she said as she handed him the folded newspaper. "We actually aren't mentioned until the second paragraph."

"That's comforting. At least our former president got mentioned before we did."

"If only the reporter had said more about President Grant and less about us," Madeline responded.

"Detective Cahill, is that you?"

Jonah looked around and found his current employer standing at the opposite end of the hall. "Mrs. Smith, yes, it's me."

"Excellent. This saves me from having you summoned. Won't you join me in the parlor. I've got someone you need to speak with." She paused to turn her gaze toward Madeline. "You as well, Miss Latour."

Madeline did as she was told, and Jonah followed a step behind. Once inside the parlor, he immediately spied Reverend Wyatt seated beside Mrs. Smith's favorite chair.

Rising, he reached out to shake Jonah's hand. "I suppose you're wondering why I am here."

"I am," Jonah said as he looked over at Mrs. Smith. "But I'm sure that is between you and my employer."

"Of a sort," he said, "but it also concerns you and Miss Latour."

Jonah helped Mrs. Smith to her chair and then took a seat nearest the door, placing the newspaper on the table beside him next to a vase full of pink rosebuds.

"First, I owe you an apology. I did not realize you hadn't told Mrs. Smith you'd been shot at."

Madeline looked down at the floor and then back at the reverend. "Detective Cahill and I did not want to worry her," she said.

"There is always the possibility the gunshots were accidental," Jonah added, but only for Mrs. Smith's benefit.

"They were not, I assure you," Reverend Wyatt said. "Although I can also assure you that they were not meant to do anything more than to frighten you."

"How do you know this?" Jonah asked.

"Because I am the one who fired the shots."

Jonah stood. "Let me get this straight, Reverend Wyatt." He shook his head as he tried to tame his temper. "You aimed a .45 caliber weapon at Miss Latour and fired it?"

"Essentially, yes."

"Reverend Wyatt," Madeline said. "When I saw you, my first thought was that I owed you an apology. I now think that apology is rather owed by you."

"And I do apologize," he said. "You see, I was keeping a promise, although it was not one I should have agreed to."

"Go on," Mrs. Smith said when his words stalled. "Tell them the rest."

"To do that, I have to go back to the beginning," he said to her.

"Then the beginning it is." She swept her gaze across Madeline and then stopped at Jonah. "With the understanding that you will not be required by any of us to say anything other than that which you are free to say."

He bowed his head as if praying and then lifted it again. "It all started back when I wasn't more than a lad. I went to sea because that's what we did in my town. I'm from south Louisiana, you know. A little town nobody's heard of. We all fished or we went to sea and that was that."

Gretchen arrived with more tea and saw to refilling the reverend's cup. She offered tea to Jonah, who declined. Ignoring Madeline, she left quietly.

"You were saying you went to sea," Mrs. Smith said gently.

"Oh, yes, and our captain was a good and fair man." He nodded to Mrs. Smith. "I was with Captain Smith for nigh on seven years before the incident back in '55."

Jonah sat up a little straighter at the mention of the year of the Smith granddaughter's birth. He slid Madeline a look and saw she had done the same. She had also thought to retrieve her notebook and was scribbling notes at a rapid pace.

"It was storming something awful, and men where lashing themselves to the ship to keep from going over. Two hadn't had the forethought to do that, and they were long gone," he said as if recalling the moment with brutal clarity. "Me, I was trying to keep the old girl afloat, what with her taking on water like she was."

"By 'the old girl,' I assume you're speaking of the ship you were on?" Madeline asked.

"I am," he said. "So it came to the point where the captain's son, well, his wife was in the family way and came to her time right in the middle of all of that. We all stayed away, but it wasn't hard to imagine by the sound of it all that things weren't going as they ought. The serving girl she'd brought with her went in and out, always asking for more cloths and hot water, things like that. Finally it got all quiet and we figured all was well."

"But it was not," Mrs. Smith said.

He looked up at her. "As you know, it wasn't."

"What happened?" Madeline asked.

"The mama, she died. We thought the little one had too until that serving girl comes out carrying the wee thing. She wasn't any bigger than a minute, probably shouldn't have come early as she had, but she had her daddy's eyes and the tiniest little mewl like a kitten. We'd have given thanks right there, most of us being God-fearing people, except that we were all about to go under right there in that storm."

"That must have been terrifying," Madeline supplied.

"Oh, we'd had worse blows, but none where we had a woman and child aboard. Some said that was why our luck went sour, what with women being considered bad luck aboard a ship and all."

"A bunch of poppycock," Mrs. Smith said, her tone pure acid.

"Indeed, ma'am," Reverend Wyatt said. "The ship, she was shuddering, and the captain, he called me to come see him. I gave him the report and he knew we were done for. There were only two boats on board, so he decided he'd send out his son with his wife to bury her on one and the baby with the serving girl on the other."

"Why take separate boats? Were they that small?"

"They weren't at all. Each held a half dozen full-grown men, maybe more. But the captain, he feared losing all his family at once if one of those boats went under. And honestly, it was a strong likelihood. So he decided he'd divide them up and hope the Lord took neither but was prepared in case He took one."

"So each of these boats had two passengers and then the remaining spots were filled with crew members?" Madeline asked.

"Not a one of the crew would volunteer to leave with the ship in distress. It isn't done, miss. We go down with her, to a man, unless our captain says otherwise. He knew this, our captain, so he picked two and sent one out with each boat to do the job of rowing. I was the one sent to row the captain's son and his missus."

"That would be Samuel and Eliza," Mrs. Smith supplied.

"It would be," he said as he dipped his head. "Mr. Samuel, he fought me for the oars. Said he needed to do something to help get us to shore in Indianola. But I told him an order's an order and I'd be the man rowing. He understood. We made it to shore, we did, though only the Lord knows how. Out in the middle of that weather with the waves pounding us and Mr. Samuel holding tight to his lady wife, well, I just stopped what I was doing and begged Him, would You just let us live? I've got orders to get this man and his lady to shore and I'd be obliged if You'd let me do that, is what I told the Lord."

"And obviously, He allowed that to happen," Jonah said.

"He did, but I promised Him one more thing before He did. I promised Him wouldn't nobody harm Mr. Samuel or his little girl ever long as I kept watch because he was good as family to me and so was she."

Jonah shook his head. "It's obvious Samuel Smith owed you his life, but what does that have to do with firing shots at Miss Latour?"

The reverend winced at the question. "I am getting to that, I do promise. You see, that storm raged on for two days. We took shelter in a boardinghouse and were thankful for the lodgings."

"Francine's?" Jonah asked.

"It was indeed. Mrs. Francine, she was kind to us. Once he was able, Mr. Samuel, must have been three or four days later, he arranged for the burial of his lady. That changed him, I'm here to tell you. Loved his Eliza, he did, and without her he was good and lost. All the worse, that boat with his baby girl on it never showed up. Every day he went out to look and see if it had arrived, and every day he came back to that boardinghouse vowing to do the same thing the next day."

"That's so sad," Madeline whispered.

"It was," Reverend Wyatt said.

Jonah tried not to let on that he'd noticed both the reverend and his employer had tears in their eyes. Instead, he looked away to give them a moment.

"So anyway," Reverend Wyatt said, swiping at his eyes with his sleeve. "It came time to leave Indianola, and Mr. Samuel, he wouldn't go. He wrote to his mama and told her he was staying until his baby girl came home to him."

"So he lived there until he died," Jonah supplied. "Which was a few years later?"

"It was 1857. By then there'd been fevers a few times. He'd recovered, but that last time, it got him. I saw to his burial beside his lady wife and then wrote to his mama here to let her know."

"What happened to Captain Smith's ship?" Madeline asked, looking up from her notes.

"It limped along until he finally got to Galveston. There he set up and waited until he got her seaworthy again. Then I understand he went home to Mrs. Smith here."

"And lived to sail another day," Mrs. Smith supplied. "But we never found our granddaughter. The one my husband called his lost treasure until the day he died."

Jonah looked over at Mrs. Smith. "Was the serving girl or the man who rowed that boat found?"

"The actual name of the man rowing the boat has never been known. My husband learned once we began searching for our granddaughter that his loyal crew member had sailed under an assumed name. It was done then, of course, as it likely is now, so that the man at sea cannot be connected to the family at home."

"So the man hid who he really was by giving a false name?" Madeline asked, her pen poised above a page of her notebook.

"Essentially, yes," Reverend Wyatt said. "Most of us reinvented ourselves when we left home. Some because of who they were before and some in spite of it. I figure this man who was charged with that baby girl just didn't want anyone to know who he used to be. Could be he had a family of quality who wouldn't have approved him shipping out with the likes of us. That happens sometimes."

"But eventually, yes, according to Samuel, the serving girl was found," Mrs. Smith said. "He wrote me all about it but said she was no help in locating my granddaughter."

"Why not?" Madeline said. "If she was in the boat with her, then she should have seen what happened."

"She saw," Madame said, "but as a woman and a serving girl, her protests were ignored when she was separated from the child."

"And this serving girl? Do you know her name?"

"I do not," Mrs. Smith said. "Nor did Samuel recall it in the letters he sent. I can provide them if you need them, but I will have to have them sent from New Orleans."

"Yes, if you would, please," Madeline said. "I would very much like to find her."

"I don't know that finding her is possible," Madame said. "She is referred to only as the serving girl in my son's letter. There is no other identifying information."

"But where could the child have gone, with or without this girl? Where did they finally land, is the question," Jonah said.

The pastor launched into a long diatribe regarding the wind and waves as he recalled them on that night. Then he described the size of the vessel and the difficulty steering due to wind and weather. Finally he admitted he had no idea where the boat went.

"But you know it went somewhere," Madeline said. "Because you have a serving girl testifying to reaching land."

"To reaching Galveston," Madame corrected.

"Yes," Madeline said. "Galveston."

"So we can agree that the trail of the child goes cold right here in Galveston," Jonah said, and all in the room nodded in agreement. "Reverend Wyatt," Jonah continued, growing tired with waiting for the chatty preacher to get back to the question he most wanted answered, "you still haven't told us why you felt you had to shoot at Miss Latour."

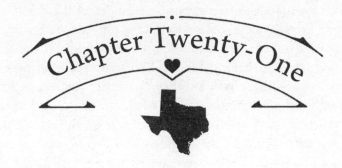

Chapter Twenty-One

Before he died, I made Mr. Samuel a promise. He was a private man, and for reasons I didn't ask, if you know what I mean. He didn't want nobody coming around and asking questions."

"Yes, that sounds like my Samuel," the older woman said. "I always appreciated his letters, but he never told me how ill he was. All those times he kept me from traveling to Indianola by telling me he would visit me soon. I only wish I hadn't taken him at his word."

"Like as not he did have plans to visit you, ma'am, but with Mr. Samuel, you just never knew." Reverend Wyatt glanced around the room and then shrugged. "Anyhow, as I told Miss Latour when the two of you visited the parsonage, I was pledged to keep his secrets, and that goes well before I changed my ways and became a preacher."

Jonah's temper spiked as he thought of how close Madeline had come to being shot by this man, all in the name of protecting a dead friend. Ridiculous.

"And it didn't matter who was asking the questions," Jonah snapped.

"Detective Cahill," Mrs. Smith said firmly, "please let the reverend tell his story in his own way."

"Yes, of course," he said evenly. "Do continue, Reverend Wyatt."

Reverend Wyatt paused to glance over at Madeline and then back at Mrs. Smith. "So when I heard somebody from the Pinkertons had been asking about Mr. Samuel and his lady wife, well, I got concerned. It's been more than twenty years since he joined Mrs. Eliza in glory, so what did a Pinkerton man want with coming around like that?"

"I wanted to get questions answered for my employer, Mrs. Smith," he said evenly. "And Miss Latour was my assistant in this endeavor."

"Oh no," he said, shaking his head. "Wasn't you who came asking first, Detective Cahill. It was another Pinkerton man, or leastwise he said he was. So when I got word from a fellow I know who works down at the wharf that another Pinkerton man was on the manifest for the *Haven* along with a young lady, I figured I needed to take action."

"Who was this man?" Jonah demanded; then he had a thought. "Did he call himself Detective Donovan?"

"No, that name isn't familiar. He was a dark-haired man, average build. Just a fellow who wouldn't stand out on the street."

"Detective Donovan has red hair," Madeline said to him, "so it couldn't have been him."

"No indeed, it could not have been a red-haired man, of this I am certain, although that name does sound vaguely familiar. I will have to check the card he gave me when I get a chance, if I still have it."

"Yes, please do that," Jonah said. "I would be very interested in finding out if another Pinkerton has been assigned to a similar matter."

The reverend once again ducked his head before lifting it up again to look over at Madeline. "Again, I do own up to shooting at you, Miss Latour, although owing to the fact I am a pretty decent shot, I want you to be sure to understand that I missed on purpose. Even as I say it, I realize that is nothing I ever thought I'd say as a pastor."

"I think I understand," Madeline said. "I can be quite fierce when it comes to defending my family as well."

The reverend turned to Jonah. "And that spent shell casing I put in your food hamper was to be another warning. I figured if you thought I'd followed you or at least knew how to get close to you, then you'd back off and stop asking about Mr. Samuel."

"Why put all the food in the other hamper?" Madeline asked.

"So I wouldn't miss the message," Jonah responded, keeping his gaze directed toward the reverend.

"Yes, that was the idea," he admitted. "I almost didn't get to hand it off to my contact at the wharf that day because Miss Latour caught me walking back from the boardinghouse and waylaid me into talking to her." He shrugged. "Anyhow, that's what happened and part of why I am here in Galveston. I do appreciate your understanding on the matter."

Understanding wasn't exactly how Jonah felt at the moment, but he was relieved that the question regarding the shooting had been answered. Knowing there wasn't someone following the reporter and looking to strike again was a huge relief.

However, he did wonder who was impersonating a Pinkerton agent. Or perhaps there truly was a Pinkerton sent to investigate, although Jonah seriously doubted that. If another agent had intelligence pertaining to this case, the captain would have already put them in touch.

No, he decided. This was a likely case of someone trying to convince this man he was a legitimate Pinkerton detective.

"Reverend, one more question if you don't mind." At the preacher's nod, Jonah continued. "What kind of questions was that other Pinkerton man asking?"

"Best I can recollect he was asking pretty much the same questions Miss Latour was. Wanting to know about treasure and such."

Madeline's cheeks colored as Mrs. Smith offered a surprised expression. Neither spoke, so Jonah continued. "Was he as relentless as Madeline?"

Chuckling, Reverend Wyatt shook his head. "I believe he tried, but no sir, Miss Latour wins on that count." He turned his attention to Madeline. "You really ought to consider becoming a Pinkerton detective. You almost had me talking back there in the parsonage."

"It's never too late to talk, Reverend Wyatt," she said in a lighthearted tone that made everyone in the room except Jonah believe she was teasing.

"Well," Mrs. Smith said before the preacher could respond. "This has been an interesting visit, Reverend Wyatt. I am most grateful to you for coming to Galveston and speaking with us."

"There's more, and to this I first owe a debt of apology to Mrs. Smith and to your late husband for not being forthcoming with this information. But you see, I was bound by my promise to your son not to tell you that, well. . ." He shrugged. "You see, though Mr. Samuel, he did miss his lady wife something terrible, he was swayed into another love match between the second and the final fever that took him."

"Samuel found love again?" Mrs. Smith said softly, her voice tender. "That's wonderful. Why would you possibly think I wouldn't want to know this?"

Reverend Wyatt shook his head. "There's more to it than that. You see, well, he took Mrs. Francine to wife—she's the widow woman who was running the boardinghouse—and they, well, there was another girl born to Mr. Samuel, though she came into the world a few months after he passed on."

"Annabelle?" Jonah asked.

"Yes, she'd be the one," he said as he glanced over at Jonah and nodded. "Looks more like her mama but she's got Mr. Samuel's eyes too. She's been striving to stay above water with that boardinghouse, but it has been a rough go with her man shipping out like he does."

"I have two granddaughters?" Mrs. Smith said, a smile lighting her face.

"And a great-grandson," Reverend Wyatt said. "That's truly the purpose of this visit. You see, I have felt terrible awful about taking those shots at you, Miss Latour, and that had me praying hard on what the Lord would have me do about it. He told me I ought to go make it right and tell the whole story, which I have now done, and to ask for forgiveness."

"Well, yes, of course," Mrs. Smith said. "Of course they understand and forgive, don't you, Detective and Miss Latour?"

"Of course," Madeline said. Jonah grudgingly agreed, knowing he'd be sorely tempted to behave the same way under the same set of circumstances.

"So where is my granddaughter and great-grandson?" Mrs. Smith demanded. "I must be taken to them." She rang for Gretchen, who somehow managed to come immediately. "Prepare my things and have passage booked for Indianola. The reverend and I will be traveling as soon as possible."

"Now hold on a minute, ma'am," he said. "That won't be necessary. You see, they're here in Galveston right now. Annabelle, she's anxious to meet her gran, and little Jordy, well, he's just the image of your Samuel."

Mrs. Smith turned her focus to Jonah, her eyes misty. "Detective Cahill, did you hear? I have *two* granddaughters and a great-grandson." She rose. "Reverend Wyatt, I want to see them right now."

He chuckled. "I thought you might say that. I can fetch us a buggy in no time and have you over to the place where Annabelle has taken rooms. It ain't far, but it certainly ain't posh like this."

Jonah spied the maid listening from the hallway just a few feet away from where Madeline was sitting. While the reporter was still taking notes, the maid seemed to be trying to read over Madeline's shoulder.

Mrs. Smith grinned. "I have an entire floor sitting empty just for them right here."

Out of the corner of his eye, Jonah saw the maid frown.

"I'm sure that would cause no end of trouble for your staff," the reverend protested.

"Nonsense," Mrs. Smith said. "My staff will provide any assistance my granddaughter needs to settle in with her son. And I insist you stay with us as well, Reverend."

The maid's expression of dismay, which included a roll of her eyes and something that looked like a swoon, almost caused Jonah to laugh out loud. Rather, he allowed her to see he had been watching her. To his surprise, the maid ignored him to continue her vigil at the door, although now wearing a decidedly unhappy expression.

"There's no need to fetch a buggy, Reverend Wyatt," Jonah said. "I would be glad to offer up mine for your use."

He looked surprised. "You don't mind?"

Jonah grinned. "Anything that gets Mrs. Smith's granddaughter and her great-grandson here as soon as possible is my pleasure."

The maid glowered in his direction and then stormed off. Madeline gave Jonah a curious look, no doubt wondering why he was chuckling under his breath.

❤

Later, after Madame and Reverend Wyatt had left in the buggy, Madeline sat on the porch swing beside Jonah while he read through the

Daily News article. "What exactly do you find so amusing?" she asked after he'd laughed yet again.

"All of it." Jonah dropped the paper on the table in front of him. "Come on, Madeline. The whole thing is ridiculous. No one will believe any of it."

"Except for the fact that you did kiss me in front of Mrs. Brown and then we danced all night."

"Well, true," he said.

"And we were supposed to be pretending to be smitten," she reminded him.

He grinned. "It worked."

Madeline shook her head. "You're not helping."

Jonah swiveled to face her. "Then let's talk about our investigation. Do you believe Wyatt's explanation for shooting at you?"

"I do, actually," she said. "And not just because he's a preacher. I think he's telling the truth."

"I have my reservations," Jonah said. "But yes, I agree. Unless he does something to change my mind, I believe he did think he was doing what he needed to do. The fact he came here of his own accord to make things right speaks volumes for me."

Madeline recalled the preacher's expressions as he told his tale and thought of the almost reverent way he spoke about Samuel. "I agree. I believe the guilt weighed on him until he was forced to confess."

"We could have pressed charges," Jonah offered.

"What would be the point?" Madeline shrugged. "Besides, once he told Madame that she had another granddaughter, that was the end of any other conversation."

"I have my doubts about that," Jonah said. "What proof is he offering other than his word? I know this isn't part of the investigation, but I have come to like that old lady and I don't want anyone to take advantage of her."

"I agree," Madeline said. "But I don't know, Jonah. What harm is it for her to believe she actually has a living granddaughter?"

"There could be plenty of harm," he said. "She's an old lady."

"All the more reason for her to have the distraction of new family.

Considering we have found nothing to support the theory that Eliza and Samuel's daughter survived," she said.

An idea occurred. Madeline jumped off the swing and headed toward the door. "Wait right there."

Jonah rose. "Where are you going?"

"Just wait right there," she said as she stepped inside. Madeline retrieved her notebook and said, "All right, let's walk, shall we?"

"We could take the trolley wherever you're wanting to go, you know."

"Yes, but it is a glorious day and I feel like walking."

"Then walking it is." Jonah fell into step beside her and then hurried ahead to open the gate. "Right or left?"

"You tell me," she said. "I want to go back to the beach. You and your sister were anxious to leave this morning, and I would very much like to go back and stay a little longer."

"Then right," he said as they walked down Broadway Avenue to the end of the block and then turned right to go east on Twenty-Third Street.

The road here formed a straight line to the beach. With the wind in their faces and the sun shining overhead, Madeline retrieved her notebook from her pocket. "Let's talk about Reverend Wyatt's story about Samuel and Eliza."

"All right," Jonah said. "Mrs. Smith didn't disagree with any of it, so I think we can take some things as facts."

"Samuel was her son and he was married to Eliza," Madeline offered as she pressed an errant strand of hair away from her face. "And Eliza did not survive childbirth."

"But where is that child?" Jonah shook his head. "The only clue is that the serving girl was found and interviewed but could offer nothing of value on what happened."

Madeline slid him a sideways look. "I don't understand that, Jonah. How do you not know what happened to the baby you've been entrusted to watch over? And how do they not know who the man was who rowed that boat in the storm? It makes no sense."

"It does if there is a reason someone doesn't want that child found. That would either be the serving girl or the rower. I can't figure why either would not want to deliver that baby to Mrs. Smith."

"Revenge?" Madeline said as they stopped to allow a wagon to pass at the intersection before they continued walking.

"Maybe," he said. "But for what?"

Madeline searched her mind, sorting through a few possibilities. "If John Smith is who I think he is, then maybe it's not revenge but rather a kidnapping that we're looking at."

"Go on," Jonah said.

"All right, I know we don't have any proof of who Madame's husband actually is. And maybe I am wrong, but you know I think he was actually Lafitte."

"I think it's possible," he said, "although I'm reserving judgment until the facts support this."

"Which is why I am looking for the facts," she reminded him. "But just for the sake of argument, let's say that is who he is. Think of the potential of getting Jean Lafitte to tell you what he knows."

"As in where he buried all that treasure over the years."

"Exactly," she said. "But the theory fails when you realize that the little girl was never returned to her grandparents. Wouldn't a kidnapper or kidnappers want to get rid of the child once they got what they wanted?"

"Let's go back to the serving girl." His eyes narrowed. "What if the ransom is somehow paid but the child isn't returned because this serving girl has decided to keep her? I mean, don't women do that?"

"Decide to keep children who don't belong to them? I wouldn't know, Jonah."

"All right. I withdraw the question," he said. "But let's think about this a little more. The way I see it, the serving girl is the key. She's the one living person who was with the baby from her birth all the way to whoever took the girl away from her."

Madeline nodded. Up ahead the beach and the greenish-brown water of the Gulf of Mexico came into view. She picked up her pace.

"In a hurry, are you?" Jonah said as he caught up to her.

"Yes, I am as a matter of fact," Madeline said. "Just look at that water. And that beach. Isn't it glorious?"

"It's, well. . .it's a beach," he said with a shrug.

"Spoken like a man who grew up with beaches." She paused to enjoy the view from this distance and then crossed the road to step onto the sand. "Humor me, Jonah. We have nothing like this in New Orleans, and I intend to enjoy this while I can."

"By all means. Don't let me interrupt." Jonah laughed as he watched her tuck her notebook back into her pocket.

Madeline glanced around to be certain no one was watching—besides Jonah, of course—and then she ran toward the surf.

Chapter Twenty-Two

Jonah stood back and watched as Madeline discarded propriety and her shoes. Unlike his side of the island where the bay met the land in a marsh filled with sea grass, the Gulf of Mexico lapped against the sand here behind sand dunes covered with sea grapes.

With the sun dipping lower toward the horizon, the tide had begun to come in, each wave daring to move a little closer up the sand. Terns and gulls screeched overhead while off in the distance a ship looked to be heading away from port.

Owing to the crisp temperature on this spring afternoon, there were few others around on this stretch of the beach. Off in the distance he spied several vendors and a crowd of maybe a dozen families, but here there was only him and Madeline.

Apparently, the foolish woman didn't care about water temperature. Picking up her skirts just enough to keep them from dragging on the sand, Madeline stopped only when the waves were crashing around her ankles.

Her laughter drifted past over the roar of the waves to catch his heart and hold it. How had he ever thought he could live without this woman?

"Come on," she called.

"No thanks. I'll just wait right here." He crossed his arms over his chest, determined to enjoy this view, and this unexpectedly playful side of Madeline Latour.

"Jonah, come look," she said, now bent down as if enthralled by something she saw on the sand.

"What is it?" he called from his safe and dry spot.

She glanced up, her dark curls dancing in the sea breeze. "That's what I need you to tell me, Mr. Beach Expert."

"Beach expert, is it?" Jonah grinned. "This expert is just fine standing over here. What you're looking at is probably a seashell."

Again she looked up to fix her attention on him. "It isn't," she said. "It's round. Some kind of circular thing."

"That would be a sand dollar. Is it white?"

"Yes," she called. "Come and see it. I'm afraid to touch it."

"Just pick it up. It isn't alive," he said, even as he knew the stubborn woman wouldn't do it. "Oh all right. But don't get my boots wet."

He picked his way across the sand and stood just close enough to see what all the fuss was about. "Yes, that's a sand dollar. It's harmless."

She reached down to touch the smooth white surface then looked back at him. "What's underneath? Does it have teeth?"

"Pick it up and see," he said as a vendor strolled past to watch them openly. Jonah shooed the vendor away and then moved closer to Madeline. "I thought you didn't rest until you got to the bottom of a story. Think of that sand dollar as a story and investigate."

She straightened and gave him a look. "You're joking, right?"

"Did it work?"

Madeline looked down at the sand dollar and then back up at Jonah. "Maybe."

"All right. Yes, it has teeth—five of them—but they are inside the shell and cannot hurt you. Just keep an eye on the surf," he warned. "The tide's rising, and some of those waves can surprise you."

"I'm blaming you if this goes wrong," she said with a broad grin as she knelt down to press her fingers into the sand.

"Madeline, you should probably stand up now. That wave looks like it is—"

A wave slammed into the back of her and then crashed past, sending Madeline tumbling forward. By the time the wave receded, Jonah was upon her.

Madeline looked up at him through a curtain of wet hair, her fancy hat dangling by its ribbons from her neck and her day dress soaked through. Without a word, she thrust her hand up.

"You're right," she said as she showed him the sand dollar clutched between her fingers. "It has no teeth on the back. Investigation complete."

❤

Madeline sat as primly as possible considering her chair was a stretch of Texas beach and her skirts were now demurely stretched across her legs drying under the last rays of the Texas sun. Tracing the circular edge of the sand dollar in her lap, she paused to dust sand off her stiffening skirts.

To her right the beach extended off into the distance with only a few families still strolling about. At the water's edge a small boy tossed a toy boat into the waves and then dove in after it, emerging from the surf in a fit of giggles.

To her left, Jonah sat beside her, his elbows resting on his knees and his boots soaked from the water she'd thrown on him. He hadn't seemed to mind when she splashed him, but then she also hadn't remained close enough to the water for him to get his revenge.

"You're not going to tell our boss about this, are you?" she asked as she glanced over at him.

Jonah smiled a lazy smile and looked up into the sky, the sun slanting across his tanned features. "I figure we're off duty right now," he said. "Although I do like the idea of holding this over your head."

"Go ahead," she said. "I'll tell Madame you were willing to let me drown."

"Hardly." He chuckled. "I warned you to watch for waves, but considering the trouble you put me through for just one sand dollar, I'm sure she wouldn't blame me." And then his face went serious. "Wait a minute," he said. "I think you might be onto something."

Madeline slid him a sideways look. "Drowning?"

"Yes, but not you." He shook his head. "Let's revisit the story of the second boat, the one that left Smith's ship carrying Samuel's daughter."

"All right." Madeline shifted positions, chasing away a small bird that had wandered too close. "So the boat leaves the ship in the storm with a man rowing and a serving girl carrying the baby. Reverend Wyatt says the rest of the crew and their captain elected to stay with the ship."

"And risk drowning," Jonah said. "But obviously the captain did not drown because he found his way home to his wife. Others likely did as well. But how?"

He waved away any response she might make with a sweep of his hand. "Let's leave that question for a minute and move to the baby. We have that ship placed in the waters near Indianola. It is approximately one hundred fifty miles from Indianola to Galveston, as we know from our trip."

"Right," she said as she tucked the sand dollar into her pocket and then felt the soggy remains of her notes on the subject. "Oh, Jonah, look," she said as she pulled the destroyed notebook out. "I've lost everything I wrote."

"No you haven't," he said as he leaned over to tap his forefinger lightly against her temple. "It's all right here. Now back to this storm and the boat. Samuel's version would have us believe the boat landed in Galveston and the serving girl was separated from the baby, never to see her again."

"But to do that, the man rowing that boat would have had to row for one hundred fifty miles," she said as she dropped her notebook with a plop into the sand beside her.

"In a storm," Jonah added.

"That just isn't possible." She paused. "So what do you think happened?"

"I see several possible scenarios. That boat could have come ashore somewhere else along the coast—definitely not Indianola because if it had Samuel would have found it eventually—but maybe Matagorda or another coastal town north or south of there."

"That is possible," she said. "But someone with a motherless child is going to stand out. The word would eventually reach Samuel, don't you think, especially considering how hard he searched?"

"I do," he said, "and that's why I don't think this is a viable option to consider."

"I agree," she said. "So what other options are there?" Her face fell as she realized one of the two. "You don't think that baby was lost at sea, do you?"

He ducked his head. "I think it's a possibility we have to consider. If that was the case, and that girl was later rescued, what do you think she would say to her rescuers? Possibly that the baby was taken from her rather than that she allowed the baby to drown on her watch."

"Why lie?"

Jonah straightened. "Panic? Fear that someone of her status might not be believed? Any number of reasons." He paused. "But let's step back from that a minute and think again about a related question. How did that serving girl and the man who rowed the boat get to Galveston?"

"We've already established they didn't row there," she said. "Unless the weather turned nice very quickly."

"Even if it did, why go north for more than a hundred miles when you are directly off the Texas coast? Why not row due west and land in under an hour, especially if there's a newborn child aboard that is likely needing to feed?"

"Oh, true." She let out a long breath. "I can only think of one way they got to Galveston and that would be if another vessel picked them up."

"Exactly."

"So someone out there, if they are still living, picked up our serving girl and the baby from the boat, and possibly our rower too. That vessel was heading for Galveston, so they continued on and deposited all three—at least we hope it is all three—at the harbor. And that is where the serving girl and baby separate."

"Yes," he said. "And using that theory, we can go to manifests and see which vessels were in port on those specific days. That narrows down which ship might have delivered them."

"It does," Madeline said, "but it still doesn't tell us what happened to that little girl. Or, for that matter, who that serving girl and rower were."

Jonah swiveled to face her. "What if Samuel knew?"

"What do you mean?"

"I mean what if he was so heartbroken over the loss of his wife that he just couldn't deal with the care of a baby?"

"Oh, Jonah, that's just not possible, is it?"

He seemed to consider the question. "I can't imagine it. If this was you and that was our child. . ." He shook his head and then straightened his spine. "Well anyway, I wouldn't react that way, but maybe he did."

"Maybe," she said slowly, "but that's out of the realm of fact, so I think we need to set aside that possibility for now."

Jonah shifted positions to look out toward the ocean, while Madeline returned her attention to the little boy and his boat, allowing the conversation to fall into a comfortable silence.

She thought of Jonah's reaction when he considered losing her and of how he could barely manage to speak about not finding their lost child. He was a good man, this Pinkerton detective who sat beside her.

A very good man.

Where would they be now if she hadn't been so stupid? If she hadn't counted her career as a reporter as more important than her fiancé's reputation as a Pinkerton detective?

"Madeline, do you ever think about where we would be if we hadn't broken our engagement?" Jonah said softly.

Madeline looked up sharply. "I don't suppose you would believe me if I told you I just was."

He rolled over on his side and leaned up on his elbow. "I might."

"Okay, well, I was."

"And what did you think about all that?" he asked.

"Oh no," Madeline said, flustered beyond trusting anything she might say, "this is your conversation. You answer first."

"It was my question, which means you should be the one to answer." He reached over with his free hand to place his palm over hers. "I think it doesn't matter where we would be."

Madeline looked down at his hand, his fingers strong and his skin as brown and tanned as his face. "Why not?" she managed.

"Because I was an idiot and you deserve better than an idiot."

Madeline lifted her head to chuckle. "Oh, Jonah, you've got it all wrong. I was the idiot. You deserved better than me."

Rather than respond, Jonah rose and then reached for Madeline's hand to help her to her feet. "Though you might disagree, I am slightly less of an idiot now, and I wonder if you might consider taking me back."

"Back?" was all she could manage as her heart rose to her throat.

"Madeline," Jonah said patiently, "all you got out of that was one word? Don't you have anything else to say?"

"Yes," she whispered as Jonah's image shimmered before her through unshed tears.

"Yes you do, or yes?"

She nodded. "Yes," she said. "As in yes I do."

"All right," he said as he swiped at the sand on her cheek. "Then say it."

"Oh, Jonah," she said. "Yes, the answer is yes!"

He gathered her into his arms and laughed. "Then why didn't you say so?"

"Shut up and kiss me," Madeline said.

Jonah leaned down and then lifted his head again. "That necklace you always wear," he said. "Were you wearing it when you went into the water?"

"Yes, why?" She reached up to touch her neck, and her heart sank. "Oh, Jonah, it's gone."

"Relax," he said. "I will look for it."

She traced his footsteps down to the shoreline and watched as he paced across the sand. Finally Madeline could not stand by and do nothing, so she joined him in the search.

"It's gone," he finally said.

"It can't be gone. I promised my father I wouldn't take it off."

Jonah shook his head. "But you weren't wearing it at the ball."

"I know," she said, "and I felt terrible about that. When I realized you had my bag in your jacket pocket, I almost went after you because I was so worried about it being lost. And now it is."

She dissolved into tears. No effort on Jonah's part to console her could stop her crying. "I've let my father down. I promised. You don't have any idea what that key meant, Jonah. In our family we take these keys very seriously."

"Madeline," he said. "You're right. I don't. But right now the tide is coming in. Tomorrow morning it will be out. I'll come back and search for it. I promise. Likely it will be right where the water took it, waiting for you once the sand is uncovered again."

"You would do that for me?" she said as she swiped at her eyes.

"I would do anything for you, Madeline Latour." He wiped her tears away with the back of his hand and once again gathered her into his arms, apparently not caring that he was up to his knees in seawater and his boots would be ruined. "Now where were we?"

Madeline looked up at him, her brown eyes now clear of their sadness. "I believe I had just told you to shut up and kiss me."

"Detective Cahill, is that you?" a familiar voice called.

"Townsend," they said in unison as Madeline rested her head on Jonah's shoulder.

"At least this time the story will be true," she said.

"Not if I break his fingers and he can't write."

"Jonah, be serious," she told him as she watched the *Daily News* reporter make his way across the sand toward them. "And don't tell me you are because even if you do want to break his fingers, and you probably do, you're a good man and I know you won't."

"We just agreed I am an idiot," he said under his breath. "Do you think that's an adequate excuse that would stand up in court?"

"Stop it," she said with a giggle as she looked up at him. "He's going to hear you."

Jonah released Madeline from his embrace then entwined his fingers with hers. "To what do we owe the pleasure, Townsend?"

The reporter was clearly out of breath, his tie askew flying over his shoulder in the breeze. When he stopped in front of them, he doubled over as if trying to catch his breath.

"I've been looking everywhere for you. I've just come from covering an accident. An old man nearly drowned when he slipped and fell into the water over by the harbor, but they've got him at the hospital." The reporter glanced down at Madeline. "He's especially anxious to speak with you, Miss Latour. Officer Pearson sent me to try and find you, and I looked everywhere until I finally spied the two of you here."

Madeline looked over at Jonah and then returned her attention to Mr. Townsend. "Whatever would he want to speak with me for?"

Mr. Townsend gasped for air. "It's his last wish to have the secrets of his past told to someone who knows what to do with them, so he says."

"Who is this man?" she said as she followed Townsend toward Beach Road where a buggy was waiting. Jonah fell into step beside her.

"Name is Horace Montlake," he said.

Chapter Twenty-Three

The confines of the loud and busy ward at the city hospital did not allow for conversation or privacy, although drapes had been drawn around the commander's bed to offer a modicum of privacy.

"Where is his family?" Madeline whispered as she straightened the blanket covering the elderly gentleman.

Jonah came to stand behind her, his arms surrounding her. "He outlived them all," he said. "Never married and his brothers were older than him."

"Then he needs us," she said.

Jonah stepped back to still her hand. "It's likely he will not recover sufficiently to know you're here."

"But I will know if I wasn't."

"I should argue against you staying here any longer. You're just going to watch this man die," Jonah said. "But given your stubbornness, I'm going to bring a folding chair and something for you to eat."

"Thank you," she said.

Jonah was back much sooner than she expected, and true to his word he brought her a place to sit and food to eat. Though she had no appetite, she did gratefully open the folding chair and place it next to the cot where the commander still lay motionless.

"The doctor came to visit while you were away," she said. "It won't be much longer now, so if you want to go, I will be fine."

Jonah reached to thread his fingers through hers. "We are staying together then, Madeline."

"You're here," Commander Montlake whispered.

Madeline jumped to her feet and then forced a smile. "We've been here for hours, Commander, just as you asked. Detective Cahill is with me."

"Cahill," he said, shifting his gaze to Jonah. "Yes, good man."

The commander closed his eyes. Madeline looked over at Jonah and tightened her grip on his hand. Until now she'd never had to watch a man die. It had seemed so easy to make such a vow and already so hard to keep it.

"Come closer, child. I have a story to tell."

Madeline returned to the chair that put her nearer to the old gentleman. "I am here," she told him.

"This story has burdened me for so long that I don't know if freeing myself of it will help, but I will try."

"Sir, don't talk and tire yourself."

"I must. You see, if I do not, then who will? Lives are at stake here. I am the only one who can right that wrong, and I will not go to my grave with this on my conscience. I cannot."

Though the doctors had declared that the commander's injuries were internal, it appeared he must have hit his head or suffered from some deprivation of breathing in the course of his accident. For truly, he made no sense.

"Shall I call for a priest or pastor?" she asked him.

"Don't want either here right now. You are the one to whom I must confess. You and the detective will know what to do with what I am about to tell you." He shifted positions to turn his head in her direction. "I was a man of war well before I made that designation official. Very few who know me know this, but now you do."

A nurse stepped into the room. "Is he awake?"

"Out," the commander managed, his voice rough.

The nurse's brows rose. "Well now, that answers my question." Her gaze swept the length of Madeline's damp and sand-covered attire.

"We were at the beach," Madeline explained.

"Generally one changes into clean clothing before visiting a hospital, but then generally one does not swim in the same clothing one would wear to a hospital." She shook her head. "I will leave you to your conversation and return later."

"See that you do," he snapped with more strength than Madeline expected him to have. "Sailors these days have no good training. In my day we'd be hung by the yardarm for interrupting a superior officer," the commander grumbled. "Now where was I? Oh yes, my story. It begins when I was forced to make a choice. You understand, Detective Cahill, that an order is an order and once given should not be questioned, do you not?"

"Under most circumstances, I would agree," Jonah said.

The commander returned his attention to Madeline. "I make no excuses. I owed a debt of life and I paid that debt back. She would have taken the child."

Madeline looked back at Jonah and saw her feelings mirrored in his expression. She gripped the side of her chair.

"Who would have taken the child?" Jonah asked him before she could.

The commander coughed and then gasped to catch his breath. "Women on a ship. Bad luck, if you ask me."

His voice had lost its dignified edge. It was as if the commander was gone and a young man was left in his place. His eyelids fluttered and then closed. At any moment, he could draw his last breath.

Madeline decided to take a risk and skip all the other questions to ask the one she most wanted answered. "Commander," she said gently, "where did you take the baby?"

"Priest said she'd be safe." His eyes opened, although Madeline wasn't certain he could see her.

"What priest? Where, sir?"

Commander Montlake fell into what appeared to be a deep sleep. She reached down to shake him but could not get the old gentleman to awaken.

"Let him rest, Madeline," Jonah said. "We could bring him back a pudding or something soft and easy to manage in case he is hungry."

Madeline adjusted the blankets and tucked the commander's hand back under them. His breathing was even and deep, his color slightly less pale than it had been.

"All right, but we're going to hurry and come back quickly."

"I promise," Jonah said as he led her away.

They found an empty table at the restaurant across the street and ordered quickly. While they waited for their meal to arrive, Madeline reached into her pocket and then groaned.

"What's wrong?" Jonah asked.

"I thought to write down what Commander Montlake told us."

"If we weren't in a hurry, I would take you down to the stationer's after we eat to buy a replacement," he said.

Madeline shook her head. "I have the one Madame gave me. I'll just have to get over the fact the jewels make it a little fancy for everyday use."

Jonah laughed, and then his expression sobered as their food was delivered. Once the waiter left them alone, he regarded Madeline with a curious look.

"Let's talk about what the commander said. If he is talking about the same baby we are looking for—"

"And we are reasonably certain he is," she supplied.

"We are. So what do you make of his comment about the priest?"

"I think it fits with our theory that either the three of them got to Galveston somehow. . ."

"Or they washed ashore and somehow found a priest at whatever location that was," he finished.

"Agreed," she said. "So where would a priest take a newborn child?"

"The orphanage," he said. "If the child was delivered to Galveston, no matter how she got here, she would have been given over to the sisters."

"Could a priest maybe bring her to someone who might already be nursing a child?"

Jonah exhaled a long breath. "It's possible."

Madeline sat back and placed her fork beside her plate. "So we really don't know that much more than we did before the commander woke up."

"That's not true," Jonah said. "We know the child was handed over to a priest, and we are left to assume that priest handed the child over to someone to care for her."

"Hold on, Jonah," Madeline said as a thought occurred. "What if the priest didn't give her to the nuns?"

"We already established that he might have taken the child to someone already nursing. Is that what you mean?"

Madeline shook her head. "Not exactly. What if he knew someone who wanted a child?"

"And gave someone else's child to them?" Jonah paused and seemed to consider the possibility. "I just don't see it happening, Madeline. Wouldn't that be against his vows?"

"Against his vows, I don't know, but if he was told who the child's parents were, then yes, it would be wrong. However, what if he wasn't told who the parents were?"

"Why wouldn't he?" Jonah asked.

"I don't know." She sighed. "I am out of answers."

A short while later, Madeline gathered up the meal they had purchased to take to Commander Montlake and walked with Jonah back to the hospital. The sun had long ago set, and the evening air had cooled. Her skirts had dried a wrinkled mess and her shoes were full of sand, but Madeline hardly cared.

They were so close to information that might lead them to Samuel and Eliza's daughter. So very close.

Turning the corner at the end of the corridor, Madeline found the curtain pulled around the commander's cot. The sound of a man's voice, deep and soft, stilled her hand just before she reached for the curtain.

She looked back at Jonah. "There's someone with him."

Jonah took the wrapped food they'd brought and pressed past Madeline. "Excuse me," he said as he pulled back the curtain just enough to see inside. Madeline crowded behind him to peer in.

"I'm sorry to interrupt," Jonah said softly. "We brought Commander Montlake something to eat if he's up to it."

A gentleman with close-cropped iron-gray hair rose abruptly and turned to face him, his eyes wide. "He is sleeping, but thank you. You're very kind."

"Jonah Cahill," Jonah said. "I don't believe we've met?"

"No, I don't believe we have," the older man said as he placed the wrapped food on the table beside the cot. "Father Brendan," he said.

"Pleased to make your acquaintance."

"Father?" Jonah said as casually as she'd ever heard him. "Are you the man who took the Smith child from Commander Montlake?"

The priest stepped back as if he'd been slapped. "I have no idea what you're talking about, young man."

Jonah studied him a moment. "I think you do."

"I assure you, I do not."

His tone conveyed his obvious confusion. Madeline decided to step in and help. "So you're the priest here in Galveston?"

Of all the times not to have her notebook. Madeline did her best to commit the man's description to memory.

"One of them, yes," he said, appearing grateful the subject had been changed.

"I wonder if we could bother you with some questions," she asked. "Just a few and we'll leave you and the commander in privacy."

"I'm sorry," he said as he opened the curtain farther and stepped around Jonah. "But I must get to an appointment. Perhaps tomorrow?"

"What time tomorrow?" Jonah asked as he followed the priest down thc hall.

Madeline returned to the folding chair she had left at Commander Montlake's bedside and reached over to adjust his blankets. The elderly gentleman seemed unchanged since they left earlier, a fact that gave Madeline much relief.

Jonah returned, shaking his head. "The priest was of no help. I told him what the commander said and why we asked if he was that priest. He agreed a child without parents would go to the orphanage but could offer nothing further, but he was vague at best on a meeting. I left him my card, and he said he would call on me as soon as he could."

"So he was not here back in 1855, then."

"He said he is newly arrived since last fall and came from San Antonio," Jonah said. "So no."

"How does he know the commander?"

"He said they are old acquaintances from childhood." Jonah shrugged. "I saw no reason to disbelieve him, but I have a feeling something isn't right."

"He seemed nice enough," she said. "And he's a priest. What could be wrong?"

"Nothing," Jonah agreed. "And yet. . ."

"And yet we back up our hunches with facts," she reminded him.

"Then tomorrow I'll go down to the church and investigate the facts. Tonight, however, I need to get you home."

"Oh, Jonah, I don't want to leave him."

"He's fine," Jonah said as he looked past Madeline to the man lying on the cot. "Look how well he's sleeping. We can come back tomorrow, but let him have his peace and quiet tonight."

Jonah was right. There was nothing left to be done here tonight. Still, Madeline rose reluctantly.

"Would it make you feel better if I asked the nurse to send for us should his condition change?"

Madeline nodded and then watched as Jonah went hunting for the nurse. He returned with the nurse, her expression telling Madeline she was not pleased.

"Are you family?" she demanded.

"Of a sort," Madeline said. "We are all he has except for the gentleman who was just here. At least as far as we know." The nurse continued to scowl, so Madeline made one more attempt. "Do you have a father?"

"I do," she said, giving Madeline a sideways look. "Why do you ask?"

"If he was ill and you weren't able to attend to him, wouldn't you want him to have a friend watch over his care?"

Her face softened slightly. "What is that on the table there?"

"We brought him something to eat in case he gets hungry," Jonah offered. "We are hoping he will wake up and wonder why his stomach is so empty."

She glanced down at the chair. "And you will leave me with a place to rest my bones?"

"Yes," Jonah said. "The chair is yours."

The nurse offered him a smile. "Then tell me how I can reach you in case you're needed."

Jonah retrieved a card from his pocket and handed it to the nurse.

"A Pinkerton man?" she said, brows raised. "Impressive."

"For ten years now. This man is important to us, so please send for me." He told her where he lived.

"Oh yes, I know that house. Built on the ashes of *La Maison Rouge*."

"That is the one," Jonah responded evenly, "but don't believe what you read in the papers about the house."

She gave him a knowing look. "No, of course not," she said as she shooed them out of the ward.

"So tomorrow, then?" Madeline said when they were back outside walking under the stars.

"First thing," he said.

They walked along in silence until they reached Broadway Avenue. "Madeline," Jonah said when they arrived at the gate. "I don't want to say good night." He grinned. "And yet, I really do want to kiss you good night."

He gathered her to him and held her then slowly lowered his lips to hers. The kiss was soft and gentle, his embrace tender.

"I love you, Madeline," he said against her ear. "I never stopped even when I was too stubborn to admit it."

"I'm glad only one of us is stubborn," she told him with mock seriousness. Then her expression softened as she looked up into his eyes. "I love you too, Detective Cahill, and I have for a very long time."

"Good night, Madeline," he said as he stole another kiss and then walked away.

Madeline walked into the house and nearly stumbled over something on the floor. She reached down to grab a stuffed rabbit that had been left in the way.

"The child," Gretchen said as she walked toward Madeline to snatch up the toy. "He is a menace."

Madeline stifled her smile until she'd reached her own room. Then she laughed out loud.

Chapter Twenty-Four

True to his word, Jonah was back first thing the next morning. What little sleep he'd gotten was filled with dreams of Madeline, first as a carefree woman dancing in the surf and then kissing him under the stars.

Marriage couldn't come soon enough for him. Whether Madeline felt the same remained to be seen. He would ask her soon enough, but first he had to write to her father for permission.

He'd done that during the night as well, posting the letter on his way to the beach to make an unsuccessful search for Madeline's necklace. Now he sat in the same swing he'd shared with Madeline yesterday and waited for her to appear on the porch.

At least he'd thought to bring a change of footwear. His ruined boots, newly wet from this morning's trek through the surf, sat drying in the sun on the edge of the porch. He'd claim them later though they were good for little else other than continuing his search for that blasted key she'd lost.

Jonah gave thought to what she claimed about the key, and something struck him as odd. She'd said that keys were very important to the Latour family, but she had not said why.

"I'm sorry to keep you waiting," she told him as she stepped outside. "I can tell from your expression that you didn't find my necklace."

"I will look again at the next low tide. I'm not giving up," he said. "I'm sorry. I know it was important to you."

"And to my father," she said.

"Why is that, Madeline?"

Her eyes widened as if she was surprised he'd asked. Then she looked away. His Pinkerton training told him he'd hit a nerve.

"Because my father told me it was." She shrugged. "In any case, I do apologize for leaving you sitting here so long, but there's a funny story to go along with my excuse."

Jonah briefly considered steering the subject back to the key but decided against it. He'd find out soon enough. "All right. Let's hear that story, then," he said as he nodded toward the walkway.

"It appears little Jordy enjoys playing with his food, a fact I was not warned about until after he'd generously shared his scrambled eggs and biscuits with me."

Jonah followed her down the front steps. "That was nice of him."

"It might have been," she agreed. "Except that he threw the entire meal and ruined my dress."

"Ah," he said. "That's different."

She grinned as Jonah opened the gate for her. "He's so cute, though. Just an adorable child, when he isn't throwing food, that is. And Annabelle seems very sweet. I know Madame is thrilled to have them staying with her."

Madeline giggled and seemed to be thinking of something that amused her.

"What?" he asked.

"While Madame is thrilled, Gretchen is not." She shrugged. "That makes having to give her extra laundry to wash almost pleasant."

Jonah shook his head as he escorted Madeline onto the trolley and to a seat near the front. Owing to the early hour, the trolley was nearly empty. They rode in silence until they reached the hospital.

"I'm hoping he's up to speaking to us again," Madeline said as they walked from the trolley stop toward the hospital.

They stepped inside and followed the hallway down to the end and then turned toward the commander's cot. The curtain was open and the cot was empty. Even the folding chair was gone.

Madeline stopped short. "Oh, Jonah," she said softly. "He's gone."

Jonah pressed past her to look around the small area and then turned back to her. "Wait here."

He found the nurse making good use of Madeline's folding chair by taking a nap in a closet adjacent to the nursing station. Once he woke her up, she explained Commander Montlake's miracle recovery and return home.

Jonah nodded toward the old man's cot where Madeline now stood. "Tell her what you just told me."

She sighed and climbed to her feet then walked down the hall to stand in front of Madeline. "The father came back to stay with Mr. Montlake, must have been about a half hour after you two left. Wasn't an hour later, I see him helping the patient out of bed. He tells me there's been a miracle recovery and his friend can go home. What was I to do? Since they were friends, I didn't think it would matter if I sent for you."

"And why was that?" Jonah demanded.

"She asked me what I would have wanted if my father was in a hospital without me and a friend wanted to help. I'll tell you what I told her. I would want that friend to help. The father, he was a friend. He helped. End of the story."

"And this was the same Father Brendan who was visiting earlier?"

"One and the same," she said.

"And you know him from the church?"

"Oh no," she said. "I'm Lutheran, but what sort of priest would lie about his name?"

Jonah shook his head. "One with something to hide?"

"You don't know that, Jonah," Madeline offered. "It's possible the commander was feeling better. When we left him last night, his color had improved and he was breathing well."

"Then we will pay him a visit," Jonah said. "Enjoy your chair," he told the nurse as they turned and walked away.

A short time later, Jonah knocked on the door of the Montlake home on Mechanic Street.

"No one is here," Madeline said. "So maybe the priest took him to the church?"

"There's only one way to know," he said as he escorted Madeline to

St. Mary's Church, where very quickly they were told there had never been a Father Brendan in the church's employ.

"Perhaps you could try St. Joseph's," the bishop's assistant told them. "Or telegraph the bishop in San Antonio. Perhaps he has a record of where Father Brendan was sent after he left there."

A trip to St. Joseph's Church on Avenue K had the same result. They then tried the Lutheran church in hopes that they had misunderstood and the gentleman was not Catholic. No one there had heard of Father Brendan either.

Other than sending the telegram to San Antonio, Jonah was now out of options.

"Perhaps he is a retired priest," Madeline offered as they walked away.

"He did look old enough, although they were adamant at all three churches that they'd never heard of the man."

"So we're at a dead end."

Jonah shrugged. "I'm going to ask around. Montlake did not have family left, but most of Galveston knew him. Surely someone will know who his friend Father Brendan is. Assuming he gave us his real name."

She slid her arm around his. "Let's think positively. We learned something from our visit, and the commander made a miraculous recovery from his accident."

"About that," Jonah said. "My gut tells me that's not the case."

Madeline looked up at him sharply. "Do you think the commander was kidnapped?"

He did, but given Madeline's affection for the old man, he decided to temper his words. "No evidence of it but I am not ruling it out."

"Fair enough," she said. "Now walk me home. Madame wants me to record more stories in the journal this morning, and I'm sure she's wondering where I am. Plus, I need to write to my editor, and I owe a letter to my family."

Jonah thought of the letter he had posted to Phillip Latour and smiled.

"What?" she asked.

"Nothing. What are you planning to tell your editor?"

"With Madame's permission, I plan to pitch a reunion story with Annabelle and Jordy as the focus and to promise to have it done in time for the Easter issue."

He nodded. Either his unrelenting reporter had thought better of exposing whatever deep dark secrets she thought Mrs. Smith was keeping or she'd found a better tale to tell. Either way, he liked it.

And her.

"What?" she asked again.

"I think that's a great idea."

He saw her home safely and then laughed when she opened the door and the noise of a giggling child drifted toward him. If nothing else came out of this investigation, the fact that an old lady was presented with a family she didn't know she had would make it a success.

"That you, Cahill?"

He turned around to see Detective Donovan walking up Broadway Avenue toward him. Though he hadn't decided completely whether the detective had told him the truth regarding the intruder in the garden, he was close to determining he had.

Friday's dinner with Pearson should confirm what he was already thinking. That Donovan handed the guy over in good faith and was simply too busy to follow up on what he assumed the police were handling.

That's what he would have done, though he liked to think he would have remembered to check. Still, though they were both Pinkerton trained, they were also both human.

"I thought you'd gone back to Chicago," he said as he offered his fellow Pinkerton detective a handshake.

"This place is hard to leave, especially given the weather here. Have you taken the time to go down to the beach?"

"I have," he said as he thought of Madeline dancing in the surf and smiled.

"From your expression, it looks like you liked it."

"Very much," he said. "So what brings you here?"

"I just left a meeting with Mr. Brown. Captain wanted me to follow up and then make a report. After that, I'm off to Chicago unless I can convince the boss to give me another job here. Where are you off to?"

"Need to send a telegram," Jonah said as they paused at the corner to allow traffic to pass and then crossed the street. "You really like Galveston."

"I do," he said. "You probably have no idea what this is like, but I get tired of not having a home to call my own. It would be nice to settle down somewhere and not have to be packing for the next assignment after just getting back from the previous one."

"What would you do?"

He shrugged. "I've thought a lot about that over the past few days. Even went down to the other end of the island and looked at a piece of grazing land that's up for sale. I've got to say I am sorely tempted."

"But?"

"But a Pinkerton's salary won't pay for a ranch house and prime coastal grazing land, so I'm left just wishing unless I find another way."

"You'll figure it out," Jonah said. "In the meantime, remember that case I told you I was working on? The lady across the street from the Browns?"

"The Smith lady," he said with a nod. "What about it?"

"I'm at a dead end on the investigation and I need another opinion. Care to give me yours?"

"Be glad to," Donovan said.

"Remember I'm dealing with something that happened twenty-five years ago," he said. "But I've got two witnesses claiming to be firsthand sources. The first one's story agrees with the second, and neither were present when the other one spoke with me. For that matter, I don't think they know one another or have spoken since the incident."

"Sounds like good testimony, then. Are you questioning the validity?"

Jonah shook his head. "More like the details. Taken separately, neither one helps me find my missing person. But put together, it makes more sense and gives me a solid direction. Problem is, my second source is less reliable, mostly due to age and health, and has not given me any details I can work with."

"Then you discard that information," Donovan said.

"On what reason?"

"Preponderance of the evidence," he said. "It sounds like you're hoping that your second guy can add to what your first guy said and send you in the right direction. But if the second guy hasn't given you reliable details, then don't go on what he said until he does. That's basic investigative theory, Jonah."

Much as Jonah hated it, Donovan was right. "Without the second guy, all I have is a general idea of what happened to the people my missing person was with. The six of them separated into parties of three and went in different directions. I can account for the members of one group but not the others. Unfortunately, the group I can locate was not with the missing person."

Donovan stepped aside to allow a mother with two boys in tow to pass and then caught up to Jonah once more. "Okay, who else can? Is there someone else who was in that second party who can corroborate?"

"There were three in that second party. My missing person, my witness, and a third person as yet unidentified. I have a dead man's word that this person knew nothing."

Detective Donovan's chuckle held no humor. "And we all know how valuable a dead man's testimony is."

"So I need to find that third person."

He nodded. "That's where I would start. Do you have any ideas on how to do that?"

Jonah stopped short. "I do, but this is where we part ways. I think the person I need to ask is the one who has me running in circles."

"Mrs. Smith?"

"Exactly." He reached out to shake Detective Donovan's hand. "Thank you for the advice. Are your travel plans set yet?"

"Taking the train to Houston on Saturday morning." He let out a long breath. "From there it's straight north and then the next assignment."

"There's always that next assignment waiting, isn't there?"

Donovan shrugged. "Until I figure out how to claim that ranch down the road from here, yes, that's true."

A thought occurred. "Say, since you don't leave until Saturday, how about joining me for dinner Friday night? A few others are coming, and we'd be happy to have you."

He grinned. "And I'd be happy to have a home-cooked meal."

Jonah told him the time. "And you know where I live?"

"Everyone on the island does, my friend," he said. "It's the house that's sitting on top of Lafitte's treasure."

"Don't believe everything you read in the newspaper," he called as he walked away.

"If I did, I'd believe you and that pretty little reporter from New Orleans were more than just friends."

"That I'm all right with you believing," Jonah said over his shoulder.

"Don't blame you, my friend."

Donovan's laughter chased him as Jonah turned to head back down Broadway Avenue. A few blocks later, he arrived back at the Smith home.

The surly maid let him inside and left him waiting by the front door while she went to fetch Mrs. Smith. There was no sign of Madeline, though he expected she was hidden away somewhere working on her letters or possibly with Mrs. Smith recording memories.

"Go to the garden," the maid said when she returned.

Jonah complied, retracing his steps onto the front porch and then following the sound of a child's laughter until he arrived at the gazebo where Mrs. Smith was seated. A swing had been hung from a tree, and Annabelle was seated on it with Jordy on her lap.

"Detective Cahill," she said as she nodded toward her family. "Is there anything better than this?"

"There is not," he agreed. "Except perhaps to find your other granddaughter. Have you considered she may have given you great-grandchildren as well?"

"I believe she will," she told him. "So what brings you here on this beautiful morning? Miss Latour is working on some things in the library if you are here to see her."

"No," he said as he sat down beside her. "I am here to see you."

"Oh my," she said with a half smile that told him she had noticed his abruptness. "How can I help you?"

"I want the name of that serving girl, Mrs. Smith. I know you know who she is, and unless I miss my guess, you know where she is."

Her eyes widened almost imperceptibly, and then a smile rose. "You are quite blunt, Detective Cahill."

"As I recall, that is why you hired me."

"Yes, it is." She lifted a bejeweled finger to push away an errant strand of silver hair and then returned her attention to her family on the lawn.

"I am at a dead end," he said gently. "That serving girl has information I need."

"Then you are in luck." She slid him a sideways look. "It happens that I may know where she is."

Jonah leaned back. "I thought you might."

Madame swiveled to face him, her smile broad. "We are nearing the end of our investigation, are we not?"

"It is possible," he said. "I feel this serving girl could give us the answers we need."

"Despite what my son told me?"

He looked down at his boots then back up at her. "I do not wish to speak ill of the dead, but I believe your son was wrong. That girl knows something. The question is why you aren't asking her where your Trésor is."

"Come to dinner here Friday night," she said.

Jonah shook his head, confused at the abrupt change of subject. "I regret I cannot. I have a prior dinner obligation."

"Then bring them."

"I couldn't. There will be at least six of us. More if my sister has invited extras. But truly, I came here to talk about this girl."

"Bring your family and any guests you wish," she insisted. "The more the merrier as we are having dinner out here under the stars to celebrate. Since you and Miss Latour are responsible for returning my Annabelle and her Jordy to me, I wouldn't hear of you missing it."

Jonah opened his mouth to protest, but Mrs. Smith silenced him by holding up her hands. "I know," she said. "I am evading the answer to the question you've asked. Humor me today. I only wish to enjoy my newfound family."

"And I wish to provide one more member of that family to you if you will just help me do that."

"Oh," she said gently. "I plan to. You have my word I will see that you are able to interview this girl, and from that interview perhaps you will find the clues that lead you to my Trésor."

"Thank you. One more question if you don't mind," he said as a thought occurred. "How well do you know Horace Montlake?"

Her smile wobbled. "He is a very old friend. Why do you ask?"

"He had an accident yesterday and almost drowned. Miss Latour and I were called to his bedside last night to hear a confession."

Her brows gathered. "What sort of confession?"

"A rather disjointed one. He made the claim that he rowed the boat your granddaughter and the serving girl escaped in."

Mrs. Smith gasped. "Why would Horace say that?"

"I don't know," Jonah admitted. "But he thought he was dying when he said it. Then an hour later, he was seen leaving the hospital with a friend. Miss Latour believes it to be a miracle recovery."

"But you don't, I can tell." She paused to wave when Jordy called her name. "Who was the friend?"

"That's where it gets interesting. He said his name was Father Brendan. He was certainly dressed as a priest, and he claimed he was recently arrived from San Antonio. I have checked the local churches, and no one has heard of him. That is all I know."

"Oh." She rose abruptly. "Would you mind helping me inside? I'm feeling a bit tired."

"Of course." Jonah did as she asked and escorted Mrs. Smith inside. The maid met them at the door, and he wondered whether once again she had been listening.

"Detective," Mrs. Smith said just as his fingers touched the doorknob. "What will you do about Horace?"

"File a police report," he said, and she answered with a nod. "Then I will see you tomorrow night."

"Very good," she said as she turned and allowed the maid to lead her away. "Good day then, Detective."

Jonah responded and then looked over to see Madeline peering out from the library door. "Hello, Madeline," he said and then grinned when she pressed her finger to her lips as if to silence him.

He waited until Mrs. Smith had disappeared down the corridor before sweeping his future wife—pending her father's approval, of course—into his arms and kissing her thoroughly.

"Jonah," she said softly, "you are incorrigible."

"Considering the other things you've called me, I think I prefer incorrigible." He stole another kiss then ducked out of the way when she pretended to swat him.

"I heard you telling Madame goodbye. Where are you off to?" she asked.

"I thought I'd send a telegram to San Antonio and see what I can find out about Father Brendan." He looked past her to the sealed letters on the table. "Would you like me to post those for you?"

Her eyes twinkled. "Actually, I have another errand in town, so I thought I might join you, unless you have other plans."

"I would like that very much." Scooping up her letters, Madeline grinned and scooted past him to head for the door. "Good, because one of us owes the other a treat from T. Ratto & Company Confectioners."

"That would be me," he said as he hurried to follow her outside.

"Oh no," she called, already at the gate. "That would be me."

"You know Mr. Ratto will throw us out again if we don't decide this before we get there," he called as he shut the gate behind him.

Madeline laughed over her shoulder at him and picked up her pace. "Then I suppose we'll just have to risk it."

He caught up to her and fell in step. "We will just end up in the alley again," he said.

She looked up at him, a smile dawning. "I'm counting on that."

Chapter Twenty-Five

By Friday, Madeline had given up on ever finding the missing key. She had also given up on hearing back from her father after she'd written asking for him to accept her apology.

Considering that letter had also informed her mother and father that she and Jonah were back together, she was anxious to know what Papa thought of it all. Mama had been near to tears when the wedding was called off, but Madeline suspected that had been as much because Madeline would not be a bride as it was in regard to who the groom might be.

But Papa, he had remained stoic. He had never much cared for Jonah and had not encouraged the relationship. It would be interesting to see if his opinion had changed, especially given the fact that he had indicated he wished her to find the right man very soon.

Because she had. Oh, she definitely had.

Madeline looked out her third-floor window at the preparations for tonight's party. Over the past twenty-four hours, Madame had become like a general directing her troops, and even the surly Gretchen had fallen into line.

As dusk approached, the back garden had been turned into a fantasyland full of lights. Torches had already been lit around the perimeter, and lamps were lit at each of the many tables.

Annabelle would have her work cut out trying to keep little Jordy out of the pink roses that had been placed all around, but the determined woman had shown she was up for the task. Madeline smiled. Though Annabelle had apparently been left alone to care for her son without her husband's assistance, she remained so serene and happy to be Jordy's mama.

Perhaps someday she would have her own child and know that feeling as well.

A knock at the door distracted her. "Come in, please."

Gretchen stepped inside, her usual scowl in place. "Hurry up and sit. I have work to do."

"Thank you for helping with my hair," Madeline said sweetly as she took her seat at the table. "You're the only one who can make anything of this mess the Lord gave me."

"Be glad the Lord gave you good hair," she said as she yanked a section of the alleged good hair into submission and then reached for another.

It was all she could manage not to cry out. Instead, Madeline bit her tongue and remained quiet.

When she was done, Gretchen stepped back and tilted her head. "Not awful," she said before gathering up her combs and heading for the door.

"Gretchen, wait." She reached into the drawer and pulled out a wrapped package. "This is for you."

Gretchen looked down at the package and said nothing. Nor did she move.

Madeline rose and crossed the distance between them to take the combs from Gretchen and place the package in her hand. "Open it," she said.

The maid did as she was told and then looked at Madeline. Her normally hard expression had softened almost to tears. "My mirror. It was broken and now it has been repaired. How did you manage it?"

Madeline shrugged. "I had it repaired. There's a glass shop just across from the post office. It was a simple thing."

"It was no such thing," she said fiercely, and then she ducked her head. "Why are you so nice to me?"

Madeline grinned. "Why not?"

Gretchen straightened. "Thank you," she said as she gathered up her things. "I like you, Miss Latour."

And then she was gone. Madeline shook her head and then finished preparing for the party. By the time she was ready to go downstairs, she could hear the musicians had begun to play a lively tune and guests were arriving.

She slipped into her shoes just as someone knocked on her door. "Come in," she said, and the scullery maid appeared with a letter. "For you, miss," she said as she hurried away. "From a Mr. Townsend."

Something inside the letter shifted as Madeline opened the seal, and then her key and its gold chain fell to the floor. She returned the necklace to its place around her neck and tucked the key into her bodice and then picked up the letter once again.

> *I confess I have kept this key thinking I might have found a story in it, but out of deference to you, I will not go forward with that. As I told you and the detective, I have a particular skill in tracking down the facts of a story of which I am quite proud. I have done as you asked and tracked down the source of the story about the Cahill property and its treasure. I'm sure you understand that information cannot be conveyed in a letter, but I will impart the details next we meet. Wonderful about the commander's miracle recovery, wasn't it?*

The letter was signed Walter Townsend.

Madeline tucked the letter into her pocket and hurried downstairs to join the party. Jonah surprised her by stepping out from behind an oleander to haul her against him in the shadows.

"A quick kiss before the inspections begin," he said as he made good on that statement.

"What inspections?"

"My mother is here, Madeline, and you've not met her yet."

Her stomach did a flip-flop. "Oh," she said. "I hadn't thought about that."

"Relax, she will love you," he said as he gave her a sideways look. "Is that your key necklace you're wearing?"

"It is. It was delivered along with this note." She handed the folded paper to Jonah, who read it then returned it to her. "What do you make of this?"

"There you are," Susanna Cahill called as she linked arms with her brother. "Mama has been asking to meet your intended."

Jonah rolled his eyes. "More like you cannot wait to see what happens when she does."

"That is not true. She's going to love Madeline." Susanna linked her other arm with Madeline's and led them away from the oleander. "It is you who I cannot wait to watch."

"And why is that?" he asked, looking over Susanna's head to make a face at Madeline.

"Because while Madeline is meeting Mama, it appears you will be meeting Papa." She inclined her head toward Madeline. "Her papa."

Madeline stopped short and nearly hauled both Cahills against her. "My papa? He's here?" she managed as her heart jumped into her throat.

"With your mama," Susanna said. "They're both here, and it gets even better. They're sitting with Mama."

"Wonderful," Madeline managed as Jonah's cheerful sister dragged her over to the table where two Latours and a Cahill awaited.

Mrs. Cahill's smile was every bit as dazzling as her son's, although she was very much an older version of Susanna. Rising to walk toward them, Jonah's mother embraced Madeline and then held her at arm's length.

"I am Gwen Cahill. I have prayed for you," she said. "About you and for you, that is, since the day my son was born. And now here you are. Welcome to our family, Madeline."

"Here I am," Madeline echoed, and then she thought to add, "thank you."

"You've overwhelmed her, Mama," Jonah said, coming to her rescue. "And it is a little soon to welcome her to the family, if you know what I mean."

"Nonsense," Mrs. Cahill said. "We're just one conversation away from that. Here," she said. "Come and meet the Latours."

"Isn't that supposed to be my line?" Madeline whispered when she came to her senses.

"Generally, yes," he said. "But not when Hurricane Gwennie rolls into town."

Just before she reached the table where the Latours and Mrs. Cahill were sitting, she stumbled forward and nearly landed in her father's lap. "Well now, I knew you would be surprised, but I expected more poise from my daughter."

"Give me time and I will manage it," she said against his ear as he rose to embrace her.

"You're perfect as you are," he said. "Now let me greet your young man so I can pretend to dislike him."

"Papa, behave," she said as she turned toward Jonah. "You remember Jonah Cahill."

"Pinkerton detective Jonah Cahill, as I recall," Papa said, and Madeline suppressed a groan at what sort of connotations that might hold.

"Yes, sir. Pleased to meet you." Jonah offered a handshake and then turned to Mama. "Mrs. Latour, it is good to see you again."

"Rose Latour is a gardener and a much sought after artist," Jonah's mother said with a smile.

Mama blushed under the attention but had no trouble making small talk with the Pinkerton detective and his mother. Madeline looked over at Susanna and her mother, who seemed to be conspiring together.

Conspiring what, Madeline was afraid to ask.

Madame Smith walked over to offer a broad smile. "Welcome. I see you have all found one another."

"We have," Jonah said with a smile that did not quite reach to his eyes. "It would have been nice to know ahead of time. Say perhaps yesterday?"

"Oh, Detective Cahill," she said. "That would have completely ruined the surprise, now wouldn't it have?"

"Of course," he said, though it was obvious to Madeline he wouldn't have minded having this surprise ruined.

"Thank you for sharing your daughter with me," Madame said to

Papa. She then turned to Mama. "She has been a delight, and I am very grateful that she has been able to assist me in recording my memories."

"And we are very grateful to have her as well," Mama said. "She has been such a blessing."

"May we have a private chat?" Papa interjected.

"Of course," Jonah said.

"Papa," Madeline warned. "Be nice."

❤

Jonah allowed Phillip Latour to lead him past the tables of guests and over to a spot near the back alley fence. As always, Jonah assessed the perimeter, and then he returned his attention to Madeline's father.

"I assume you received my letter," Jonah said.

"I did." Phillip Latour studied his expensively tailored sleeve and then returned his attention to Jonah. "I do approve, but you knew I would."

"I had hoped," Jonah said. "But considering the clash between what I do and what you do, I didn't count on it."

Phillip looked amused. "What would you have done if I said no?"

He looked the old man in the eye. "Probably married her anyway if she'd have me."

"She would, and we both know it." Phillip leaned back against the fence and draped one arm atop the rail. "Don't be so certain we clash, you and I. Our work is not so different."

Jonah regarded him evenly but said nothing. He'd done some personal searching into the family business but found nothing untoward regarding Latour & Sons. Thus, when Madeline accused him of opening a Pinkerton investigation into her family, he could honestly say that was not true. Someday he would admit to her that he had done a little snooping on his own, though.

He had received a telegram this evening that shed a whole new light on the Latours, however. "Not even back in '55?"

Phillip's casual demeanor disappeared. "What do you know about that?"

"Not enough," Jonah said.

"That you, Cahill?"

Jonah spied Thomas Pearson coming his way from the alley. "We're not finished with this, sir," he told Madeline's father. "Pearson, come and meet my future father-in-law," he said and then made the introductions.

"Nice party," Pearson said as he closed the gate behind him and joined the pair.

"Mrs. Smith does nothing halfway," Jonah said. "I wonder if you've got any news on that shovel." He looked over at Phillip. "Somebody thought it would be a good idea to dig up our property looking for pirate treasure. They left behind a broken lock and a shovel in the cellar."

"Bad business, that," Phillip said.

"Especially with my mother and sister at home without a man to watch them." He clasped a hand on Pearson's shoulder. "I'm grateful to this man for seeing to their safety."

"I've enjoyed it, actually," Pearson said as he patted his belly. "They keep insisting I stay for dinner, and I keep agreeing."

All three men shared a laugh. Then Jonah sobered. "Miss Latour got a note from Townsend letting us know he found out who wrote that article about buried treasure on Cahill property."

"Oh?" the police officer said as his brows rose. "Did he say who it was?"

Jonah shook his head. "He didn't want to put it in the note. Said he would divulge the name the next time we met."

Pearson shook his head. "Ignore him, Jonah. He's just a reporter looking for a story, and you know how they are." When both Jonah and Phillip scowled, Pearson continued. "No insult to Miss Latour intended. There are good reporters, but this guy Townsend is definitely not one of them."

"Excuse me."

Jonah looked past Pearson to see Annabelle and Jordy walking toward them. The young lady looked beautiful this evening in a dress of pale green and a hat to match. Mrs. Smith had obviously spared no expense in transforming her granddaughter from harried mother to well-dressed young woman.

She stopped to allow Jordy to catch up then hauled him into her arms. "My grandmother would like us all to take our seats."

Pearson turned around to look at Annabelle and froze.

"You," she said with obvious venom. "What are you doing here?" She looked past him to Jonah. "This is the Pinkerton man who was hounding us in Indianola. Ran off all the paying boarders with his threats, he did."

"No," Jonah said. "This is Officer Pearson of the Galveston Police Department. He's a friend of mine. You must be mistaken."

Pearson turned his back on Annabelle and shook his head. "Woman's crazy," he said.

She set Jordy on the ground and sent him off to play on the swing and then came to stand by Jonah. "You're him, all right. Are you working a case here, or did you decide to shake them down too?"

The officer's face blanched, but he said nothing. Then Annabelle turned her attention to Pearson.

"There never was treasure there," she told him. "Not when you first showed up, and definitely not after you practically destroyed my mama's boardinghouse thinking you might find it. But you wouldn't listen, would you? You figured that Samuel's daughter was bound to know where it was."

"What's she talking about, Pearson?"

He held his hands in front of him as if to profess his innocence. "I told you, she's got me mistaken for someone else."

"I disagree." Reverend Wyatt walked toward them holding Jordy, who was covered in something pink. "I found this little guy helping himself to the cupcakes on the dessert table. You might want to wash him up a bit."

Annabelle took her son from the pastor without removing her attention from Pearson. "Don't let him fool them, preacher man," she said as she turned to walk away.

"I won't." The reverend clasped his hand on Pearson's shoulder. "Why don't we talk about this out in the alley where we won't be overheard?"

"No." Pearson shook off the older man's hand. "Look, I don't know what kind of joke you all are playing, but I do not have to stay here and let you play it on me." He turned to walk away.

"Still got that scar on the palm of your hand where you gouged yourself pulling apart floorboards in Francine's parlor?"

"Show me your hand," Jonah said to him. "So I can prove to this man he's wrong."

Pearson muscled past him and headed for the gate. "If you don't trust me enough to take me at my word, then I'm not staying to dignify this conversation."

"You're not getting off that easy. Where's Montlake, and who is that priest?"

The police officer made it to the alley before Jonah tackled him. The younger man fought back, but Jonah easily bested him.

"Your hand, Pearson," Jonah said as he grabbed for Pearson's wrist. "Show it to me."

Even in the dim light of the alley, a deep, pale slash could easily be seen in the center of Thomas Pearson's palm.

He looked up at Madeline's father. "There ought to be some rope in the carriage house. Would you get it for me?"

Phillip nodded and headed off as Jonah spied Detective Donovan bounding up from the alley. "Backup is here, Pearson. Answer."

"Priest is a guy who owed me a favor. He's got Montlake at my place," he said as he swung at Jonah, connecting with his jaw.

Jonah swung back and knocked him to the ground. "Since you like treasure hunting, did you dig those holes on my property too?"

"Wasn't anything there. Kind of a shame I bothered to write the article. I was hoping it might attract others who knew more than me."

"So you could steal what they found?"

Once again Pearson aimed his fist at Jonah. This time the police officer landed a blow that sent Jonah to the pavement. He quickly jumped up and hit Pearson between the eyes, causing him to fall backward, where he remained, eyes closed.

"What are you doing here, Donovan?" Jonah asked.

"I was invited to dinner, remember?" Donovan looked down at the unconscious police officer then back at Jonah. "What's the story with this guy?"

Jonah filled him in.

"Is this the guy who's been impersonating me?"

"I don't know," Jonah said. "You tell me."

He knelt down and dug through Pearson's pockets until he found what he was looking for. Standing, he pressed a stack of cards into Jonah's palm. The policeman groaned, and Donovan pushed his boot against the man's chest.

"How did he get those?"

"I came down here last fall for the initial meeting on the Grant security project, and I realized when I got back to Chicago that a box of my Pinkerton cards was missing. A month or two later, the agency got a couple of inquiries asking about me. Since I wasn't working on anything down here, they dismissed the reports as false."

"Why didn't you mention it?" Jonah asked.

"Same reason I forgot about that man in the rose garden. I got busy and just didn't think about following up on it." He shook his head. "See, I'd make a better rancher than Pinkerton."

Donovan stepped back as Phillip returned with the rope. Together they made short work of tying Pearson just as Townsend walked up.

"I see you figured it out," the reporter said.

"He admitted it. Help us with him and maybe I'll give you first chance to write the story," he told Townsend with a grin.

Phillip nodded toward the carriage house. "There's a back entrance to the carriage house right over there. I think we can carry him over there and lock him in the tack room until someone can fetch the law."

"Thinking like a Pinkerton man, sir," Donovan said as he grabbed Pearson's feet.

Jonah couldn't miss the older man's expression. When he and Donovan had Pearson settled behind a locked door in the tack room and the stable boy headed for the police station, he finally laughed.

"You may have just insulted my future father-in-law."

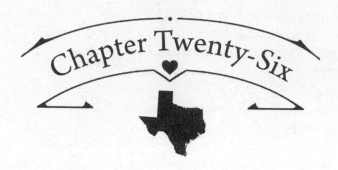

Chapter Twenty-Six

"What took you so long?" Madeline demanded when Jonah settled beside her at the table.

It seemed like an eternity since she'd been left alone to endure the company of these three inquisitive females. From Mama's unending questions to Susanna's quiet and measuring stare, Madeline felt as if she were walking a tightrope in a stiff breeze. Thankfully, Mrs. Cahill had reached over to squeeze her hand.

"It will all be quite fine," she had said softly.

Now that Jonah was back, Madeline knew it would be.

"Nothing to worry about," Papa said, returning to offer Mama a kiss on the cheek. "What did we miss?"

Madeline spied something that looked like a smudge of dirt on Jonah's jaw and retrieved her handkerchief to swipe at it. To her surprise, the smudge remained, but Jonah winced.

"Where were you?" she demanded softly, being careful not to speak loud enough to interrupt her father's description of Madame's lovely climbing rose on the back fence. "And you need to tell me the truth right now because that looks like a bruise on your cheek."

"No," he told her firmly. "I do not need to tell you the truth right now. I need to tell you something else." He nodded toward the distance where Madame was walking their way. "No matter what happens, remember that everyone at this table loves you, most especially me."

"What in the world does that mean?"

"Are you enjoying yourselves?" Madame said as she joined them. The other ladies responded in the affirmative, but Madeline couldn't help noticing Papa staring at her. Finally Madame joined him in looking her direction. "Have you told her yet?"

Jonah shook his head. "I wanted to wait until you were here." He turned to Madeline. "We found the Smith grandchild."

"What?" She grinned. "That's wonderful." Then she sobered. "Wait a minute. We were supposed to be a team. How did you find her without me?"

"Remember the day we fought over who paid for the treats?"

She grinned. "I am paying next time."

He gave her a patient look. "Anyway, I had an occasion to speak to Mrs. Smith before we left, and something she said made me think. I sent a telegram to someone in New Orleans who I know to be the keeper of quite a few secrets. Her name is Bess, and she was my grandfather's housekeeper. This telegram is her response."

YES. YOU GUESSED RIGHT. LETTER TO FOLLOW.

Madeline looked up. "I don't understand."

Jonah looked around the table. "Who wants to answer that since you're all involved?"

Papa rose. "I should. Since the dealings with Lucius Cahill started with me. Unlike his grandson, Lucius was not a completely honorable man, and for one terrible moment, neither was I."

"Papa," Madeline managed. "What did you do?"

"Cahill showed up on my doorstep with a maid and a baby. Said the baby belonged to Samuel Smith. How he knew our firm had done work for Samuel's maternal grandfather, I have no idea. But he did, and he knew we had information on where certain, um, valuables were hidden. Discovered through the course of the investigation and certainly nothing we would have profited from."

He looked over at Madame. "I doubt you were ever told this, but it was that information that caused your father to relent when he found out you'd married John. He knew you'd be taken care of."

He paused, and Mama patted his hand. "I will tell the rest of this," she said, her tone surprisingly fierce. "That man," Mama continued, "he threatened to harm that innocent baby."

"So you saved her," Madeline offered.

"At the cost of trading secrets I should not have traded." Papa looked over at Madame. "Have you something to say?"

Her gaze swung across the group and then landed on Papa. "Had you not, I would have."

Madame's answer seemed to satisfy Papa. He dipped his head, and Mama settled closer to him.

"My husband and I knew what Lucius had done, and we tried to reason with him," Mrs. Cahill said. "I wanted to find the child well before Jonah was hired for this purpose. I always wondered what happened to her, and I wrote my father-in-law often. When Lucius died, I thought that secret went with him."

Mama came around the table to kneel before her. "We wrote Samuel, and he was afraid for the child's safety should she be returned to him. We pledged to care for the baby. He came to visit twice before he passed away."

"And I was not told upon Samuel's request," Madame said. "He feared I would lead Cahill to the baby, and in retrospect, I agree."

Mama smiled. "Yes, what better place to hide a child than under the man's nose? What a tiny thing she was. It only took a bit of work at the beginning, but after a while there was no question."

"So what happened to her?" Madeline turned to Jonah. "You said you found her, and Mama and Papa, you obviously placed her somewhere that Mr. Cahill would never find her. Where is she?"

"Madeline," he said slowly. "She is you."

"Me?" The breath went out of her. "That isn't possible. I was not born in 1855."

"You were, child, but you were so tiny that no one questioned your age when your mother and father signed the registry in the spring of '56 and gave you a new birthday." Madame said. "I have known for some time. From the moment I found out," she said to Mama, "I gathered nothing but pink roses for my parlor. With each rose I said a prayer for the woman who was now mother to my granddaughter and the girl who was flesh of my flesh."

Mama began to cry. Papa reached over to wrap his arm around her.

"Do you know how many ads I had to place before you answered?" Madame threw up her hands. "More than I can count, but I had followed your articles in the newspaper and I knew what would get your interest. How does it feel to be related to the man you've been trying to quiz me for information about?"

Madeline tried to respond but found the words would not come. Instead, Jordy came running and launched himself into Madame's lap. Annabelle followed close behind, apologizing and laughing.

"I have a sister," she managed and then shook her head. "And all of you too."

Jonah wrapped his arms around her then looked down into her eyes. "Hello, Trésor."

❤

Once the tears stopped—admittedly, his included—Jonah rose to command attention. "I can think of no better place to do this than in front of our families." He turned to Madeline and then dropped to one knee. "Madeline, you've now got a sister, a nephew, and a grandmother right here at this table. I'd be honored if you'd agree to have a husband too."

The clapping and cheering drowned out Madeline's response, but Jonah was pretty certain she said yes.

❤

September 19, 1880

Everyone at the reception said theirs was the most beautiful wedding ever held at the Cathedral. They'd chosen to marry in New Orleans on Madeline's birthday so that Bess could be there to see them and have a happy memory associated with that day. She wasn't much for traveling now, and none of the rest of Madeline's family and friends minded the trip.

Besides, Madeline wanted to walk where her grandfather had walked, now that she knew who her grandfather truly was. And while this was an article she would never write, the truth was enough.

She looked around the room and spied Horace Montlake in an animated conversation with Papa. Beside her father, Mama and Mrs. Cahill were no doubt plotting names for the grandchildren they would soon demand. Gretchen was seated beside Madame, and they both smiled and waved.

"That man needs to back off a little."

Madeline looked up at Jonah, who was currently leading her in a lovely waltz, this time wearing boots instead of proper formal shoes. "Who? What are you talking about?"

"Donovan," he grumbled. "Ever since he bought that property on the island, he's been coming around acting like he wants to court her."

She giggled. "I think your sister feels the same. Look at them. Besides, it was awfully nice of you to loan him the money."

His smile was dazzling. "I need someone to keep my sister busy, and it sure wasn't going to be Walt Townsend."

"Are you admitting to matchmaking?"

"I admit no such thing. Unless you want to admit you recommended Townsend to your editor to take your place at the *Picayune*."

She spied Mr. McComb and Walt Townsend holding a spirited conversation next to the punch bowl. "The fact that Mr. Townsend will no longer live in the same town as us is merely a coincidence."

Jonah laughed and then nodded toward the edge of the dance floor. "It looks like I'm about to have to give up my bride for the next dance." The music ended, and Papa cut in. "Take care of her, sir."

"I always have," Papa told him.

"And I always will," Jonah said before he walked away to take Mama's hand and lead her to the dance floor.

"Thank you for saving the Bible for me," she told him, thinking of the small book she'd tucked under her bouquet for her walk down the aisle.

The Bible had been the one thing that her paternal grandfather had been insistent should be kept for his granddaughter's wedding day. Because Papa knew the Cahills wielded enough power to have any deposit box in New Orleans opened at their request, he had chosen a favored bank in Galveston, one owned by the Montlake family, to house the treasure. The key to that box, the one numbered fourteen, had been around Madeline's neck.

"Have you found the treasure map yet?" he asked with a grin.

She looked at him askance. "Are you serious?"

Papa shrugged. "Truth is, I never knew if John was or not. He was often a man to joke, although he never did joke about his treasure."

Madeline smiled as she rested her head on Papa's shoulder for the remainder of the dance. Then her husband returned for her and it was time to leave.

Gathering the Bible and her flowers, all pink roses, she left the reception on the arm of her husband. Only later when they had retired to their room at the most beautiful hotel in all of New Orleans did the reality of the day, truly of the past six months, cause her to stumble.

Jonah scooped her into his arms. "Tired, my beloved?"

"Overwhelmed," she said, "but in such a good way."

The roses fell from her arms, and the Bible tumbled with them. "Oh Jonah," she said as the world tilted and she landed in the middle of a pile of pillows on the bed.

❤

Jonah retrieved the roses and tossed them toward Madeline and then reached for the book. The binding was old, and its collision had caused the spine to crack.

"Did I break it?" she asked.

"No, I think it's fine. Just a split in the binding, but I think that can be repaired." Jonah brought the Bible over along with pen and ink. "You write it," he told Madeline. "My handwriting is terrible."

Madeline smiled as she took the book and turned to the page listing the family weddings. Beneath the entry listing the marriage of Samuel Smith and Eliza LeBlanc, she wrote their names and then the date.

He took the pen and ink and set it aside then came back for the Bible. Placing it carefully on the dresser so the ink would not smudge, he noticed something odd about the split binding.

Fumbling with fingers too large for the task, he pulled a folded slip of paper out and looked to see what it was.

"Find something?" Madeline asked.

"Just an old page that fell out," he told her.

Tomorrow he would tell her what it was. Would show her that her grandfather had more than just the heritage of a family Bible in mind when he insisted Phillip Latour put that Bible away in a safe place.

Tonight, however, he would show this woman just how much he loved her. He would show her he would have married her even if she hadn't inherited an extremely detailed treasure map.

He folded the paper and returned it to the hiding place in the Bible. Then he turned around to smile at his wife.

"Hello, Mrs. Cahill," he said with a grin. And then the pillows scattered.

Bent Facts: Acknowledgments and an Author's Note on Actual Galveston History

I hope you have enjoyed your historical trip through one of my favorite cities in the world, Galveston, Texas. Because I am a historian at heart, I take the factual events of history very seriously. For that reason, I am deeply indebted to Dwayne Jones, executive director of the Galveston Historical Foundation, for providing answers to my many, many questions on life in Galveston in 1880.

As a tenth-generation Texan and former property owner in Galveston County, I wanted to honor one of my favorite places on the planet by getting the history right and not guessing. Any errors in this book, not counting the "bent history" I mention below, are mine alone.

In addition to being a history nerd, I am also a novelist, so upon occasion I have had to bend the facts slightly to allow my fictional characters to live, work, and fall in love in a "real" world. As you read through this novel, you may or may not have realized a few of these "bent facts."

I must, however, endeavor to keep true to the record of history by disclosing the following (and offering a few interesting historical tidbits):

By 1880, Galveston was the largest city in Texas. Census reports showed more than five hundred businesses, ten hotels, and a port that received and shipped more than a half million dollars in goods. At one time, Galveston was known as the Wall Street of the South.

While Jonah's grandfather is mentioned as a surveyor who helped create the grid of streets on the island, in actuality, Robert C. Trimble and William Lindsey were hired by the Congress of the Republic of Texas (yes, Texas was its own country before it was a state) to do the work of turning the island into an actual city.

As his last act of defiance on the night of his escape from the island, Jean Lafitte burned *La Maison Rouge* (Red House) to the ground in 1821. In 1870, Hendricks Castle—owned by a ship's captain of the same name and not the man I created as Jonah's father—was built over the cellars and foundation of Red House. Although it was destroyed during Hurricane Carla in the 1960s, the remains of this real-life home can be seen on Harborside Drive between Fourteenth and Fifteenth Streets.

T. Ratto & Company Confectioners was an actual store located at 159, 161, and 163 Strand, using the old numbering system. The owner, Thomas Ratto, was an Italian immigrant who arrived in Galveston sometime before 1871. While I could not locate the actual date the shop opened or discover what the interior looked like, I did find research that says it was definitely in business at that location by 1881. A Galveston City Directory dated 1871 lists several locations for the confectioner, including one on Tremont Street. For the purposes of this story, I have located the shop at the location where it remained until the 1890s.

From September 17, 1855, through September 19, 1855, a hurricane hit Matagorda, Texas, and its effects were felt in Galveston and elsewhere in that part of the Gulf of Mexico. Vessels were sunk, businesses were flooded or destroyed, and the town of Matagorda was leveled. After the storm came a yellow fever epidemic that killed many residents of the area.

The Galveston Historical Society with some of Mrs. Brown's original pieces at 2338 Broadway Avenue, called Ashton Villa after Mrs. Brown's maiden name, has preserved the 1859 Brown family home as a museum. Said to be the oldest brick home on the island, it's an amazing place to visit. The Browns raised five children—three boys and two girls—in the home, with the Browns and their daughters residing on the second floor and the Brown boys and their maternal grandparents living on the floor above. Moreau Brown, the real-life version of fictional Jonah's childhood friend, grew up to be a prominent physician. President Lincoln's letter freeing the slaves, then known as General Order No. 3 and later known as the Emancipation Proclamation, was indeed read by General Granger of the Union army from Ashton Villa's second-floor balcony on June 19, 1865.

As an aside, it is true that former president Ulysses S. Grant visited the Browns at Ashton Villa on March 25, 1880, although there is no evidence that the Brown family or anyone else on the island hired Pinkerton agents to prepare for the visit or had a ball in his honor. Nor is there any research that shows what Mrs. Brown's rose garden looked like, so I happily made it all up!

What I didn't make up was the Indianola hurricane of 1875. On September 15, 1875, a hurricane unexpectedly slammed the coastal Texas town of Indianola. When the storm finally cleared two days later, only eight buildings were left in this once prosperous city, and somewhere between 150 and 300 people had lost their lives. While I have tried to be as factual as possible concerning the city of Indianola, the locations and names of characters I mention, including Mrs. Francine's Boardinghouse and Sheriff Pake Simmons, are completely fictional.

Morgan's Louisiana and Texas Railroad and Steamship Company operated trains and steamships between Galveston and many parts of Texas and beyond. In their advertisement in the *Galveston Daily News* of March 1880, the company advertised steamers leaving daily at midnight (yes, midnight!) for New Orleans and on Sundays and Thursdays at 4:00 p.m. for Indianola aboard the steamship *Harlan*. Passengers to New Orleans could plan on sleeping two nights on the vessel while Indianola-bound passengers slept one night aboard. It was the *Harlan* that transported former president Grant and his party from Galveston to New Orleans during his visit to Texas in March of 1880.

When Madeline mentions to Jonah that a female Pinkerton saved the life of President Lincoln in Baltimore before his inauguration, she is referring to Pinkerton detective Kate Warne who foiled an assassination attempt on the president-elect's life in 1861 by going undercover as a wealthy Southern woman and infiltrating a group suspected of wanting to cause Lincoln harm.

I have already made mention of the *Galveston Daily News*. As impossible as it might be to believe now, the *Daily News* was once one of the largest papers in the nation with offices in four major Texas cities by 1880. Except for the fact that the reporter Mr. Townsend is completely fictional, as are some of the newspaper articles I have mentioned, I have done my best to keep as close to the facts as possible regarding this newspaper.

When Jonah refers to the Korean incident of 1871, he is speaking of a real incident where American Naval ships were sent to Seoul in search of an apology for the murders of several shipwrecked sailors and to try and negotiate a treaty that would protect shipwrecked Americans in the future. Negotiations failed, and though there was a small skirmish, the American fleet had to withdraw without any solution to the issue when typhoon season hit.

Regarding the mention of the article in the *Galveston Daily News* about the party Madeline and Jonah attended, the story chronicling the benefits of Dr. C. McLane's Liver Pills and the advertisement for the Hazard Powder Company Blasting and Mining Powder actually appeared in the March 26, 1880, edition on the third page. Obviously there was no gossip about my fictional characters in that edition, although there were other interesting articles and advertisements, including one for Jenkins's Annihilator cure for rheumatism, gout, and neuralgia, and another assuring readers that a cure for opium addiction could be found by purchasing morphine from the doctor who placed the ad. The name of the doctor in the opium cure ad is too blurry to read, which is probably just as well.

During the fictional ball at Ashton Villa, Jonah references Mrs. William Ballenger. Mrs. Ballenger (maiden name Hallie Jack of Brazoria County, Texas) was a real-life philanthropist who served on boards and charities throughout her lifetime.

When Jonah and Madeline discuss possible pirate treasure at Three Trees, they are referring to a place near 14520 Stewart Road that was once the site of a battle between Jean Lafitte's men and a tribe of Karankawa Indians in February of 1821. The site, also called Lafitte's Grove, is commemorated by a marker erected by the State of Texas in 1936 near the gates of a property called Stewart's Mansion.

Beginning in 1867, the Sisters of Charity of the Incarnate Word operated an orphanage and infirmary in Galveston. Because the child in my story would have been delivered to the orphanage in 1855, I chose to bend history by a few years so that I could include an orphanage in the story.

Regarding the Smith home, if you are curious as to what Madame's rented home on Broadway Avenue in Galveston looked like, be sure and look up the Trube Castle. This grand three-story home was actually not built until 1890, and it wasn't located on Broadway Avenue at all. Rather, the home is located at 1627 Sealey and is now a private events venue. Sadly, the location of the fictional Smith home is actually the site of a loan agency and a laundromat.

And finally, BOI is the term Galveston natives use for people who are Born On the Island.

If you've read this far, great! You're a history nerd too! Scoot over to my website at www.kathleenybarbo.com and email me to let me know! And when in Galveston, be sure and check out the Galveston Historical Society to find out all the cool history behind one of my favorite cities in the world!

Bestselling author **Kathleen Y'Barbo** is a multiple Carol Award and RITA nominee of more than eighty novels with almost two million copies in print in the US and abroad. She has been nominated for a Career Achievement Award as well as a Reader's Choice Award and is the winner of the 2014 Inspirational Romance of the Year by *Romantic Times* magazine. Kathleen is a paralegal, a proud military wife, and a tenth-generation Texan, who recently moved back to cheer on her beloved Texas Aggies. Connect with her through social media at www.kathleenybarbo.com.

Coming Next in the Series. . .

My Heart Belongs in Gettysburg, Pennsylvania
(November 2018)
Clarissa Avery Ross has everything a young woman ... on of the ... med a war ... And she ... ck again

... his ... n in the ... vers a ... amily. But ... ong the

F... BOUR